ILLICIT CONNECTIONS

ILLICIT MINDS #2

REBECCA ROYCE

Illicit Connections (Illicit Minds #2)

Copyright @ 2019 by Rebecca Royce

Original Publication 2016 called "Embraced" by Rebecca Royce

Ebook ISBN: 978-1-951349-12-7

Print ISBN: 978-1-951349-13-4

Cover art by Glowing Moon Designs

Content Editing: Heather Long

Copy/Proof Editing: Jennifer Jones

Final Proof Editing: Meghan Leigh Daigle

Formatting: Ripley Proserpina

Published by Rebecca Royce

www.rebeccaroyce.com

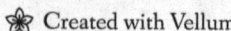 Created with Vellum

PROLOGUE

ONE YEAR SINCE THE ADDISON WADE INCIDENT

Every damn news outlet had covered the Addison Wade–Spencer Lewis debacle. Every damn one. The President loosened his tie and glanced down again at the paper he'd been trying all night not to focus on. He had no choice but to sign it. The public outcry in favor of the administrative changes the Committee had set forth had been almost unanimous. Everyone was terrified that a Conditioned uprising was on the horizon. Hysteria was at an all-time high.

Still, the new rules sterilizing all Conditioned females over the age of twenty and putting them to death by forty? It seemed downright cruel. Why couldn't they simply increase the security everywhere? Why not put them to death at birth? They had no rights under the Constitution. They weren't even people. He closed his eyes for a moment. The Conditioned were profitable to the Institutions for the first forty years of their lives, before health issues took over and they couldn't work as much. They earned their own keep. It was either eliminate them at forty or make sure they were better nourished and taken care of in their earlier years.

He sighed as he put his head in his hands. It was not his fault this had happened, but how he responded to it would be his legacy. Yes, the few freedoms the Conditioned had would be cut back. Even the policies to let them live would have to be limited.

They were too dangerous—that was all there was to it.

ONE

October in New Orleans was a blessed month. Not too hot, not too cold, just perfect for being outside and doing nothing strenuous. The sun shone down on City Park, illuminating the currently empty children's playground that Ben Lavelle was sure would be busy later in the day when the kids got out of school. For now, it was the ideal place for his semi-illegal meeting with the most notorious person Ben knew: his brother, Gene.

"What you're asking for, Benedicte, is next to impossible these days."

Ben took a deep breath and held back the sharp, insulting remark he wanted to throw at Gene. Only his brother still called him Benedicte. Not to mention that virtually nothing was impossible for Gene to accomplish. The fact that his brother pretended that he couldn't do this was insulting to both of them.

Normally, Ben refused to play Gene's games. But in this case—for Ben's daughters, neighbors, and entire community —he would let Gene run him through his emotional obstacle course.

"Surely, for your *boss*, it can't be that much of a problem. I know someone is getting them out still, and it's not like we don't have a real need."

Eugene was eighteen months Ben's senior, but he looked ten years older. Not surprising, considering he worked for the Mob. The Giallanis had been illegally running New Orleans for at least five generations, and Eugene had pushed and pushed until he'd become part of their inner circle. That kind of self-serving devotion to criminal activity took a toll on the body and soul.

Gene took a seat on the park bench Ben had just vacated. It was a beautiful day and, given other circumstances, Ben would have loved to spend it sitting on that park bench just thinking. Today, however, was not for quiet contemplation.

Eugene rubbed his nose. "If y'all are seeing ghosts, perhaps you should take yourselves down to the Institute Evaluation Center and have yourselves checked for the Condition."

In his head, Ben counted to ten, searching for the patience he'd once had before the weight of the world had settled on his shoulders. "All thirty of us can't be Conditioned. Besides, I haven't heard of any instances of the Condition showing up for the first time in adults. Have you?"

In general, it was a problem that manifested in childhood. Just one more thing for parents to worry about all the time.

"No." Gene closed his eyes for a moment. "I don't suppose I'm in any position to start moralizing to you. Am I, brother?"

Ben shook his head. There was no point in disagreeing. Considering Gene's line of work, he really wasn't in any position to judge anyone. Besides, it wasn't as if he was asking Gene to do anything illegal. He just wanted use of one Conditioned Ghost Talker. That was all. One day with the strangely afflicted individual so he or she could tell him how to get rid of the ghost that was haunting the three-block radius around his house.

Gene sighed and opened his eyes. For a second, Ben could almost see him as he'd been as a child. His older brother had always been the sensitive one of the two. Whereas Ben had ignored the constant taunting about their "weird" eyes and their "Jap" mother as nothing more than stupid ignorance, Gene had clung to the idea that he looked more Caucasian than Asian, desperate to fit in with the racist morons who'd taunted him. He should have wanted to stand out as much as possible from that small group.

It hadn't mattered one lick to Ben that their mother had been born in Japan. To Ben, she'd been the epitome of grace and beauty. To Gene... well... his brother had never said anything directly, but Ben suspected he'd almost been ashamed. It had been hard. They'd been the only family at school and church who weren't completely white.

Ben could almost see Gene as he'd been then. But then he blinked and the image passed away. Instead he was presented with his sort of criminally-inclined brother who existed in so many shades of gray, Ben wasn't sure he would know if Gene fell into the darkness completely.

Not that Ben should judge. Right now, he needed his brother's abilities to make things right at home.

"How long will you need the thing?"

Ben sat down next to him. "I can't imagine it'll take very long. Is there a time limit?"

"Well, you know, ever since Addison Wade ran off last year with that freak from Safe Dawn, things are a lot harder out there." He looked up, his eyes gazing out at something on the horizon. Ben wondered if Gene was really looking at anything at all. "They're killing them. They're not even letting them live anymore."

Ben touched Gene's arm. "Eugene, I wouldn't ask if it wasn't important. You know that. The girls, Gene... Daphne and Ella..."

"Done. I'll make it happen." Gene stood. "You know I would walk on water for the girls. In this case, I won't have to do anything miraculous."

Ben knew that Gene meant every word he said. Uncle Gene was completely devoted to his nieces and had been since they'd first arrived in the world, two minutes apart, with black hair stuck to their heads as they'd wailed like banshees.

"They're not Conditioned." Ben spoke quickly. "They're suffering through the same weirdness we all are. I mean, maybe it isn't a ghost or a poltergeist or whatever it is..."

Gene put his arm on Ben's sleeve. "It's fine. You're doing the right thing. There's so much strange shit out there..."

"Yeah."

An uncomfortable silence grew between them, as it always did when they got together and Ben didn't have his girls with him to talk Gene's ears off. Cars passed by on City Park Drive, marring the otherwise pastoral feel of the moment.

Gene pulled a cigarette out of his coat pocket, and Ben shook his head. "Do I need to tell you how disgusting it is that you still smoke?"

His brother shrugged, ignoring his remark as he always did.

"Doing anything for the anniversary?"

Ben didn't follow. "Anniversary?"

Gene leaned back on the bench where they sat. "Seriously?"

"What?" Somewhere along the line, Ben had lost track of the conversation.

"Benedicte Lavelle, I'm asking you what you're going to do to mark the death of your wife? Four years ago, tomorrow? Ring some kind of bell?"

Ben put his head in his hands. "Jesus Christ." He'd fucking forgotten. He'd been so distracted by the ghosts that he'd forgotten Dana's death. What kind of monster was he?

Gene changed the subject. "So, the weather is nice today, isn't it?"

Ben walked into his house, shutting the door behind him with a thud. He stood silently and listened to see if he could catch anything unusual. Nothing greeted him but the *tick-tock* of the old grandfather clock he'd inherited from his father, and he let go of the breath he'd been holding.

His own ghostly encounters had been limited to strange feelings and sounds. He hadn't seen the apparitions his neighbors claimed to have witnessed, and was glad as anything that he hadn't.

As it was, since he'd been "elected" to take care of the problem, he hadn't paid one hoot of attention to his law practice all week. This visit to his brother and contact with the Institutions was the last attempt he could make. After this, someone was going to have to find an exorcist, which was way above Ben's pay grade.

His nanny refused to work—she was too spooked to even come inside the house—which meant he also had to take the girls back and forth to school and be with them afterward. He looked toward the sound of the ticking. It was one o'clock. He still had two hours before he had to get them. *Enough time to obsess.*

His phone rang, and he picked it up, surprised to see Gene's number flashing across the screen. "Hello?"

"If you can take her in an hour, the Institute will drop the best Ghost-Handler they have off at your house. She happens to be out doing a job, and she's on her way back to the Institute. It has to be now, because she's scheduled to be put down when she's returned." Ben listened to his brother's fast talk on the phone.

"Benedicte? Are you there?"

Ben cleared his throat. "I'm here. An hour? I have to get the kids in two—"

Gene interrupted him. "Great, then you can do it."

"Did you say she's going to be put down?"

"Gotta go. I've got to get back to Tony and tell him it's a go. You owe me for this."

Gene hung up and Ben stood, staring at his cell phone in disbelief. How had this happened so fast? He'd thought he'd have weeks to prepare. Where was she going to sleep? Did they sleep? He cursed as he stalked over to the fridge to get out a soda—a real soda, with actual sugar, like he let his daughters drink on special occasions, not the diet stuff he usually restricted himself to. He took a swig, letting the sweetness fill his mouth.

Moments like this were why he needed a housekeeper. He was going to have to bite the bullet and dish out the money to get cleaning help in addition to the nanny—if she ever came back. As soon as he finished his drink, he was going to have to go upstairs and make up a bed in the guest room. Did he even have clean sheets? And where the hell was he supposed to get the money for a full-time house-keeper? If he doubled his billable hours, which he couldn't even do if he didn't have the nanny, he would never see the kids—

The grandfather clock fell over, smashing onto the floor. The noise was so deafening that for a second, he couldn't even move. Instinctively, he'd covered his ears when the first smash had sounded, which meant he'd dropped his drink all over the floor. He could only hear his fast breathing in his ears. What the hell had just happened?

He grabbed a towel to clean up the spill. The grandfather clock... that was too huge. He couldn't deal with that now. Not yet. The drink, yes. That he could handle.

What the fuck had knocked over the clock?

He rose, holding the wet towel in his hand as he clenched his fists. This was the same crap that had been going on for weeks. Something he couldn't see had knocked over his ancestral clock. *What the hell?*

Knowing he wouldn't be able to express any of this once the girls came home, he took the opportunity to scream at the top of his lungs, loud and unabashed. Anyone who would care if they could hear him was at school. This would be the one time today he could lose his mind.

His screaming was short-lived. It wasn't solving anything. He still felt like hell.

A knock on the door made him groan. So much for no one hearing him freak out. In two strides, he made it to the door and pulled it open. The sweet, plump sixty-year-old woman who greeted him made him grin. She was his favorite neighbor and a pseudo-grandmother to his girls.

Annie spoke very fast. "I was walking to my car and I heard—"

He interrupted her. "Yes, I was screaming." He tried to give her a sheepish grin.

"Is everything okay, Ben?"

"My grandfather clock fell over."

"The old one, that you've had forever?"

"Yes." He turned to regard the mess on the floor just to assure himself it had actually happened. "Would you like to come in, Ms. Annie?"

"Maybe for a minute. I'll help you clean it up."

"Thank you." He gestured for her to enter and closed the door behind her when she finally did.

"This has to stop, Ben."

"I know." Walking to a narrow closet, he pulled out the broom and dustpan. He'd have to get the large, wooden part of the clock up first before he could even attempt to handle the glass. "I spoke to Eugene. He's gotten us one of the Conditioned, as we discussed."

"Oh, good." Annie's face brightened significantly. "We all knew we could depend on you."

"Yes." He smiled. "I'm very... dependable."

"Are you going to keep the girls here while *it's* here?"

Ben's thoughts stuttered. He hadn't thought of moving the girls out of the house, but Annie was quite right. Not having expected such fast service, he hadn't had time to dwell on the particulars. He was bringing—inviting—a dangerous Conditioned person into his home, where his daughters slept.

"Annie, I'm not sure what to do." He closed his eyes. "I think I might be losing my mind. Until Gene reminded me this morning, I'd forgotten it's the anniversary of Dana's death."

His neighbor placed a gentle hand on his shoulder. "You've got a lot on your plate. Your sweet wife wouldn't have wanted you to stop life every year on October fifth."

"In this case, it's not about what she would have wanted but what my girls need. They were two. Talking about her, recognizing the date... it's the only way we can keep her in their day-to-day lives."

He gave up and sat down on the floor.

"Well, you would know best." She cleared her throat. "If you'll pick up the big piece of the clock that's too heavy for me, I'll clean the rest of this up. And the girls can stay with me."

"I couldn't possibly impose."

She interrupted him. "Of course you can. Hugh will love it, and you can't have them there with *it* until we're certain it's safe."

"I don't know what to say but thank you."

Annie laughed. "Thank you for handling the difficult part of this whole thing. I wouldn't want one of those things in my home." She took the broom from his hand. "I'll get them from school for you today." Before he could speak, she held up her hand. "Don't you dare say thank you again."

An hour later, with Annie's persistent help, he'd gotten the house put together enough that they could receive visitors. Even if, in this case, the visitor wasn't exactly a visitor. He wasn't even sure what to think about what was happening.

Annie hadn't left. He suspected she wanted a glimpse of the Conditioned person and was too polite to say so. Right now he couldn't be sure, but he thought she might be making lemonade. A knock on the door sounded. Neither he nor Annie moved.

"I'll be honest, Ben, I never thought to really see or meet one in person."

He hadn't either, and he had good reasons for not wanting to meet them. But there was a first time for everything. He walked forward and opened the door.

In front of him stood a tall, redheaded woman. She was

exactly his height, which made her about five feet, ten inches tall. Her eyes were blue with dark, almost black smudges of exhaustion underneath. She wore an orange jumpsuit that resembled the clothes he saw prisoners wear on the side of the road when they worked cleaning up the ditches. She was in both wrist and ankle cuffs.

He sucked in his breath, because all he could think was how lovely she was. Her hair was like a sunset and her blue eyes, as exhausted as they were, reminded him of the Gulf of Mexico in the summer, where he took the girls on vacation. Internally, he tried to jar his thoughts from the direction they'd taken. She was Conditioned. She couldn't be lovely. Or shouldn't be.

"Benedicte Lavelle?" From behind her, a man stepped forward.

He was clearly the guard. Dressed in a blue-and-gray jumpsuit—their uniform—with the word Crescent on the pocket to indicate which Institution he'd come from, he had a sidearm visible on his left hip. If Ben had to guess, he'd have bet he was armed elsewhere, too.

"Ben."

The guard looked down at his paper. "It says Benedicte Lavelle."

"Yes, but I go by Ben."

The guard nodded. "Oh. I see." He shrugged. "We got a call that we're supposed to bring Seven-Two-Four here."

Ben stepped back so they could enter the house. He heard Annie suck in her breath at the sight, but he didn't turn to look at her. She'd be embarrassed if she knew he'd noticed.

Not sure what to do, he pointed at the woman's cuffs. "Is she dangerous?"

"Nah." The guard shook his head. "This one is as gentle as a puppy. This is protocol, that's all. Come here, girlie."

The woman moved at the guard's bidding, and he took off her cuffs. In all his life, Ben didn't think he'd ever seen someone stand so silently or so still as the Conditioned woman now in his kitchen.

"You must really be *someone* to have gotten her here. She's scheduled for removal. Almost nothing stops that."

Ben's gaze flew to the woman's face again. Nothing. She had no reaction to hearing she was going to be killed as soon as she returned home. A headache formed between Ben's eyes.

"I'm not important."

"Well."

Now the guard didn't seem to know what to say. They stood in silence. Ben wasn't going to speak first. There was no way he was going to tell this person how he'd managed to get the woman there. His brother might be a crook, but he was *his* crook, and Ben didn't betray family.

"There are some rules. I'm going to tell you what they are, and then you'll sign girlie out."

Ben held out his hand to take the contract from the guard. He was a lawyer. In this respect, he felt right at home.

"It's real easy. You have to feed her once a day. You have to give her somewhere to sleep. The kitchen floor with a blanket will be fine. Nothing fancy. She's not used to fancy, and she won't know what to do with it. You have to give her someplace to use the bathroom. You can't touch her sexually. Madame Joan will inspect her when she gets back, and if she's been abused, there will be a fine to pay." The guard looked down at the list to see if he'd forgotten anything. "When you're done with her, call the number here. And—

oh—if anything goes terribly wrong, you're being watched by the Fury, so don't worry—someone will show up to help."

He had no choice but to push that thought from his mind. The Fury was the stuff of nightmares.

"But you won't have a problem with this one. Like I said, gentle as a puppy and good at what she does."

Ben signed the contract before he passed it back to the guard. He felt a little bit sick to his stomach. Why was he doing this? Why was he deliberately sticking himself in this situation? He turned to regard the place where his grandfather clock had once stood. That was why.

"What's her name?" Maybe he should have asked her, but he wasn't sure what the protocol was.

"Madame Joan doesn't give them names. She blames that treatment for what happened at Safe Dawn. We don't have any incidents at Crescent like that. Don't make them human and they don't get ideas. She's Seven-Two-Four."

With that, the guard turned on his heel and left the way he had come in. Ben looked at Annie. She was pale as she leaned against his kitchen counter, not uttering a word.

She was obviously not going to be any help. He had a woman in his house—a Conditioned woman who didn't have a name—because he had a ghost problem.

How the hell had any of this happened?

TWO

Seven had never been in a house like this one before. Usually the places she got sent to were large mansions where very, very rich people lived. Or wanted to live. Or, in the case of her most recent trip, wanted to sell for a very large profit. She looked up at the wall. There were pictures of two little girls hung all over it.

They weren't identical twins, but they were definitely sisters who looked a great deal alike. Still, they might have been twins, because they seemed to be about the same age. They had the same long, black hair and high cheekbones. Their noses were different, though. Seven squinted to try to get a better look but couldn't make out exactly how they appeared. She needed glasses, badly. But she wasn't going to get them this close to termination, no matter what her profit margin was.

Her guard left, and the click of the door closing behind him caught her attention, pulling her back into the here and now. The room fell silent as the two other occupants regarded her. She wasn't sure how long they were going to make her stand there, not moving, but she would find a way to endure the time. Speaking first was out of the question, since she didn't crave a beating at the moment.

"My God, Ben, she's a baby." The older woman took two steps forward. "I thought Eugene said she was scheduled to be put down."

Ben must have been the handsome man with the kind eyes. Seven made a mental note of that. Not that she would ever be addressing Ben as "Ben." If she spoke to him first, for some reason, she would call him "sir." Still, it was nice to know.

"Um..." Ben obviously didn't know how to answer the older woman. Seven could have, if she'd had any inclination to do so. She could have told her that Madame ended the lives of Conditioned inmates whenever she saw fit. There wasn't a particular age for execution. Why would the woman think there was?

Ben took a step toward her. "You're Seven-Two-Four, that is correct?"

Seven cleared her throat. "In the past, sir, some people have found it simpler to call me 'Seven.' Since we are not around any other Conditioned here, it is not likely to get confusing if you choose to shorten the numbers."

"Seven." Ben exhaled a loud breath. "Is there anything I can get you?"

"No, thank you." He could tell her she could move, or show her where she should put herself until he wanted her services. But get her something? No, she was just fine.

He motioned toward the sofa. "Would you like to sit down?"

She would have kissed him in gratitude if it wouldn't have gotten her shot.

"Yes, thank you."

Seven tried to walk normally toward the living room

without her legs giving out beneath her. She nearly stumbled but caught herself before, she hoped, anyone noticed. Finally, she positioned herself on the floor next to the couch. This would be the point, she knew, when they would tell her about their paranormal issues and she would figure out how to solve them.

This was to be her last case, which was a gift to begin with. Her last assignment had gone so badly that she had almost gotten physically ill thinking it would be the last thing she would do before she died. If there was any Heaven for people like her—and everyone told her there was not—she didn't want to have to make a case for herself with God after failing so terribly down on Earth.

Ben moved forward. "Why are you on the floor? Please, feel free to sit on the couch."

"Thank you, but Madame prefers us not to use luxuries whenever possible. It is not our lot in life to be comfortable."

She wasn't sure what the look that passed between Ben and the other woman, whose name she still didn't know, was about. Like with most things that went on outside the walls of Crescent, she found herself confused by the way people related to each other. It didn't bother her to be out of the loop. She'd gone through most of her life that way, and now that her days were ending, it mattered even less.

After a moment, they sat down on opposite ends of the brown couch. Hoping they wouldn't notice, she reached out to touch the material. It was soft, not hard like most of the couches she'd secretly felt in people's homes.

"Well, I'm sure you have lots to discuss."

The woman who had just sat stood back up again. Seven scratched her head.

Had she done something to make the other woman leave?

"Ben, don't worry. I'll see myself out."

Seven didn't want to strain to see the woman leave, so she focused instead on the shuffling of her feet as she moved away. The door opened and closed, leaving Seven alone with her quiet employer.

"So... I'm Ben Lavelle." He drummed his fingers on his gray pants. "Look, I understand that Madame doesn't like you to use luxuries or whatever, but in this house, furniture isn't a luxury, it's a necessity. Could you do me a favor and at least sit on a chair?"

No one had ever asked her to do that before. She stood up on unsteady legs and took a seat on the opposite side of the couch from Ben, in the seat the woman had vacated.

Ben nodded. "Thank you. That's better."

The couch felt like a dream beneath her, and she wanted to sigh in relief. Her aching body had been crying out for a moment of comfort.

"How old are you, Seven?"

She rubbed her head. Personal questions were the worst. Despite her abilities, she hated feeling like a freak. The only reason people wanted to know anything about her was so they could talk about her afterward to their friends or gawk at her. Madame had told them it wasn't their job to be concerned with what normal, non-Conditioned people did. Her role in life was simply to serve, and pray for redemption in the end.

"I'm not sure how old I am."

That was the truth. They didn't exactly celebrate birthdays. Even her file, which she had once managed to convince a guard to read to her, stated that she'd come to them when she'd been around two years old. That was vague enough to be completely unhelpful.

"I see." He nodded, and she wondered if he actually did understand.

She dared to look him straight in the eyes. He wasn't purely Caucasian; she could see that. Crescent was filled with people of all races and colors. If she had to guess, she would say that somewhere in his background there had been an Asian ancestor.

She'd seen it a few times on a globe. It was a world away from where she was.

Maybe, if she got to go to Heaven, she'd get to look down and see Asia.

The strangest urge to reach out and stroke the side of his face with her hand nearly overtook her.

Ben spoke. "You're so quiet, and I'm not certain exactly what I'm supposed to do with you."

"We're not supposed to speak to Madame's clients unless we are spoken to."

Discomfort made her want to stand, so she braced her legs instead. Inside her shoes, where no one could see, she moved her big toe. It had always been her little rebellion. She was expected to stay completely still, and no one had to know she disobeyed.

"Surely no one is here to watch us. You can talk to me. Tell me what I'm supposed to be doing with you. This has all happened so fast. I'm not prepared."

Seven had heard about these instances before. Clients were paid to trick the Conditioned to break the rules. She narrowed her eyes. Was that what was happening? Why would Madame bother? Seven's termination date had come up.

Why waste the time?

"Are you testing me?" She stood up from the couch, which she never should have sat down on in the first place.

Would Madame make her termination harder? Was there a way to do that?

He rose as well. "What?"

"I'm not going to break any rules. I'm not."

Ben nodded his head. "Okay."

He paused, and she had no idea what to do, so after a moment, she sat down on the floor. It wasn't nearly as luxurious as the couch, but it was more familiar.

"Was I asking you to break some rules?" He moved forward until he stood right in front of her. Slowly, he lowered himself until he was sitting across from her on the ground.

She looked up until they made eye contact. Silent, as she'd learned to be over the years, she stared into his eyes, wishing she held some of the freakish abilities her friends had. Mind-reading would have been a real helpful ability right now. Still, she didn't see any deception in his eyes. Ben's dark depths spoke only of confusion and kindness.

Seven sighed, looking down at her hands. "There are things I'm not supposed to do. Things that, if I were to do them, would be... bad."

Bad was not the most articulate word she'd ever used, but it was the only one she could come up with at the moment. One of the things she wasn't supposed to talk about was what went on at Crescent. *Bad* would have to suffice.

"How would anyone find out you did them?"

He loosened his tie as if it were choking him. She wanted to reach up and rub his shoulders until he unclenched his teeth.

"You would tell them. Or the Fury would."

"Unless you do something to endanger me or someone else when you're with me, I'm not going to tell anyone anything. I'm a lawyer. I'm really good at keeping people's secrets." He lowered his head to match the lowering of his voice. "And the Fury is not in my house. I'm not one hundred percent certain they're real."

Before she could stop herself, she reached out and took his hand. He didn't pull away or gasp, which was good. A lot of people wouldn't want to be touched by the Conditioned.

"The Fury is quite real, sir. Everything you think you've heard, it's probably happened."

He squeezed her fingers. "You would know better than I would. Either way, they're not here in this house."

"The Fury is everywhere."

Ben shook his head. "They're not here."

He was wrong, but you didn't argue with the client. She believed that he wasn't going to report on her, but he had no idea how capable the Fury was of being anywhere and everywhere they wanted to be. If they set their eyes on her, she was a dead duck. The likelihood was they'd leave her alone—she was already marked for death—but she still had to be careful.

Ben spoke again. "I don't know what I'm supposed to do, how I'm supposed to treat you. Perhaps others have time to prepare for this kind of thing, but I didn't. I only asked to get some help this morning and they sent you right over. I'm a little in over my head."

"I see." And she finally did. She let go of his hand and stood up. "Why don't you show me where your ghost problem is?"

He rose to his feet. "It's many places."

She raised an eyebrow. It was, apparently, a strong energy. That was fine. She had dealt with them before. There wasn't much she hadn't seen since she'd opened her eyes sometime in her second year and seen things that others didn't think were there. She was the most sought-after Conditioned for what she did—that was what Madame had told her. She was the best at a skill that went against nature, that was a slight against God. The only thing she could do was try to help as many people as possible and hope it was enough to earn her redemption for her sin.

"Show me."

He scratched his head. "I can show you the many places in this house where we've had incidents, but I can't take you to the other places, because they're in other people's homes."

Had she heard him correctly? "Are you saying that there are ghosts in many different homes, and that I'm taking care of all of them?"

Her head spun. She was in no rush to get back to Crescent and her death sentence, but she wasn't sure she had the resources to handle such a large case.

Seven felt exhausted, that was all there was to it.

"We assume it's the same ghost."

She crossed her arms over her chest, wishing she could crawl into a hole. "Why would you assume that?"

"We'd never had these kinds of problems before, and then we all started having them. It seemed logical."

Seven shook her head. "No."

It really shouldn't have surprised her. Outside the others with her particular problem, people didn't know that much about ghosts. Or energies, which was what they really were. Why should they? From what she gathered, people either pictured floating white sheets or something out of a horror movie. In her life, it wasn't anything like that.

"What do you suppose it is, then?" Ben's gaze pleaded with her for answers.

He'd clearly been through a lot.

She sighed. "I'm just guessing, since I haven't seen anything yet and Madame doesn't like us to speculate. If we don't know, she prefers we say so."

"Madame has a lot to say, doesn't she?"

Seven wasn't sure what to say to that. Was he being sarcastic? What would be the point of that?

"About many things." She gasped and covered her mouth as soon as she'd spoken. Had the Fury heard her?

Ben patted her on the arm, sending tingles through her body, which was more than a little odd. Touch didn't usually have that effect on her. She'd placed her hands on his earlier and it had had no effect. Was it because he'd touched her and not the other way around?

"Don't worry. No one is here to hear you except me."

If only she could have believed him. Even if it was true, it didn't exactly follow that she should be saying bad things about Madame. The woman had the right to do bad things to the Conditioned, but she also kept them fed, clothed and functional, which was more than what would happen to them if they lived in the outside world. In some ways, the woman should apply for sainthood. It couldn't have been easy to have to spend your life surrounded by the damned.

"Why don't you show me where the ghost is here?" It would at least give her a chance to find her feet in this place.

She'd only been there a short time, and she was already unnerved. This beautiful man with his dark eyes and direct gaze threw her off her game, which couldn't be a good thing. The last thing she needed in this phase of her life was to disregard her path, the one she hoped would lead her somehow to divine redemption.

Sighing quietly, so no one else could possibly hear, she followed where he walked. A few feet farther into the hallway and she stared up at blank space on the wall. Here? Something had happened here?

"Right before you got here, the grandfather clock that had been in my family for generations crashed to the floor like someone had shoved it over. I was alone in the house."

It would have to have been one heck of a ghost to manifest such a maneuver. "Are all the people in the three-block neighborhood having such dramatic encounters?"

"Some people are having it worse. Some people swear they can see things moving. I haven't had that yet. My girls have seen..." His voice trailed off, and he looked away.

She nodded. "I'm sure they're not Conditioned. In extreme circumstances, even the non-inflicted can see manifestations of the energy."

"How is that different from what you do?" Ben stepped closer to her. They stood side by side, staring at the blank wall together. She could feel the heat off his body, and it was comforting in a way she'd never felt before.

"Trust me, it's different. In a few seconds you're going to see how different." She looked over her shoulder to silently admire his profile. It was solid. He had a strong chin and an aristocratic nose, both of which spoke of power and resilience.

She forced her attention back to the task at hand.

"Your wife? She's gone."

It wasn't really a question. None of the recent pictures of the girls included a woman, although their baby pictures did. It seemed a fair guess she was gone.

He sighed and rubbed his forehead. As he did so, his arm gently collided with hers. She stifled a gasp at the contact. "She died four years ago."

"I see."

She really hoped that the energy signals she found were

not those of his late wife. That would break her heart. That would mean the woman hadn't been able to transition her entire spirit on to the next world, that part of her had stayed behind here. She didn't want to have to tell Ben that his wife had never really left the house.

He turned to stare at her, and she felt heat rise in her face. She really, really didn't want to blush. It was a big problem with her skin tone.

"Do you think it's her? Dana?"

Seven didn't want to lie, not this close to her own end. "I have no way of knowing who it is just yet. But I will know when I find the ghost, and if you want, I'll tell you who it is. Only if you ask me, okay?"

He nodded, and a strand of his dark-as-midnight hair fell over his eyes. He blinked and pushed it away, causing her heart to flutter. "Fair enough."

"Your daughters? Have you sent them away from here to avoid me?"

She wasn't sure why she had asked the question, except she felt compelled to sort out the complex picture Ben presented of himself.

"Daphne and Ella—they're six." He cleared his throat. "I couldn't know what having you here would mean for them. I hope you're not offended, but that's how it had to be. They're with Annie."

Annie—she must have been the neighbor. The older woman who had visited earlier.

"It's totally understandable. You can't know what kind of danger bringing a Conditioned into your home would mean."

Even though it was true, the thought that Ben shared the feelings of most of the world stuck in her gut. She pushed it away. It was important information to have.

Always better to know when she was surrounded by real hate versus minor curiosity. She would have put Ben in the latter category. No matter. She'd been wrong before.

"If I'd known you were so nice, I would have let them come home."

She wasn't sure whether he meant it or was being polite. Either way, it warranted a response from her. "Thank you for saying that. It's not necessary. I'm actually good with children. My job in Crescent is to help in the nursery."

"The nursery? I thought they were no longer letting you guys have children."

"Madame never let us have children." Seven turned her attention back to the wall. "The nursery is where the babies who are brought to us are kept. It's where I was raised. You were right to keep them away, sir. What I'm about to do... it scares adults. Probably best for your kids never to see it."

He paused for a second. "What are you going to do?"

"Find your ghost."

It took only seconds for Seven to transition her gaze into the netherworld that was the energy field where ghosts—or energy signatures, as she thought of them—were found. When she'd been a child, it had happened as easily as breathing, but now she controlled the pull into that dimension and had to work at opening it up.

When she was sure she was fully integrated, she turned to regard Ben. She wanted him to see what she looked like so he wouldn't freak out later when there would be people around. Most people screamed when they saw her. She'd never seen herself, but she knew what he would witness. Her eyes—the entirety of them—had turned completely black. They were her demon eyes, the sign to the world that she was cursed beyond redemption.

THREE

Ben reached out and grabbed the side of Seven's face. He wasn't even aware he was going to do it until he had. It was as if his hand had a mind of its own. She had the most incredible blue eyes, and now they were blacker than the night sky when he couldn't see any stars. He should have been afraid, except he wasn't. Not at all.

He was drawn to them like moths to the buzzing light he hung on his porch to keep the mosquitoes away. The moth shouldn't fly into that light; it was the wrong bug. All the same, the bug would die, even though it shouldn't be there at all.

There was no way he should have been reacting this way to this woman and her eyes that changed from sky-blue to black in an instant.

"You're not screaming or running from the room."

No, he was touching her, embracing her cheek with his hand. Did she not notice his skin on her skin?

"I'm not frightened."

She raised a strawberry-blonde eyebrow. "You're not?"

"I've never seen anything like it. But I'm not afraid."

Seven blinked a few times without speaking. "Are you touching me?"

"Can't you feel it?" His instinct was to drop his hand from her face, but he stayed where he was. It was like when one of the girls fell down and hurt themselves. He had to hold onto them until he'd reassured himself that they were fine, and maybe a few moments past that, too, just for safe measure. He couldn't hold Seven—had no business wanting to—but he was touching her just the same.

"It's hard for me to feel things when I'm like this. It's like living in two different worlds. In a second, when I focus, I won't be able to speak to you at all."

He didn't like the thought of that. What if something happened? Like the kitchen spontaneously caught on fire. He shook his head. What the hell was wrong with him? His brother had presumably called in a huge favor to get this woman here. He needed to let her do her job. Where had all these protective instincts come from? She was nothing to him.

As he dropped his hand to his side, he moved a few feet away from her. "By all means, do what you need to do."

In two strides, he had made it to the counter. What he needed was to be busy. His hands needed a task to keep his mind where it was supposed to be. Reaching over, he grabbed the cup Annie had left on the counter earlier. There was a little of the lemonade she'd made left inside. He took a long sip from the cup, letting the beverage take his mind—sort of—off what was happening.

"There's nothing there."

Hearing her voice, he nearly choked. As he turned around, he set his cup down on the counter. The clink of the cup hitting the granite was the only sound in the room.

She was two shades whiter than the pale shade she'd been before.

Instinct drove him forward. Before she even swayed, he knew she would fall. She'd half-collapsed onto the floor before he grabbed her arm, hauling her against him.

"Sorry." Her voice was barely a whisper, and her eyes, once again blue, were unfocused.

He swept her into his arms and carried her over to the couch. She weighed almost nothing, and she wasn't a short woman. It was hard to tell exactly what she looked like under her orange jumpsuit, but he now suspected she wasn't properly fed.

"Does it take this much out of you every time you do it?"

"No." She raised a dainty hand to rub at her eyes. "I was already tired. I shouldn't have attempted it. I wanted to give you the services you're entitled to. I don't want to fail at this job. Not right before my death."

His stomach turned at the thought. She didn't know how old she was, but in his mind she couldn't be more than thirty, and maybe she was even younger.

"I don't want you doing anything that might cause you pain. I'm responsible for your welfare."

She nodded, her blue eyes sad as they looked at him. "Okay, sir."

"Ben. Please call me Ben."

"I can't do that."

He brushed her hair out of her eyes. "You can. What can I get you? Water? Food?"

"I know it's very early, but I really need some sleep. I'd rather save my meal for tomorrow, if that's okay?"

His heart broke every time she spoke about her expectations. "Seven, listen to me. While you're here, I'm going to feed you three meals a day. Maybe a snack, too, if you want one. I'm in charge, right? You have to do what I tell you, and I'm informing you that despite what Madame says, you will eat a lot here."

The smallest smile formed on her lips. "Really? I don't want you to get into trouble."

He helped her to sit up, feeling sorry he had to let her go at all. She was a young woman—and he didn't care who disagreed, she was, in fact, a woman and not an *it*—and she was in his home. Ben was responsible for her wellbeing. God help anyone who told him how he was going to care for someone who lived within his walls. No one would abuse her here.

"I won't get into trouble. I'm a lawyer. You can trust me to know what I can do within the law." He stood up. "You're welcome to go to bed. I'd also be glad to feed you."

"Where should I sleep?" She looked down at the floor and he followed her gaze. Suddenly, he understood what she was thinking.

"Not on the floor. No way." He extended his hand and was relieved when she took it. "We have beds in this house. You'll use one."

"Thank you."

The simplicity of her gratitude made him stop in his tracks. Who might this woman have been if she hadn't been Conditioned? The thought made him remember something else. "You said there was nothing there?"

She nodded. "That's right. No ghosts. No leftover energy."

He took her arm to lead her up the stairs. She smelled fantastic, like cherries and coffee beans. He wondered where she'd picked up those scents. In other circumstances, he would have closed his eyes and drowned in the aroma for a few moments. Not since Dana had a woman's mere presence affected him like this. If he wasn't careful, he was going to have to adjust his pants.

Sex was the last thing he should have been thinking about.

He made himself move again, taking her with him toward the stairs. "You keep talking about energy."

"That's what ghosts are—leftover energy. Something the person left behind."

"Oh." His mind whirled. Apparently, whatever it was Seven saw, it wasn't a floating spirit waiting to make amends for wrongs done to them or by them in their lifetime. "So how can you tell who they are?"

"That's a complicated question."

The lawyer in him hated that answer. "That's vague... deliberately, yes?"

She smiled as she made a noise that was somewhere in between a laugh and a groan. "Most of the time when I don't answer questions, it's because I have found that people don't want to know the real response. They think they do, but the reality of it keeps them up at night."

"Don't consider me most people. I have an obsession with the truth. I need it beyond almost anything else."

It had driven his brother crazy when they'd been children. Gene wanted to exist in the shadows, never to be bothered with the total truth of anything. Maybe that was why Ben had gone so far to the other side of the issue. He hated lies, detested them. Not answering was akin to a lie for him.

"I take the energy inside me and, for one moment, I can see who the energy once belonged to, who they once were."

They climbed the stairs slowly. He could feel her

exhaustion ripple through her body. Under his grasp, her bones felt fragile. "How about I get you some milk?"

He cringed as the words left his mouth. She wasn't one of his girls. There probably wasn't any way he could feed her problems out of her. A multi-vitamin wasn't going to fuel a change in her health.

"I'm not thirsty, thank you."

"You're welcome." Frustration slammed through his insides. He wanted to fix this, damn it. "Please stop thanking me."

"Okay."

She was too easy, too accepting of all that went on around her. They reached the top of the stairs, and she sagged against him. He wasn't sure he'd ever been around anyone who was so tired before. He bent over slightly, scooping her into his arms.

Seven didn't complain or even comment, other than a murmur of something he couldn't make out. Her eyes were open, giving him the chance to gaze into them, but he suspected she couldn't really see him.

The guest room was right at the top of the stairs. With one hand, he managed to finagle the door open. In two strides, he'd reached the bed. He laid her down upon it gently.

She smiled up at him. How was it that despite his knowing her for only a little while, she'd managed to thaw out his emotions and break his heart at the same time?

"This is a very nice room."

He sat down on the edge of the bed. "Your bathroom is right there." He pointed at the closed door. "Tomorrow, I'll see about getting you some clothes."

"I'm not supposed to wear anything but this."

He touched the ugly, orange jumpsuit that made her

look as if she'd committed some kind of felony. Technically, she had. At birth.

"What did I say about what would happen while you're in my house?"

She smiled and pulled the pillow up against her until she embraced it as if it were a teddy bear. "Your house, your rules."

"Exactly. Get some sleep. I'll see you in the morning."

He left the room and crossed the threshold into the hall. Closing the door behind him, he stood for a moment, listening for any sound within the bedroom. Silence filled the hall, and when he eventually felt foolish, he made his way back down the stairs.

Not wanting to dwell too long on the reasons why he was doing so, he hurried into his office. At first, when Dana had been alive, he'd resisted the idea of having a space to work in at home. He spent so much time in the office. When he was home, he wanted to be home. But his wife had thought it would be better if he didn't have to take job-related phone calls in the same room where screaming toddlers played. She'd been right, of course. After she'd died, and he hadn't been able to go to the office as much, it had been a gift to have the space at home to get things done. At least his daughters got to see him.

He sat down on his leather chair and picked up the phone. Before he did anything else, Ben needed to check on his little ladies, who had to have been freaked out that they hadn't come home from school today but instead, were staying at Annie's.

Quickly, he dialed Annie's number. She picked up on the first ring. "Has something bad happened with *it*?"

"It?" He opened his desk drawer, his mind already moving to his next task.

His favorite pen sat in its assigned spot, and he pulled it out.

"The Conditioned in your house."

"She's not an *it*. She's a she. That's why I couldn't understand what you meant." He knew he was opening up a can of worms by speaking his mind to Annie. Still, he couldn't seem to help himself. How could she have been in the room with Seven and still refer to her as an *it*? Annie had been the one to point out that Seven was a "baby," although there was nothing about Seven that said baby to Ben.

Annie was silent on the other end of the phone. He closed his eyes. The woman was currently watching over the two most important people in his life. Why couldn't he control his damn mouth?

"I have to keep reminding myself, Ben, that the young woman who walked through your door is dangerous. A means to an end, as they say." He could hear the tightness in her voice.

"Ms. Annie, you'll have to take my word on this, but Seven is more a danger to herself than she is to anyone else." He was certain about that. She took the ghost energy into herself? How the hell did that work? "Now, how are things going on over there with y'all?"

Annie sighed. "I hope you're right. I hope we're all not being naïve about *her*." Ben didn't miss the way she enunciated "her," and it made him roll his eyes. "Your girls are delightful, as always. They were both a little worked up about why they weren't going home. Daphne, in particular, was worried something bad had happened to you. I've reassured them as best I can, and they're reading books with Hugh right now as we speak."

Ben looked at the clock. It was four-thirty in the afternoon, which meant that Annie had performed a miracle if the girls weren't begging to watch cartoons or eat ice cream. He smiled at the thought. "I hate to interrupt, but can I speak to them, please?"

"Absolutely. You just hold on a second, dear."

He leaned back in his chair. If Daphne worried, then Ella worried, too. Daphne was just the more vocal of the two of them. Ella would internalize her pain until she couldn't take it anymore and threw up. He'd gotten to know their coping mechanisms very well in their brief six years on the planet.

"Daddy?" Daphne's voice came onto the line.

He could hear the concern radiating in her high-pitched, little-girl voice that always made him smile. "Hiya, bébé, ask Ms. Annie to put the speaker phone on so I can talk to both of you at the same time."

In the background, he could hear Daphne do as he asked. Seconds later, both Daphne and Ella were saying hello again.

Ben grinned. They spoke in unison so frequently that sometimes he wondered if they even noticed.

"How are my princesses?"

"Daddy?" Daphne's voice sounded determined. "Why aren't we at home?"

"Daddy has someone over tonight, princess, talking about grown-up things, and Ms. Annie thought you might like to have a visit with her."

He hoped that would suffice as an answer even as he doubted it would. His girls were as sharp as tacks, as their mother had been. They didn't miss a trick.

"Someone is staying at the house?" Ella piped in.

"Yes. Someone Daddy is working on a project with."

Ella clicked her tongue. "Then you need us to come

home and help take care of him. Someone needs to see to the guest."

He covered his mouth to keep from laughing. Ella was serious, and she wouldn't take well to being mocked even if his amusement fell into the "I'm amused because you're too cute for words" category. She didn't like to be the object of anyone's jokes.

When he could speak, he did. "I appreciate the offer, but Daddy has it under control this time."

They spoke in unison. "Are you sure?"

"I'm sure." He picked up his pen, twirling it through his fingers.

"Will we see you tomorrow?" It was Daphne's turn to talk again.

"It's Saturday tomorrow, sweet pea. You'll see me. You can come home in the morning." *Yes,* he silently agreed with his statement. If Seven didn't murder him in his bed tonight, he would feel confident in knowing his instincts had been correct. She was safe, and his children could be around her. He'd bet money she was trustworthy.

"Okay, Daddy—we'll be over first thing in the morning."

They said their goodnights, and he smiled. It would be hours until they went to bed. Annie and Hugh would need the patience of saints to wrangle them down on a Friday night. His girls had a way of getting what they wanted out of unsuspecting adults.

In the meantime, his brain itched to become an expert on Conditioned law. He'd never paid that much attention to the subject before. It wasn't as if there were any contracts drawn up for the Conditioned. As far as he understood it, they didn't have any rights to speak of, which was surprising in Louisiana. Whereas the rest of the country existed under one legal system, Louisiana had stuck with its Napoleonic code.

In some ways it was antiquated, but in others it granted more rights to people than the other state laws did. When he'd studied at Tulane, it had only been the students planning to remain in Louisiana for their careers who had bothered with taking the code classes. He'd been born in New Orleans and meant to spend the rest of his days living within its city limits, even if he had to prepare to evacuate for impending hurricanes.

He'd come back and do it all over, again and again.

But he hadn't ever cracked a book to read about the rights of the Conditioned. He hadn't needed to—it wasn't on the bar exam. Civil Rights wasn't his field, and in any case, he doubted that too many lawyers were spending any time on the Conditioned. Especially not after Safe Dawn had burned to the ground last year. The idea of dealing with the kind of people who could kill you with only their thoughts didn't make anyone rest easy.

Booting up his computer, he opened his LexisNexis database and began his search. It wouldn't be easy. It never was. While television showed attorneys having big courtroom dramas, most of his work was done this way—sitting in front of a computer reading case law, preparing briefs and harassing associates to get what he needed.

Today, he wouldn't be asking anyone for any help. In fact, he'd prefer it if no one knew he'd spent any time doing this. They might think he'd lost his mind. Maybe he had.

He started to read. It wasn't easy. Half the cases had been written in the late 1980s, early 1990s. Almost no one had tried a case for the Conditioned in nearly twenty years. After the Safe Dawn fiasco, the President had signed into law some Committee recommendations that tightened

restrictions. That was all. No one had challenged the constitutionality of it, and he doubted they would.

A strange set of occurrences had started taking place
around 40 years ago. Children born with weird abilities—
psychic phenomena, as they'd been called then—had
screwed up some serious political negotiations. Then there
had been deaths. One boy had accidentally set his father on
fire. The government had finally intervened and the word
"Conditioned" had been coined. Ultimately, families had
been given no choice but to turn their Conditioned children
over to the government, where they were institutionalized
for both their own and the general public's safety. Occasionally a Conditioned who had abilities—like Seven—
could be sent out to serve the interests of those who could
afford to pay the Institutions for their use. If anyone tried to
resist these circumstances, a special Conditioned police
force, the Fury, was supposedly sent out to handle them. Of
course, it wasn't entirely clear whether the Fury really
existed.

Hours felt like minutes as he lost himself in statutes he'd
never read before. The sun went down outside his office
window, and he turned on another light so he could
continue reading. If he had his facts correct—and he had no
reason to doubt himself—then the law stated that Seven
should be put to death at forty years old. This was a new
requirement, one that had been put in place since Addison
Wade, granddaughter of a wealthy industrialist, had run off
with a Conditioned man named Spencer Lewis. The irony
was double. Not only was her grandfather a member of the
Committee that ran the Institutions, Addison Wade was,
herself, Conditioned, and that fact had been hidden from
all. Somehow, Addison Wade and Spencer Lewis had
managed to burn down an Institution in their escape, and

authorities still hadn't gotten all the missing Conditioned back.

But kill them all at forty? That didn't make any sense. The details of exactly why this was thought to be necessary were vague at best. Besides, there was no way Seven was ten years older than him, or anywhere near forty. He bit down on his bottom lip. If the statutes had been followed, she should have been made barren at the age of twenty. Leaning back in his chair, he closed his eyes.

Had that happened to her? "Sir?"

His eyes shot open. Still wearing the orange jumpsuit and leaning against the door of his office, Seven waited for him to acknowledge her. If it was possible, and apparently it was, she was even more beautiful than she'd been earlier. There was something ethereal about her, as if she'd been dropped from Heaven into his hallway. It must have been the lack of the dark circles under her eyes.

"How long were you standing there?" He stretched his arms over his head, wishing he could miraculously work the kinks out of his neck. "I get kind of engrossed when I'm working."

"Not long. I didn't expect to find you awake."

"Why?" His eyes sought the clock on the wall. It was midnight? He stood up. "I guess I lost track of time. What are you doing up?"

"I get about five hours of sleep a night, so I've had more than my allotted amount now. I decided to believe you that it was fine for me to eat." She looked down at the floor. "Then I saw your light on, and I thought maybe I could cook you something. A late-night something."

She was vulnerable in that moment. He wanted to pull her in his arms and...

And what? He sighed. What could he possibly do for

her? He couldn't even find a legal way—yet—to keep her from dying.

"I didn't eat dinner. You cook?"

Her head jolted up, her eyes bright and excited. "I can. Really well."

He turned off his computer monitor. No more of that tonight. He needed to eat and go to bed. Ben knew he'd been kidding himself. Solving major life-and-death problems was not his domain, no matter how much he wished it could be.

Feeling selfish, he let himself touch her arm. "You remember where the kitchen is?"

FOUR

More awake than she'd been earlier, Seven could admit to herself what she'd suspected. Ben was amazingly handsome, like a man on the cover of some of the books the female guards read. She couldn't read—it was against the rules at Crescent—but she'd always imagined those stories were great romances filled with wonder and adventure, something other than the horrors filling her head. Regular people didn't live like she had to, that much she understood. So why would they read books that were anything but light and fluffy love stories? That's all she would read if she were given the choice. People who weren't Conditioned got to be in love.

Ben reminded her of those men on those covers. She smiled at the thought. Meeting him at this stage of her life was a gift she hadn't thought she would have.

"What are you smiling about?"

His voice sounded inquisitive, not harsh, and she was actually tempted to tell him. But that might have gotten her thrown out of the house before her job was done, and she couldn't have that. Completion of the task at hand was pivotal to her wellbeing right now.

"I'm not sure I could explain it."

Usually people—non-Conditioned people—left her alone when she said that. They really didn't want to know the workings of the Conditioned mind.

Ben sat down on a stool in his kitchen. "I'm really smart. Try me."

Was that amusement in his eyes? She wasn't sure. "I was thinking about what a nice place I've ended up in for my last job."

Seven didn't have to feel terrible about that little fib. Ben probably didn't want to hear she'd developed a crush on him.

This spared them both the embarrassment.

"Don't ever lie for a living." He tapped his hands on the counter. "I won't push you to tell me. Your thoughts are your own. We're all entitled to that."

"Not in Crescent." She gasped as she realized what she'd said. At this stage in her life, she knew better than to talk about

Crescent to people outside its walls. "I could make pancakes."

"I have a mix." He jumped off the stool and walked into the pantry, pulling out a box. "I can make it for you."

She shook her head. "No, let me."

He nodded, and she smiled. She liked to cook, not that she was given much opportunity to use her minuscule skills in the kitchen. But she had made pancakes before for the children at Crescent, under the watchful eyes of the guards, of course.

"I can't read. Can I assume the directions on the box are the same as the ones I've used in the past? The guards taught those of us not deemed a threat to cook some basic things. But by memory not by a recipe."

Ben was silent, and she cursed herself for admitting she was illiterate. It wasn't exactly her fault. It went against the rules at Crescent for the Conditioned to learn. Madame had made it forbidden to teach them.

He took the box from her. "I'll read it aloud to you."

"I think it's the same as what I've done before." She stared at the package. The woman looked the same as the one who had been on the cover of the boxes at Crescent. "If you see me doing something wrong, just stop me. Would that be okay?"

Ben leaned against the counter, staring at her. His gaze heated her insides, and a melting sensation she was unaccustomed to spread throughout her body. Her cheeks warmed up, and she was sure he would be able to see their red hue. That was the problem with being a redhead—you could never really hide your feelings.

"I'm sorry." She looked down at the counter. There was no choice; she had to say something to address what had happened. "I think I'm reacting to you this way because I've reached the end, and I'm not entirely in control of myself. Not as well as I should be, anyway."

Ben walked toward her. "I'm the one staring at you, Seven."

He brushed her hair off her shoulder, and she shivered. As his hand caressed the side of her face, she met his dark gaze and knew she was lost. In the past, she'd always managed not to fall in love with anyone. She'd gotten good at protecting herself from that level of exposure. No one had tempted her to take that risk.

In a few measly hours together, Ben had managed to

break down all her defenses so that her silly heart had let him inside.

His hands were rough. She closed her eyes and decided that for one second she would pretend she was just a girl letting a man flirt with her in the middle of the night.

"I keep trying to tell myself that you're off limits to me." Ben's voice sounded hoarse.

She opened her eyes to regard him. His hair was disheveled. The blue-and-white tie he wore fell loose around his collar.

"I spent the better part of tonight trying to learn about Conditioned law. It basically amounts to one legislative document after another talking about how you are all monsters." He traced the side of her face. "You seem like a woman to me. That's all. A beautiful, sensitive, abused woman who smells like coffee beans."

His mouth was right above hers. She could feel the heat from his body radiating into hers. Ben was the sun, and for just a moment, she was going to let him heat her cold soul.

The sharp pain on the back of her neck made her stagger, and she fell forward into his arms.

"Seven?" He shouted her name as he caught her. "What's wrong? I'm sorry. I shouldn't have said those things..."

Gasping as she tried to catch her breath, she held tight to his shirt. "There's something here, in the room with us."

It didn't usually happen like this. She closed her eyes and willed the pain to stop. Most of the time she couldn't tell when negative "ghost" energy existed in a room. It was a faint sense of something being off. Only once—in a very dark and dangerous place—had she ever felt something like this. She'd been fifteen at the time and on her second assignment.

It had made her catatonic for a week. But she was stronger now. She didn't have to go down like an amateur. Somehow, she would control it. On her last assignment, she would prove she could handle really dark energy, even in an onslaught like this.

"Seven?" Ben shook her slightly, and she realized she'd dug her fingers through his shirt into his skin.

She gasped as she let go. "I'm sorry I hurt you."

He shook his head, scooping her up in his arms. "You didn't. I'm worried about you. What's wrong? Negative energy?"

"Something came into the room." She needed to breathe, and forced herself to take three deep breaths, in through her nose, out through her mouth. "It's overwhelming me."

With a determined gait, he was across the room, taking her with him to the living room and out of the kitchen. He placed her gently on the couch and sat down next to her. "What can I do to help?"

His touch made a huge difference. She didn't want him to stop. It kept her there, kept her from going in after the energy without preparing herself.

"I'm going to have to go see what this is. It shouldn't be like this." She took another deep breath. "Last time it was this bad I kind of went away somewhere for a while. Can I ask a favor?"

His eyes were huge. "Anything."

She actually believed him. He said things to her that no one else ever had. It made her feel as though she might be able to handle this.

"Hold my hand. I need to feel something keeping me here. I can't allow myself to get too deep into this, not while I'm so vulnerable."

He squeezed her hand, and she wanted to melt into the situation. "I won't go anywhere. I won't let you disappear."

Seven knew that was unrealistic. If she got lost in the energy, there wasn't a thing Ben could do to bring her back, no matter his best intentions. Still, she appreciated his wanting to help her. No one had ever offered before. The last time this had happened, she'd woken up in Crescent with no memory of what had occurred between the time she'd chased the ghost energy and the second her eyes had opened.

She couldn't allow that to happen this time. They'd never let her wake up again, and that would mean she'd failed in her plan to go out on such a positive note that they had to let her into Heaven, even with her dark soul. "I'm going to go under and see what this thing is."

Ben squeezed her hand. "I'll be right here waiting for you."

She hoped that was true more than she could ever admit. It would be nice to have someone waiting for her when she got through with her task, someone who would care about what had happened to her during the time when she had to be alone.

Her arms tingled as goosebumps appeared on her sensitized skin. It always hurt to transition, but today it felt particularly painful. She supposed she shouldn't have been surprised, considering the amount of dark energy pulsating in the room. It wasn't odd that Ben's clock had fallen over, not if it had been hit with a force like the one assaulting her right now.

As she took a few deep breaths, she let her mind travel into the part of the world that very few would ever see. She blinked, letting her eyes adjust to the change in her surroundings. Everything around her looked darker, the shadow version of what existed in the "real" world. The couch that she and Ben sat on looked less vibrant. Instead of being a chocolate brown, it was a dull, lifeless shade that wouldn't inspire anyone to buy it.

The only things that looked interesting in this space were the energies people left behind when they died. She had heard that some Conditioned people could actually see the energy of the living, too. They were called Locators, because they could use that energy to find the missing. But that ability had never been her gift. Only the signatures of the departed appeared to her.

Seven gasped as she looked around. Earlier, she had scanned the room and it had been empty. Not one bit of energy to see. Now it was filled with colors from ghost energy. Blues, purples and reds danced and exploded around her. She stood up to move closer to the source. She knew Ben would be concerned on the other end about what was happening, and she wished she could explain it.

She had no memory of what had happened to her the last time she'd been around this much intensity. Energy signatures usually looked like small dots of light floating in the air. She could breathe deeply, take them inside her, and then send them on to wherever it was they should go. But this? She wasn't sure she could handle this—not even on her strongest day. It was as if she had stepped into an energy storm that wanted nothing more than to destroy her.

She shook her head. No, that wasn't true. Ghost energy wasn't personal. It was leftover "stuff" that the dead hadn't taken with them. It had nothing to do with her whatsoever. The fact that she was there to witness and handle it was nothing more than a simple twist of fate. The energy didn't have thoughts. It didn't care if she was there or not there.

Steeling herself, she breathed in a little bit of the orange light just to see what it would feel like. Her lungs burned, but not much worse than they usually did when she had to use her powers to disperse ghost light. If it was all like that, then she could absorb it and survive the experience.

Nothing could have prepared her for what happened next. The lights in the room exploded in front of her like the pictures of fireworks she'd seen on the walls of Madame's office. Not even seconds later, they boomed a deafening sound that made her fall to her knees as her hands instinctively reached to cover her ears. The whole room shook.

Oh God, what's happening?

Her mind felt disjointed, and she tried to convince herself that she wasn't under attack. It wasn't working. This felt personal, even if it shouldn't. Colors swirled in front of her eyes, and she knew she would faint. This was exactly what had happened to her the last time she'd seen this much power in one room. She hadn't remembered it, had blocked out the experience, but going through it again brought it all back to the front of her mind.

Seven couldn't let herself lose consciousness in the shadow dimension. She wanted to be able to open her eyes to sunlight again. When Madame put her down, her last memories shouldn't be of the place that was a constant reminder of her own darkness.

Forcing the shift of consciousness back to the real world, Seven panted hard breaths as she tried to regain control of herself. Immediately, she became aware that she was in Ben's lap. Well, her head was, anyway. The rest of her body sprawled out on the floor. He ran his hands slowly through her hair.

"There you are." Relief sounded in his voice. She tried to sit up, and he stopped her, holding his hands on her shoulders. "Don't move just yet. I have to imagine something really bad happened in there?"

She swallowed, wishing the room would stop spinning. "How did you know?"

She wasn't the type who wept with strong emotions, but if she had been, she would have expressed how fantastic it was that she'd made it out of the shadows fully conscious.

"I knew because every mirror in the house seems to have exploded, and you screamed like you were being murdered."

She gasped. *Every mirror exploded?* Now, she needed to sit up.

"Easy." His voice sounded authoritative, and she could easily imagine him as one of the guards in Crescent, ordering everyone around. Except that where they were frightening, he was kind. Still, she'd guess that people listened to him when he spoke.

"I need to see what happened here." She blinked to try to stop the spins. "Nothing I did in there should have affected anything out here."

Or at least it never had in the past. Then again, this ghost energy had been strong enough to knock over clocks and move through houses.

"Well, it did. I was really worried you weren't coming back."

She blinked a couple of times as she let his words travel through her soul. He had worried. Hoping she could hide the emotion in her voice, she finally spoke. "Thank you. So was I. Can you please help me sit up?"

"Sure."

He moved his hand behind her neck and pulled her into a sitting position. Before she knew what was happening, she was sitting upright in his lap. In general, embracing was a bad idea for the Conditioned. Non-Conditioned didn't like to touch Conditioned people. The guards could touch them. But no one wanted that, for a number of reasons.

Seven shook her head. "That was a rough one."

Once upright, she felt as if the room straightened itself and ceased its relentless spin. Well, that would teach her to touch bright-orange energy. It really had felt as if the signatures had been out to get her. That was impossible, but when they'd exploded, it had been all she'd been able to think. Seven bit down on her fingernail, a disgusting habit Madame had beaten out of her fifteen years earlier.

Maybe she was simply regressing on all levels.

"Want to tell me what happened?"

She looked up to meet his gaze. Sitting on his lap, she could smell the scent of safety she could feel coming off his body—the fragrance was like cinnamon but different. Maybe she should have known what those aromas were, but she didn't. He just smelled as if she could finally take a deep breath around him.

"What do you smell like? I don't know those scents."

Her question made him grin. The heaviness she'd noticed, the constant burden in the dark depths of his eyes, relented a little. After a second, he started to laugh.

It was a small sound that quickly developed into downright hysterical bursts.

Seven felt her skin heat up to the point that it was actually painful. She'd never been so embarrassed in her life. What had she been thinking, getting so personal?

She'd made him lose his mind.

"I'm sorry, sir. I never should have asked you that. Please, forgive me."

"Seven." He grabbed her cheeks in his hands. "I'm not upset. I'm... well, delighted with you. Sometimes you say things that just make me so downright happy with your lack of a hidden agenda and your innocence, when you should be so completely guarded."

Seven wished she could look down, but his hands held her face in place. "I know better than to ask something like that. I guess I'm a little out of it because of what just happened."

His face fell into the serious expression she was used to seeing.

"Seven, I have to ask you something."

She gulped. "Okay."

"Do I smell bad?"

"What?" Now she wanted to throw up. "No, I didn't mean that. Not at all. I..."

He interrupted her. "I'm teasing you, that's all. I'm just having fun."

The laughter started again, and after a second, she joined him. Laughter bubbled inside her until tears sprang from her eyes. He pulled her even closer until her head rested against his chest; his heaving laughter fed hers.

"Sandalwood."

She pulled back to look at him. "I'm sorry, I don't know what you just said."

"I bought some soap from a fundraising activity at the girls' school. I don't really like scents, but this I thought smelled okay."

He pulled up his shirt to sniff it. "Is it too much? Kind of girly?"

"No." She would never call anything about Ben girly. "I really like it." She sniffed again. "It's called sandalwood?"

"That's right. It comes from a specific type of tree with the same name."

She smiled. "I like it."

"Me, too." He ran his hands through her hair. "What happened to you? Can I assume you took care of it? That's why everything exploded?"

She sighed. It would have been nice to be able to tell him she'd done that. "No, I'm afraid it exploded around me. I barely touched it. But, Ben, it's serious stuff. In my life, I've only seen it that bad once before."

"Did it hurt you?" His tone told her he hated the idea.

"The last time it was so intense I went into a coma for a week. This time it hurt but not as devastatingly as the first time. That was a real accomplishment for me."

Ben moved her gently off his lap before he stood up. As he stared down at her, his eyes were hard. "I'm calling the Institution and having you go home. I won't have you hurt working on this."

Her heart pounded hard as she jumped up. "No, please don't do that."

"I can't live with it if you're harmed because you're doing this for me. You have a number of years left, and I'll work on getting that stopped for you. But, I can't let you just die here instead."

She grabbed his arm. It was absolutely pivotal that he understood what was at stake here. "I'm going home to die, Ben. I need to do this first. I must prove to God that I did good things here on Earth."

His silence hung between them for long moments before he spoke. "I'm more than aware of what's going to happen to you. I spent the whole night reading Conditioned law."

She wanted to cry, to weep with frustration. "Did you find anything that might help?"

He shook his head. "No."

"I don't have rights. I'm not a person. I just need to get

this done. I want to achieve something spectacular before I go." And she wanted to do it for him. She wanted to make his home safe for the beautiful little girls who were pictured, smiling, all over his walls. "Let me do this. I'll find a way."

Ben didn't say yes to her request, but he didn't say no. He took her hand and led her back to the kitchen.

"Make yourself something to eat while I clean up the mess of all the mirrors. It's a good thing I don't believe in bad luck."

Seven knew there was a lot of bad luck out there, more than most people could ever digest. But she could handle it —because meeting Ben and coming to his home was the good variety. She would make sure it was. There was no other choice.

FIVE

Ben hadn't slept a wink all night, not that he'd tried. He took a swig of his way-too-bitter-even-for-chicory coffee and sighed. Seven had gone to bed four hours earlier, and he hoped she rested well, even though she'd said she wouldn't be able to sleep anymore. She had looked wiped out. As for him, he wasn't sure he even wanted to imagine what his dreams would look like in the future. Exploding glass, screaming, and Seven so pale he'd been sure she would die in his arms.

He rubbed his eyes. They burned from fatigue. Truth was, he had no idea what he was going to do. If he let Seven stay there and combat the ghosts, then it was likely he'd doom her to injury or, God forbid, death. If he sent her home, she would definitely die. Of course, if he let her stay and she succeeded without hurting herself, she would go home to die anyway. There wasn't a damn thing he could do about that, and that fact made him angrier than he could remember being in a long time.

He picked up his cell phone. For the second day in a row, he started his morning with a phone call to Eugene.

His brother might not be able to fix anything that was going on, but Ben could at least vent to him without having to worry about getting arrested for talking inappropriately about helping the Conditioned. His brother would never turn him in to the police. Not unless he wanted Ben to report everything he knew Eugene had done.

They might have had a screwed-up family relationship, but it worked for them.

His brother picked up on the first ring. "How do you like your Conditioned girl?"

Although their father had spoken with little in the way of a New Orleans accent, Eugene had picked up a strong one over the years, seemingly by choice. Ben didn't know whether he sounded that way or not. Eugene's twang was one of the things that amused him about his brother, rather than some of his other affectations, which made him crazy.

"She's going to be put to death." It was first thing in the morning, and he already had a migraine forming. "You sent a woman to my house who is going to be executed right after she leaves."

Eugene was silent on the other end of the phone. Ben wondered if he'd shocked his older brother into a lack of speech for the first time in his life.

"Don't you go and get involved in this, Benedicte. You needed help. I got you help. The girls will be better off without whatever is going on at your house. Other than that, stay out of Institution business. Nothing good can come of you getting involved."

Ben's leg shook. It was a nervous habit he hadn't ever really managed to rid himself of, which was why it was a good thing that he rarely got anxious enough for it to occur. Now he was too tired to care.

"It's too late, Eugene." He sighed. "I'm involved. She's a

sweet young woman. *Young* being the key word of that sentence. They're not supposed to be killed so early, and I'm starting to think that if I'd ever thought about the fact that they get murdered at all, I would have objected before now."

He hoped he would have. He liked to think he was the kind of person who would have said something.

"To whom would you have objected?"

Ben could hear his brother inhale on his cigarette. It was a sucking sound; a kind of *woop-woop*. Sometimes he wondered if, someday, he'd have to help his brother hook up an oxygen machine. Of course, they could all drown in a hurricane any day, too, so who really knew what was going to happen? God, when had he become so fatalistic? This whole problem with the ghosts had brought up all kinds of issues for him.

"I don't know." He didn't like his brother challenging his moral indignation. It made him feel ineffective. "Someone."

"Do yourself a favor, okay? Use the girl. Let her do her job. Send her away. Forget about her."

There was a click as Eugene hung up the phone. Ben stared at it as if it were a foreign object. Had Gene just hung up on him? He wanted to dial him back and tell him what he thought of his rude behavior.

Turning to the left, he saw the picture of Dana that sat on his desk. She was smiling, holding both the girls on her knees. They'd been tiny, barely over a year old and so petite. Half him and half her. Lately, Dana had become a distant memory to him. For the first years after her death, he'd lain up at night, missing her with a pain he hadn't thought he could endure. Now he could think of her and smile, even as his love for her became something he remembered with quiet joy—different from feeling the pain of its absence every second of every day, as though he'd lost a limb.

The girls would always remind him of her, but he knew there was life to be lived. She would have wanted that—had told him as much before she'd died—and he wanted to give the girls a complete existence, not one lost to endless grief. Even so, what the hell was he doing spending his night thinking about a Conditioned woman? Why bring her into their lives? Maybe he should have found another way.

The front door opened and slammed closed. The sound, so unexpected, jarred him out of his stupor of self-doubt.

"Hello."

He heard his daughter Daphne's voice. Who was she talking to, and what was she doing here so early?

"Who are you?" Ella's soft tones reached him next.

The girls were home, and the only person they'd have been speaking to like that was Seven. He stood up so fast that he knocked his chair backward into the desk. It made a loud bang before it toppled over onto the floor.

"Shit." He almost never cursed, but then again, lately he was doing all kinds of things he didn't normally do.

Within two seconds, he was out the door of his office. A million questions pushed through his mind. How would he explain Seven to the girls? How would he explain the Conditioned in general? Should he explain?

The scene he walked into made him stop short. Seven sat on the floor, each of his daughters sitting on her lap. He blinked a few times as he regarded them. His daughters weren't, in general, all that social with strangers, and yet there they were—on the floor—seated on Seven's lap.

"Hello." His voice cracked, which he hoped no one noticed. "What's going on?"

His daughters' two heads shot up to look at him. Nearly identical smiles appeared on their two dear faces.

"Daddy!"

Ella jumped up and threw her arms around him. He pulled her closer against him. Her dark-haired head barely reached his midsection, and he had to resist the urge to scoop her up as though she were a toddler and twirl her around. His heart pounded hard, as if he'd run a marathon, and he couldn't make sense of it.

"Hi, Daddy."

Daphne didn't rise from her place on Seven's lap. Instead, she scooted over until she was more fully comfortable where she sat, an option available to her now that Ella had given up her spot.

"The girls were just telling me what they like to eat for breakfast."

He scratched his head. "They were?"

Seven laughed, a small giggle. "They ran in. Daphne doesn't think Ms. Annie from next door knows they've come home. They snuck away."

Wow, the woman would be terrified when she realized they were gone. She'd be really worried.

"I'll call her so she's not concerned." He stopped. This was one of those times that required him to stretch his parenting skills. His mother would have called it a teaching moment. "Girls, it's never okay to run away. The adults around you love you very much, and we would all be terribly worried about you if you vanished. Please, promise me not to do this again."

Ella sighed, letting go of him. "Daphne said that you needed us."

He picked up the phone. Well, that was an interesting piece of information. First things first, however—he had to call and let Annie know he had the girls. His neighbor picked up on the first ring, which didn't surprise him, since he suspected she was already running through the house in a nervous frenzy.

"Hello, Ms. Annie." He leaned up against the wall as he spoke. "I have the girls."

"Oh, thank God." His neighbor spoke so fast that her words all stuck together like they were one word. "I woke up and they were gone. Ben, I'm so sorry."

"No, don't be sorry. They can be a handful. I've taken care of them their entire lives, and they still get around me." He glared at Daphne, who smiled at him, making his heart melt a little. He was going to be in so much trouble when they got older if they could already manipulate him so well.

Annie gasped. "Have they been around *the monster*?"

He didn't have to ask who "the monster" was. He was only mildly surprised that Annie had reverted to speaking of Seven that way after having called her a girl the night before.

"Yes, but everything is fine. Everyone is safe." *Except for me.*

He looked over at the scene before him. Ella seemed to be drawing Seven a picture, and Daphne was laughing. It was downright homey.

"Ben, I can come pick up the girls—"

He interrupted her. "No, I've got it." He cleared his throat. *Sort of.* "Gotta go."

After he hung up the phone and meticulously placed it back on its holder, he took a deep breath. How in the hell was he supposed to handle this?

"Daddy," Daphne called his attention as she stood up. "She needs a name. Give her one."

"She has a name, Daphne. It's Seven." He moved

toward them. There was no point in pretending he didn't know to what his daughter was referring.

Ella sighed. "Daddy, seven is a *number*. It's not a *name*."

"In her case, it's both." He opened the cabinet that had the cereal in it. Pouring milk onto pre-made food was about all he could handle at the moment. "And to be technical, it's not her full name. It's just the first number in her name."

"That's dumb."

Ben glared at Ella. "That's not nice language and not how well-brought-up young ladies speak."

"I'm not brought up yet." She grinned. "I'm six."

He couldn't help the laugh that escaped him. She sounded so much like his brother when she got argumentative. In contrast, Daphne was so serious, so much like Ben had once been.

"That's true. So don't make me punish you." He whirled around to finish pouring the milk. "What did you mean that I *needed* you, Daph?"

She laughed as she shrugged. "I don't know. It just seemed to me that you needed us to come home and help you and Seven look for the ghosts."

He whirled around, spilling some of the milk onto the floor.

"What?"

Seven's eyes were huge. "I didn't tell them anything about anything to do with that." She paused. "I swear it."

Even in his intense fury over the idea that his daughters knew anything about the Conditioned mess he was in, he could hear the quiver in her voice. She wasn't lying. She was terrified.

After nudging Daphne gently from her lap, Seven stood up from the floor. "I mean it, Ben. I would never do anything to harm a child, and these are *your* children. I wouldn't tell them anything without your permission."

She backed up a few steps, and he felt the distance between them as if she'd plunged a dagger into his heart. Was she afraid of him? No. That wasn't acceptable. Not after the night they'd spent together and the sensual, completely inappropriate thoughts he was having about her on a regular basis.

"I believe you." He stalked to her, knowing his temper was probably not helping her to feel less afraid of him. He grabbed her arm, pulling her forward until she was pressed up against him. His reasons for needing to touch her were not going to be examined while he was in the room with his daughters. "Come on, we'll all eat breakfast."

She looked at him as though he had two heads. "Breakfast? We never did end up eating those pancakes. I guess... we forgot."

"Things got a little crazy last night. We left them undone. So, yes, first meal of the day. You're familiar with it?"

When he'd made sure she was seated on the stool, he let go of her arm. He hadn't hurt her, but even he knew he'd crossed some kind of line by grabbing her as he had. Hopefully she'd gotten what he was trying to silently communicate. She wasn't to be afraid of him, and she wasn't to run away.

"I know what breakfast is."

He'd forgotten that he'd asked her that question. "Good. Then you won't have any problem eating it."

He placed one of the bowls of cereal in front of her as his daughters hopped up onto the stools next to her. They were content and had, hopefully, missed some of the undertones of aggression he'd just displayed.

After he set bowls down in front of his daughters, he grabbed a towel to clean up the mess he'd made on the floor.

"Where did you get the idea that we are looking for ghosts, Daphne?"

She answered him with her mouth full, which he would normally have corrected her for but at the moment he really didn't care about. "Because that's what you're doing."

"Yes." He had to find his patience or get a nap. Or do something to fix his temper before he really lost his mind. "But who told you about it? Was Ms. Annie discussing it around you girls?"

"No, Daddy." Daphne shrugged. "Sometimes I just know things."

The room was silent except for the sounds of crunching cereal in his daughters' mouths. Seven had stopped eating and regarded him with sad, quiet eyes. He closed his.

Ben had found that, sometimes in life, moments that were really important took a few seconds to register in his mind. He'd had a few of them. When he'd heard he was going to be a father—*surprise*—that had been one of those moments. The news that his wife had only months to live had been a less happy one. His daughter announcing that she was probably Conditioned, in a room with a Conditioned person, felt like the same sort of jarring to his soul those other times had been.

"No, you don't."

Seven's voice made him look up from the space on the tile floor that had occupied his gaze since his daughter's announcement. Had it been only seconds ago? It felt like hours.

Daphne turned in her chair, still eating. "What?"

Ella sighed. "She said you don't know things sometimes, but you do. You do."

Seven nodded, taking both girls by the hands. "Yes. That is true. It's a real... talent." She turned her head until both girls had stared at her eyes for a few seconds each. "But that is going to be our secret. You are never, ever, in a million years, going to tell anyone outside the four of us what Daphne can do. Promise me, Daphne. Promise me, Ella."

Daphne's grin had fallen. "Why are you afraid, Seven? Has someone done something to you? Daddy didn't mean to grab your arm. He only does that when he's scared, and he's never hurt us."

Seven placed her hands on Daphne's cheeks. "No, I'm not afraid of your daddy. He's a gentle soul."

He was? What was it about this woman that so consumed him? He hung on her every word as if it were gospel.

"There are some people in the world who won't like that you know things. It's important that they never know. We will all keep it our secret. Can you do that?"

"I can." Daphne looked so serious for a moment before she launched herself into Seven's arms. The woman he'd been fantasizing about hugged his daughter as though it were the most natural thing in the world.

"Good." He stood up from the floor. "And I am sorry I grabbed you, Seven."

She met his gaze over his daughter's shoulder. "That's okay. I kind of liked it."

She had? His mouth fell open, and he guessed that he looked a bit like a landed fish.

"What are we going to do today? It's *Saturday*." Ella enunciated the last word like it was important he hear it.

"I know what day it is." He laughed and leaned against the counter, amazed at how many things had happened in such a short period of time. "I need to get Ms. Seven some clothes, and then she and I need to go about finding our... ghosts."

"I can stay in what I have on," Seven said.

"No." He looked at her orange jumpsuit. He didn't think in his entire life he'd ever disliked an article of clothing as much as he hated that. "You're much taller than my wife, Dana, was, so I don't think anything I have here will fit you."

Ben had given most of what she'd had away a few months after her death. Some things he'd saved, thinking the girls might like to have some of their mother's clothing someday. Still, it wouldn't do them any good right now.

"That sounds like a good idea." Ella nodded. "Daphne and I will come with y'all."

He supposed they would have to. There was no way he could leave them here alone, and he needed Seven to come with him to try on any clothes he picked out.

That meant it was a family outing.

"Go get dressed."

The girls jumped off their seats and charged up the stairs as if they were being chased. Maybe they were. Maybe, at their age, every moment that wasn't filled with fun was somehow motivating them, making them move faster.

"Don't ever let them get her."

Seven's voice jarred him out of his thoughts and he stared at her. He didn't need to ask her what she meant.

"Do you think she'll keep her promise?"

Seven stood up. "Make her."

"What will they do to her if they catch her, Seven?"

He had almost been unable to bring himself to ask her that question. It was too real, and keeping his head in the sand about Daphne's Condition was one of his favorite activities. If he pretended all was well, and Daphne managed to keep from blurting out things in front of the wrong people, then nothing bad could happen to them. He had to believe that.

"You don't want to know, Ben." Her eyes flashed when she answered him.

"Yes, I do." He did. More than anything. He needed to hear the truth of what could happen to his baby. Of what had happened to the woman standing in front of him.

She reached out and took his hand. "Before they're done with her, she won't remember any of this." Letting go of his hand, she waved her arm to indicate the room. "She might not ever know again who you are, who Ella is. Everything about who she is now will be gone. She'll be Conditioned. That is *all* she will be."

He could hear the underlying meaning of what she said. If all Daphne would be was Conditioned, then that was all Seven thought she was as well.

"How can that be? I can't believe that. They'd never be able to kill all that is the human spirit."

She laughed, a bitter sound that seemed foreign coming from Seven's mouth.

"In the Institutions, there is no such thing. We're not human. We're Conditioned."

"You're human."

Everything about her was human and very, very female. His libido was keenly aware of just how feminine she actually was. It was all he could do not to slam her against the wall and be a much more aggressive lover than he'd ever been in his life.

"Don't let them take her. They'll turn her into me."

SIX

It was obvious to Seven that Ben was uncomfortable—well, maybe *uncomfortable* wasn't a strong enough word. He was downright horrified about what was going on around them. She wasn't sure what he'd expected. Taking her out in public was always a bit of a problem. In her bright-orange jumpsuit with the Crescent insignia on the side, everyone knew she was Conditioned.

Some people stared. Some people gaped. Some even ran away—fast. But Seven was pretty sure that being escorted out of two stores the second they walked in had been the biggest horror for Ben thus far.

They'd ceased trying to buy clothes and sat in the car, watching his girls eat ice cream. The six-year-old beauties, who were a combination of Ben and his late wife, chatted happily as strawberry ice cream dribbled all over their faces.

"Ice cream for lunch?" She tried to smile, hoping it would make Ben smile again. It was better when he was happy. His joyfulness made her feel soothed in the depths of her being.

He didn't seem to hear her as his fingers drummed

lightly on the steering wheel of his car. "It's like that movie with Julia Roberts. You know the one? Where she's the prostitute? What is that called?"

"I've never seen a movie in the Institutions. They don't let us watch television."

In the last house she'd been in, which had unfortunately ended badly, the owners had enjoyed movies where people got naked and had hard, painful-looking sex. She hadn't liked being forced to watch those at all. Ben watched movies about prostitutes? Maybe he liked those kinds of movies, too. Did everyone?

"It's called... *Pretty Woman*. Yes, that's it. My wife loved it." He grinned. "Anyway, they won't let her buy clothes in one particular store because she's a hooker."

Seven nodded, trying to find a way to follow his conversation. "And that reminds you of this because we can't seem to get inside any stores to buy me clothes?"

He smiled. "I'm making very little sense to you, aren't I?"

"As much as anyone makes. It's hard to talk to me because I can't follow cultural references, and I can't read or write."

"You can't read?" asked Ella.

Seven smiled. She'd known them only hours, but she wasn't surprised that Ella's sharp hearing hadn't missed that little tidbit.

"Nope." She smiled as if it were no big deal and gazed at them for a second before turning back around. Truthfully, it was her biggest regret, even if the lack in her education wasn't her fault. She'd always wanted to read.

Daphne smiled, sitting forward. "Then we'll teach you."

"No." At the child's simple words of sweetness, Seven's

voice cracked, and she was shocked to feel that tears had formed in her eyes. "It's not allowed."

Ella was clearly not going to let this go. "Why?"

"Your father will explain it to you someday." She looked back at Ben, hoping to change the subject. "So what shall we do, then? I think the best course of action would be to leave me as I am in these clothes and let me go and find your ghost energy."

A tap on the window had them both jumping. Ben lowered the window, his gaze guarded, and Seven wondered if he expected trouble from the woman who stood outside.

"I bought her clothes." The woman, who had graying hair and a round, sweet face, spoke in hushed tones.

"What?" Ben grabbed Seven's hand and squeezed. She took that to mean he wanted her to be quiet. At least, she thought that was what he wanted. That was what she was doing, either way.

"I saw y'all inside, and you couldn't get served." She shook her head. "They wouldn't even let you buy her sweatpants."

Ben laughed. "I never would have suspected a mall in Metairie to be so afraid of one woman, but apparently she's too much for the salespeople."

Tears sprang from the woman's eyes, and Seven gasped. She had a sudden urge to dart from the car and throw her arms around her. Ben squeezed her hand more tightly.

"My son... they took him from me when he was ten. I'm not even sure how they knew he was Conditioned. No one had seen him do what he could do, but somehow they knew." She sniffed. "I'd like to think that if he could somehow get out of wherever they put him, that someone would buy him clothes."

"Oh." Seven couldn't stand it anymore. She had to say something. "I'm not out, I'm just on assignment, and Mr. Lavelle is trying to be nice to me by buying me some clothes to wear."

"Well." The woman sniffed again. "I hope he somehow found a way to get out."

That was doubtful, but this woman was too nice for Seven to disillusion her. Maybe, somewhere out there in the world, there was someone who worried about all of them, who thought of them in quiet moments, who regretted the life fate had given their loved ones.

"Anyway, I guessed, but I think you're a size four. Is that right?"

Seven looked at Ben, but he shrugged. "I really have no idea, ma'am. I've never had clothes that had sizes on them."

"Well, my best guess is that these will fit you. You're so tall and thin. Really, you have the most lovely figure."

Ben interrupted. "Thank you." He pulled out his wallet.

"How much do I owe you for the clothes?"

The woman passed a bag of clothes through the window to Ben. "Consider it a gift. I insist."

Money. Seven didn't understand it. She'd never even handled any. But it meant something to Ben, as he continued to argue with the woman about needing to pay for the clothes and she kept insisting a gift was a gift.

Not sure what to do, Seven turned around to regard the girls. "How is your ice cream?"

Ella smiled as Daphne nodded. "Good," they said in unison.

Well, that hadn't distracted her for very long. Seven sat back in the seat. Ben continued to try to hand the woman some money. Finally, Seven placed her hand on his strong arm.

"I think she really wants this to be a gift."

He regarded her silently, and she wished, not for the first time, that with Ben she had the ability to read minds. It would have been a much more useful Condition when dealing with him. She wondered if his wife had been able to read all his expressions and how long it had taken her to learn how to do that.

The thought jarred her. There was no way Seven would be around him long enough to learn Ben at all. This wasn't her family—it never would be—and wishing that it could be, even in the deepest, most hidden place of her heart, would not make it so.

Wishes were for people with futures.

"Ben, take the clothes, please. I really want to get my job done. If Madame finds out I'm sitting in the parking lot of a mall not being occupied with actual work, she's likely to pull me out of here altogether, and then I'll never fix your ghost problem."

Ben turned to the woman who still stood outside the window. "Thank you for the clothes, Ms. Mary."

Apparently, at some point in their discussion he had learned the woman's name. That was a good thing, she supposed.

Mary's face lit up. "You're welcome, and I hope you do the right thing here."

Ben sighed. She could tell he didn't want to ask the obvious question by the way his free hand gripped the steering wheel. "The right thing?"

"Run away with her, of course."

Seven gasped as she leaned over Ben. "No, that would be the wrong thing, Ms. Mary. The very worst thing Ben could possibly do. Thank you so much for the clothes. I'll never be able to repay you."

"It was my pleasure. If you ever meet my son—his name was Guy, Guy McKidd. They took him far away from us."

Seven doubted she'd be meeting too many new people in the immediate future, but she still smiled and waved as Ms. Mary walked quickly through the parking lot.

"Everyone at my Institution is a number. If I know Guy McKidd, I know him as something else entirely."

Ben nodded, his brow creased. He didn't turn to look at her as he stared straight ahead. "Are you buckled?"

She had put on her seatbelt as soon as they'd gotten into the car and not taken it off. "Yes, thank you."

"Great." He looked in the rearview mirror. "Girls, are you buckled?"

They both answered that they were, and Ben pulled out of the parking lot as if he were being chased. Seven suspected he was. Her friends at Crescent had always been envious that she got to leave. Most of them were considered too dangerous to be given passes to work on the outside.

But Seven knew the truth. As much as it was nice to be allowed to see a bit of the outside world, it was hell on the people around her. She'd never been with anyone as kind-hearted as Ben before. Her presence alone seemed to be doing bad things. She was sure he hadn't slept at all the night before, and now he looked as if he were in physical pain.

"I'm sorry." Seven sighed. "If I wasn't certain that you were all but under attack by this ghost energy, I would insist that you send me back right now. I'm clearly causing you a tremendous amount of grief."

"You're not causing me grief." He looked at her sideways. "You're causing me a certain amount of moral reflection, and that's always uncomfortable. Also, other feelings that I haven't had in a while."

She wondered if she should know what he was talking about. He was so handsome. Clasping her hands in her lap, she forced herself not to touch the side of his face. She wanted to stroke away his worry lines. She wanted to know what his breath felt like mixed with hers.

Instead, she looked out the window. Most of the area they drove through looked suburban, like a million little towns she'd traveled through in her journeys about the country. The only difference was the canal that paralleled them as they made their way through.

"The first house I have to take you to is the home of an older couple. The Pellangros. Susan and Doug. They're fine people, I suppose, but they're not going to be home when we go in." He rubbed his head. "They don't want to be there while we work."

Seven turned to look at Ben. He was being kind, but she knew what he meant.

They didn't want to be there with *her*. That was just as well. The longer she sat in the car, surrounded by Ben and his daughters, the more exhausted she felt. More people would only make it worse, because every single person she encountered reminded her how alone in the world she really was.

"Good." She rubbed her nose. "Maybe we can get through this fast. I'll clear their house."

"In a hurry?"

She wasn't sure, but she thought she heard sarcasm in his voice.

"Yes and no." If he didn't get it, she wasn't going to explain it to him.

"Daddy, tomorrow can we take Seven out on the boat?"

Ben sighed. "I don't know if Seven likes boats, and I don't know if it would be a problem for *Madame*."

Now, that time, she'd heard the sneer. "Have I upset you?"

"No. Don't be ridiculous. How could you upset me?"

"I'm not sure." She wanted to yell but kept her voice level because of the girls in the backseat. "I frequently don't understand what people want me to do or not do. If I've offended you, I'm not sure how."

The car jolted to a stop as Ben pulled it into a short driveway that led up to what looked like a thin house. Seven glanced to her left and saw that Ben's house was three away from where they were located.

She pointed at the brown house in front of them. "How old is this house?"

"Not too old by New Orleans standards. Houses in this city can be really, really ancient." He scratched his head. "Most of the houses on the block were built around the same time, in the fifties. This one is called a shotgun house. It might be slightly older than the others."

A shiver racked her body as she stared at it.

"Something wrong?" Ben regarded her coolly.

"I think this house is scary." Daphne's voice was barely a whisper. "And I don't like Mr. Doug and Ms. Susan."

"Daphne." Ben unbuckled his seatbelt. "One place is not more scary than anywhere else. It's only our imaginations that lead us to believe they are."

Seven noticed that he didn't comment on Daphne's remark about the home's owners. She quickly unbuckled her seatbelt and got out of the car.

The humidity of New Orleans hit her square in the face. It seemed to her it never got as humid near the Institution as it did here.

The brown "shotgun house," as Ben had called it, had white-and-blue shutters and a covered porch. There was nothing inherently frightening about it, so why was she—and Daphne—so freaked out?

As they walked forward, the door swung open and a woman stepped out. She was medium height, blonde-haired and blue-eyed. Dressed plainly in jeans and a white T-shirt, it was her bare feet that startled Seven. Her head held high, her stride confident, she could have been wearing a ball gown—as Madame sometimes did before she left for fundraisers.

Suddenly, Seven was acutely aware that she still wore her orange jumpsuit. She had no idea what Mary McKidd had bought her, but she wanted to wear it right now. Seven shivered again. Whoever this woman was, she was powerful.

Right now, even walking next to Ben, Seven was terribly vulnerable.

A smile formed on the woman's face, one that didn't reach her eyes. "Ben, so glad you got here with the help." Her eyes scanned them, and Seven wished she could vomit. "And I see you brought the kids, too. How lovely. It's been such a long time since I saw them."

Seven thought it was a tribute to how polite the girls really were that they didn't turn tail and run for the car.

"Susan." Ben broadened his leg stance. "I thought you and Doug didn't want to be here while Seven worked."

Whatever the woman's reasons for changing her mind about attendance, Seven wished she'd change it back.

"Doug and I talked. We decided that since it's our home, it would be best if one of us attended."

She sighed and smiled as though everything in her world was just fine. The woman was a liar, and Seven had no idea why she was so certain, except that she was absolutely hiding something.

"I'm less squeamish than he is, so we decided I'd stay. He took the boat out. You should join him one of these days. You guys can race out on Lake Pontchartrain."

"Oh well, Susan, there are rules for when you can and cannot race on the lake. They keep us all safe out there, as you know." He squeezed Seven's shoulders. "This is Seven, and nothing she does should make you feel at all squeamish."

For a split second, Susan narrowed her eyes before she smiled again. Seven tried to imagine what she saw. If she were Susan, she would see Ben and his girls walking along with a Conditioned Ghost-Hunter who was dressed in an orange jumpsuit. So what had made her narrow her gaze with so much venom?

That was when she realized Ben had put his hands on her shoulders. He was touching her. *In. Front. Of. Susan.*

She'd gotten so used to him touching her. It was odd. In general, she didn't like to be handled. But she liked Ben doing it. He was a beautiful, sexy man, and she wished she were a normal woman so she could know what his strong fingers felt like all over her body. But the trouble was that she *had* gotten used to it.

Seven stepped away from his hold. He was such a sweetheart—and he was going to get himself into massive amounts of trouble if he wasn't careful.

Lowering her head in her usual manner, she avoided Susan's eye contact. "Mr. Lavelle has been very kind to me, and I am enormously grateful for his faith in my ability to get the job done. If you're comfortable with my entering your home, I would be happy to take a look at your ghost problem."

"Ben has always had the biggest heart. I was a friend to his late wife. We all adored her, and the whole neighborhood feels protective of the girls. Frankly, if we weren't desperate, I wouldn't want an aberration like you anywhere near any of us."

Seven nodded. She'd expected the woman to say something like that.

Ben practically growled. "Susan, that is enough. My so-called big heart aside, I assure you I am capable of deciding who should and should not be around my family. Seven is safe, and she is helpful."

Pretending she hadn't heard his words, Seven continued, "I would be happy to provide you with Madame's phone number—the head of Crescent, who can vouch for the safety of your premises."

"It certainly knows what to say, doesn't it?"

"Susan." Ben spoke through clenched teeth.

There was nothing about this situation that was new to Seven. Even though people asked for her help, they still felt entitled to begrudge her existence. That was fine. She was used to it. But Ben's girls...

Seven didn't dare turn around and look at Daphne or Ella.

They'd been silent.

"With your permission, I'll go inside and get started."

She hated this with a passion. Never before had she felt this exposed. It mattered to her what Ben's girls thought of her. She didn't want them to hear her referred to as an *it*. Thinking that they might come to regard her that way made her heart clench.

Truth was, it mattered to her what Ben thought of her, too. So far, he seemed to like her—he treated her so nicely. She wanted to see him smile at her, not get that pained look from constantly having to work to make people treat her well.

This whole situation felt fraught with trouble. Better to go in, find the ghost, and get out.

Susan nodded her consent, and Seven scooted past her through the front door. The shivers she'd felt in the front yard were nothing compared to what she endured entering the house.

"Why did Ms. Susan call her *it*, Daddy?" Ella's voice wafted into the house.

Seven braced herself. It was going to be a long day.

SEVEN

Seven had been in the house for fifteen minutes. Susan stood like a sentry by the door and, with one hard look, had made it clear that he wasn't to pass through. Ben was a patient man, but his tolerance was running out—fast. She got another few seconds, and then he was going to retrieve what was his.

"Daddy, is Seven okay?" Ella's voice broke through the fog of anger that had overtaken his good sense. He'd made Daphne go wait in the car. It was too risky to have her out and about with Susan watching every move they made.

"Yes, baby. I'm sure she's fine. Seven is very, very good at her job."

He spoke for his own benefit as well as his daughter's. Ella had refused to go back to the vehicle.

"Susan."

His neighbor tapped her foot on the porch, glancing occasionally over her shoulder. "Yes, Ben?"

Her smile looked vicious. He'd never liked the woman, who had been his least favorite of his wife's friends, but today he wished he could throw her off a cliff.

"What's going on inside? Perhaps I could assist Seven?" *Perhaps I could commit homicide and hide the body where no one would ever find it.*

"I don't know how you could help her. Unless you can do the freakish things that she does?"

Susan stepped forward, her bare feet really grossing him out. He didn't usually notice other people's feet, but in her case, they were veiny and old-looking. Susan was in her mid-thirties, but her feet—they looked ancient.

"Can you, Ben? Can you make your eyes turn black, like the thing inside the house, and see things that are ungodly?"

Anger surged through his veins and, before he could help himself, he'd fisted his hands. "Ella, go get in the car with Daphne. Lock the doors and don't open them for anyone but me. Understand?"

Ella's only response was to rush toward the car. He stared up at Susan. At first she made no move, but then he watched her swallow, her neck muscles straining over her apparent hidden nervousness. Ben loved external signs of internal conflict. In a courtroom, they were frequently the only small signals of discomfort from the opposing counsel.

He stomped forward until he stood directly in front of Susan.

"Move, or I will move you."

"Might I remind you, Benedicte Lavelle, that you are standing on my porch, and that I get to decide who does and does not come into my home?"

He placed his hand on Susan's arm. "Let me ask you something. Do you think you could get the very busy New Orleans police department down here fast enough to stop me from pushing you to the side and leaving with Seven? Even if you could, I'm friends with most of the guys on the force. If that didn't work, I don't think it's a secret who my brother is."

In his whole life, he had never used Gene as a threat before. But the real kicker of the situation was that he meant it. If Susan didn't get out of his way, or caused him any issue, he would sic the fury of his older brother on her before she could blink.

She stepped aside. "Well, well, well, Benedicte. I never would have thought you were the kind to have such a sick fascination with one of *them*."

"Yeah, fine." He moved her aside. "Call me deranged and depraved. I don't care."

Except that just the day before, he would have cared. How was it possible to change so much, so quickly? He shook his head. Right now, he needed to check on Seven, not dwell on some kind of moral change going on inside him.

Susan had her air conditioning turned all the way up, and his body shook for a second when he stepped through the door. When was the last time he'd been in this house? Come to think of it, he wasn't certain he'd ever ventured inside. It was more likely he'd politely waved from the driveway when he'd dropped off his wife.

The walls were dark, and the pictures that seemed to cover every free space were strange, psychedelic-looking. They hurt his eyes, and he forced his gaze from the strange decorations.

"Seven?" he called out into the house, distressed when she didn't immediately answer. After a few seconds, he heard a whimper. "Seven?"

Ben moved in the direction of the small sound. Last night, he'd watched her topple over based on the ghost energy. She could be hurt or nearly dead. Damn Susan and whatever games she was playing. This wasn't about being prejudiced about the Conditioned. This was something else. She'd been venomous on the porch.

Seven was huddled on the ground in a fetal position.

"God *damn* it." He rushed to her side and scooped her up in his arms. Her whole body shook, and her skin was covered in sweat.

He pulled her up against him as he ran for the couch. "Seven?" Her eyes were open but black, like they had become the night before when she'd been in her "dark space," seeing the ghost light.

Ben shook her. "Seven, can you hear me?"

"It's everywhere..." Her voice was barely a whisper, and he suspected she didn't know she was speaking to him, but rather was just talking aloud. "How can it be?"

Susan walked slowly into the room. She leaned in the doorway, a gun pointed at his head. Ben had never had a weapon drawn in his direction before. His mouth went dry, but it wasn't terror that fueled his adrenaline. It was rage.

"I almost feel sorry for her." She shook her head. "It's too bad you insisted on entering the house. She could have died and no one would have known what had happened. A fluke. It happens to them all the time." She walked closer to Ben, leaning over Seven even as she kept the gun leveled at his head. "They're such fragile creatures, these devil-ridden abnormalities."

Ben laid Seven gently on the ground. In a move that surprised even him, he launched forward, throwing himself on top of Susan. He didn't care about the gun. He was bigger than she was, and size alone gave him advantage. There was no way in hell he was going to sit still and get shot by a lunatic. As they hit the ground, hard, he heard the air thrust from her lungs. The gun flew across the room.

"You stupid bitch. I have never laid hands on a woman in my life. But if you don't stop this, whatever it is that you've done, I'll kill you. Do you understand? I'll choke the life out of you."

Behind him, Seven gasped for air, which only fueled his anger.

"Make it stop," he yelled.

Susan laughed, a strangled sound. "I can't. Once it's started, it can't stop." She choked. "Besides, you can't kill me, Ben. Doug will destroy your girls if you do."

His anger cooled to an utter rage, the likes of which he had never known. Gene might have been the criminal in the family, but Ben realized he was capable of committing multiple murders. Boom—he'd end Susan and Doug's lives without another thought. Hell, he could use their own gun.

He might even enjoy it. How dare they threaten his family, which seemed, at the moment, to include Seven?

"No, Doug won't be hurting the children, Susan."

Ben's head shot up. A man he'd never seen before stood in the doorway, calmly watching him hold Susan on the ground. Where had this man come from? Had Ben been so clouded by his own rage that he hadn't heard him arrive? As Ben watched, the stranger stuck the gun into a holster on his belt buckle.

"Please." The blond man strode slowly toward them. "Don't kill her, Mr. Lavelle. I have her husband locked in the back of my car. It would be my pleasure to take Susan in as well. Imagine a hidden Conditioned couple spending their life targeting other Conditioned."

Ben breathed hard as he stared at the stranger. "Who are you?"

"My name is Roman Lewis." He smiled, a mirthless grin. "I'm a Fury."

Suddenly awash with fear for Seven on the floor and Daphne in the car, Ben got off Susan. He backed up a few steps until he kneeled in front of Seven.

"I don't understand. How can Susan be targeting Conditioned? She's been here for years and years."

Roman sighed. "She and Doug travel a lot for business. I had a hard time figuring them out, which is unusual for me. In that way, Susan, I'm quite impressed."

The Fury rolled Susan over until she lay on her stomach. In two swift moves, he had her cuffed. She struggled and cursed, regaining full use of her voice again. Roman laughed. "Now, now, Susan, I've never heard language quite like that."

He looked up at Ben. "How do you like having a regular Conditioned serial killer living down the block?" Roman placed his hand on Susan's head. "Sleep," he instructed her. Seconds later, Ben heard a loud snore emit from her mouth. "There, now, we shouldn't have any more problems with her."

"I'm confused." And Ben was not used to feeling out of his element.

As Roman nodded, he looked at Seven. "Of course you are. And unfortunately, I'm not allowed to illuminate too much more for you. It goes against the rules."

"I see." Ben stood up. "The rules, huh? I was up all last night reading the so-called rules about the Conditioned. As far as I can tell, there is no such thing. It's just a bunch of the Institutions doing what they want, getting away with it, and no one complaining because what is supposed to be the law is horrendous anyway, so why should anyone bother to make a stink?"

Roman regarded him steadily. The man had no external

tics, nothing to show Ben what he thought or felt. He was the most still person Ben had ever seen before.

"Most people don't feel as you do, Mr. Lavelle. Most people are glad to have them locked up, glad people like me exist who hunt out stray Conditioned and make sure they *stay* locked up."

"Yeah, well." Ben ran a hand through his hair. "Most people are morons, apparently." He pointed at Seven. She was still in so much pain. It made his heart clench. "Can you help her?"

Ben didn't know if he'd just doomed Seven to an earlier death by asking Roman. He might have made things worse for her. But he couldn't leave her as she was. If she could have come back from the ghost light, she would have.

"I can." Roman placed a hand on Seven's shoulder. "She's pretty, isn't she? For a Conditioned, that is."

"She's pretty no matter what she is. She's the prettiest woman I've ever seen." *And I want you to get your fucking hands off her.*

It seemed a good idea to keep that last thought to himself. The man was helping Seven. After she was awake and fine, Ben might decide to use some of his pent-up aggression to tell Roman where he could shove his rules and regulations.

Seven's eyes fluttered open, and she groaned. Ben threw himself down on the floor next to her. Roman had pulled away his hand, which had been on Seven's shoulders.

"Are you okay?"

Seven tried to sit up, and Ben reached out to help her, his hands under her neck. She closed her eyes as if they pained her.

"It might take a few minutes for your body to reorient itself."

Her eyes flew open, and she gasped. "Fury."

Seven said the word like all the horror in the universe could be contained within it. To Ben's surprise, Roman smiled and a hint of humor lit up his eyes.

"Roman Lewis, at your service."

Seven grabbed Ben's hand and squeezed. "I didn't mean to mess this up. I've never seen so much energy. It was everywhere, and it kept coming and coming. I would clear it and then it rushed back."

Roman nodded. "It was a trap. It's been handled. None of this is your fault."

"A trap?"

"I can't explain it. I'm sorry. It's Institution business." He scratched his head.

"Do you remember me?"

Seven blinked. "Have we met before? I'm so sorry, sir, I don't remember."

"It's okay, Seven. I don't think he's going to skin you alive for not being able to recall meeting him." Ben looked up to hold Roman's steady gaze. "Are you?"

"I would be surprised if she did remember me. It was a long time ago."

Seven shuddered in Ben's embrace. "When?"

"The last time you got into a mess like this."

Ben hadn't asked for much clarification on this before. He needed more now.

"Seven, you've had this happen before?"

"When I was young. It nearly killed me. I woke up from a coma, back in Crescent, a long time later."

Roman shook his head. "I worked on you for days and days. I've never seen someone so close to being gone. But I brought you back."

"I had no idea. No one ever told me what happened."

"Well, I've never forgotten it. You're clearly much stronger now. That level of distress would have killed you back then. I'm interested in why it's happened to you twice. Susan and Doug didn't start their antics until a few years ago." He laughed. "But I suppose it doesn't matter, since I understand you're to be terminated very shortly."

Seven pulled herself to her feet. "Yes, I suppose it will be very soon now that I've failed at this and it's over."

Ben shook his head. "It's not over."

Roman exhaled a long breath. "Not nearly, no. There is still the matter of all the ghost energy left in the homes here. It should be pretty easy for you to take down now that it's not being fueled by psychopaths."

There was something going on with this man, and it made Ben's skin ache that he couldn't figure out what it was. For a Fury, and Lord knew he'd heard enough about the Fury over the years, he seemed incredibly caring toward Ben's girl. He would always be immensely grateful to him for bringing her back from wherever she'd gotten lost—something Ben was well aware he could not have done himself—but Roman didn't act how he was pretty sure the Fury should act.

Why was he being gentle?

"Seven is, I understand, slated to be killed as soon as she's returned. Why bring her back at all? Why save her when she was younger? I don't think I understand your motivations here, Mr. Lewis." A thought dawned on Ben. "And I feel like I know your name from somewhere. Lewis. Was it in the news recently?"

After picking up Susan and swinging her over his shoulder, Roman stalked to the door. "I have no idea what you're talking about. It's a fairly common name." *Liar*.

Ben might have been out of his depth, but he knew a lie

when he heard one. It left a bad taste in his mouth. Until that moment, Roman had restrained himself completely, but something Ben had just said to him had clearly thrown him off his game.

"And my reasons for saving the girl are my own."

Ben chased after him. "They matter in whatever way they relate to Seven. Everything about her matters to me. I have to stop the execution."

He couldn't believe he'd just admitted that to a Fury—a member of the organization that would be seeing to her death. But he'd done it, and he wasn't going to take it back. Roman had affection for Seven, and Ben was willing to use every advantage he could get in his drive to save Seven's life.

Roman stopped moving and whirled around. "There is nothing I can do about the girl's death. Not a thing. And I have to tell you that in the Conditioned world, I can do just about anything. I've asked myself for years why I can track people across continents and perform tasks that most mere mortals can't even imagine, but I can't stop the girl's early execution."

It was driving Ben crazy that Roman kept calling her "the girl."

"She has a name. It's Seven."

Roman laughed, a cold, hard sound. "Seven isn't a name, Mr. Lavelle. It's a number. If you can save her life, I wish you good luck. Madame is determined she will die. The most beautiful girl I've ever seen is to die next week, and I can't do a damn thing to stop it."

As if he'd made some grand statement, Roman turned on his heel and left the house as silently as he'd entered it.

"It was a good question."

Seven's voice sounded hoarse. He turned around to look

at her. "What was?" Ben had asked so many questions he wasn't sure which one she meant.

"Why does he *bother* to keep saving my life? He should have just left me in the dark to die years ago, surrounded by that life sucking energy, and saved everyone the trouble of dealing with me."

He heard the hitch in her voice right before, to his utter horror, tears streamed down her face.

Oh, hell.

Somehow, he'd just made her cry. "Seven?"

"I don't know, Ben. I thought we were friends. I thought you cared about me. I know, stupid. Non-Conditioned never really care about us. It's always a nightmare. What was I thinking?"

She covered her face with her hands. Oh no. He couldn't stand it. Within two seconds, he had her in his arms.

"Seven, no. You misunderstood."

She sniffed as another sob rocked her body. "I sat right here. I heard every word that you said." She tried to pull out of his embrace, but he had no intention of letting her go. Instead, he pushed her up against the wall. "Let me go. Please."

"First of all, you have no need to be afraid of me. I'm not going to do anything to you that you don't want. Ever. I don't treat women that way. You were safe last night in my house, and you're safe now. Do you believe me?"

She nodded. "I'm not afraid of you, Ben. I'm just hurt, which I don't need you to tell me is really dumb."

"No, you have every right to be feeling bad if you really think that's what I meant when I spoke to Roman. But that wasn't it." He shook his head. "I don't trust Roman. He has a game. I can feel it, but I can't pinpoint it."

"What does that have to do with anything? I know I can't follow a lot of stuff, but this I should be able to understand."

He brushed her hair off her forehead. God, it was so soft. Everything about her felt visceral to him. He wanted to touch, to feel, to breathe in her unique scent. "You understand things on a whole level that I can't follow. I can't even begin to grasp what your life has been like."

"Ben, I—"

"Listen, here's the thing. You're mine. That's all there is to it. You shouldn't be. I know it's dangerous for me, for you, for my girls—who have to come first in my life. And yet..."

That was all there was to it. *And yet*. She was. As impossible as it should have been.

EIGHT

Seven lay in the dark, listening to the utter silence of Ben's house. *You're mine.*

She could still hear his voice as he'd said those words to her. Husky, possessive. And then his girls had burst through the front door of the house. She and Ben hadn't gotten to continue their discussion.

As she grabbed the pillow, she rolled over onto her stomach. This might be one of her last nights sleeping on a bed as comfortable as this one, and she was wasting it obsessing over something that couldn't possibly be true. She couldn't be *his*. She was Conditioned. He wasn't. Plus, he had to hide dear Daphne from the Fury or anyone else who wanted to harm her. Seven was the last person who should be in his life.

She threw the covers off herself, exposing her legs to the air conditioning. The blue-green nightgown Ms. McKidd had included in her purchases barely covered her thighs. It was much different from the full-length white sleeper gown she wore in the Institution. She pushed on a pair of slippers that she'd found in the clothing bag and padded her way softly out of the room.

It would be better to get this idea out of Ben's mind sooner rather than later, before he went and did something stupid that got his whole family in trouble. She was one little Conditioned girl, and her time on the planet was limited. It was dumb that she'd cried over Ben's comment. Her hysterics had forced him to make a statement he never should have had to.

Of course, she couldn't deny that his heated words had done funny things to her insides. Before the horror of what he'd said had dawned on her, she'd actually felt warm in places she hadn't known could feel like that.

The girls' room was on the left. The door was slightly cracked, and she poked her head inside. They each had their own bed, but Daphne was curled up next to Ella in the same bed. The scene was so familial, so sweet, that tears sprang out of Seven's eyes before she could stop them. Quickly, she wiped them away.

As she forced herself to move from the sight of the girls sound asleep, she crept farther down the hall to Ben's room. She touched the door handle and froze. Could she do this? Could she enter his room uninvited? Her hand shook slightly. It wasn't as if she was in the Institution. Ben wasn't going to beat her. He might yell, he might throw her out, but it wasn't as though she was going to be taken to task physically for intruding on his sleep.

She turned the handle. The room was completely dark except for some light creeping in from outside the window. Ben hadn't closed his shades. He lay on top of the covers, dressed only in his dark pajama pants. Lying on his stomach with his face turned to the side, Ben breathed in and out with a soft sound.

Seven waited for a second to see if he would wake up. When he didn't budge, she stepped into his room and closed the door quietly behind her. Wow. Ben was a really sound sleeper. In the Institution, it was important to be able to wake up in an instant and be fully alert. She never knew when they were going to do a random inspection, or if Madame was suddenly going to insist they all get up and clean the place from top to bottom.

She crossed quietly to the side of the bed. It was all she could do to keep from crying again as she looked down at him. He was so beautiful. It wasn't fair. Men shouldn't be that breathtaking to regard. Of course, he had told her that she was *his*. Did that make him hers as well?

Even though she was about to dissuade him of either idea, it was nice that for the brief period of time she had left on the planet, she could think of herself that way.

"Ben." She whispered his name. It felt silly that she was being so quiet. She wanted him to wake up. Still, he looked so peaceful, and there was a part of her that really didn't want him to wake up to the millions of burdens she knew he currently shouldered. Maybe she should leave him alone.

His eyes flew open. They were dazed and unfocused. "Seven? Baby? You okay?"

She felt herself tugged down onto the bed next to him. He scooted slightly over until he'd pulled her up against his body.

His hand immediately started tracing circles on her back.

"Couldn't sleep? I'm glad you came in here."

Okay. So he wasn't going to yell at her for disturbing him. This was almost worse. She hadn't braced herself for this kind of reception. Kindness was always harder for her to take than abuse. She had so little experience handling it.

"I couldn't sleep, and I thought we should talk about it."

He pressed his forehead against hers. "Talk?"

"Yes." She paused. "Is that okay?"

His voice was barely a whisper. "I don't know how coherent I am, sweetheart, but I can try." He rubbed his eyes. "Is this the type of conversation I should go make coffee for?"

"I have no idea how to answer that. I've never had coffee."

He laughed, a low guttural sound that made shivers of pleasure travel up her spine. "We can remedy that in the morning. What time is it, anyway?" He lifted his head to look over her shoulder. It took her a moment to realize he was staring at the clock. "It's three in the morning. Whatever you want to talk about, can it wait until six or seven?"

Ben was right. This was a really bad move on her part. It was the middle of the night. He needed his sleep. She tried to pull out of his arms.

"Don't leave." His voice was low, soothing, like the sound of rain on the rooftop of the Institution dorms. "I like having you here. I'm even willing to talk, if that's what you need right now." He brushed her hair out of her eyes, and she sighed.

The man was like a drug that she couldn't let herself get addicted to.

"Did you have a bad dream?"

"I haven't been asleep."

He kissed her nose, and she gasped, but he only grinned at her reaction. "Too much tension today, maybe?"

"No. I can't sleep because of what you said."

Her eyes must have been adjusting to the dark, because she clearly made out one of his jet-black eyebrows lift in confusion. "What I said?"

"That I'm yours. I can't be yours."

Ben fell silent. Okay, she knew what would happen next. Now he would start to scream.

"Do you not have those feelings for me?"

That hadn't been what she'd thought he would say. Not even a little bit. She blinked a few times to try to find her focus. "That's not the point. I'm dangerous for you."

"I asked you something, Seven."

He had, and she wanted to answer him, because she was obviously losing her mind. "I do. Of course, I do. How could I not? I'm lying here in your bed in the middle of the night, and every time you touch me it makes me want to wrap myself around you and never let go."

He stroked a hand over the side of her face. "If you're trying to make me leave you alone, what you just said is not going to do it."

"I'm trying to be honest."

Ben nodded. "Good."

"I'm not good for you. You need to think of the girls, and if you're serious about your feelings, then you need to protect your own heart. I'm going to be dead in a few days."

He sighed and pulled her closer until her head pressed against his chest. She could hear his strong heartbeat. "You're not dying."

"Yes. I am." Had he not been paying attention?

"I'm going to delay your return to Crescent as long as possible, and then I'll think of something else and something after that, too. No one is going to hurt you, Seven. I can assure you of that."

She closed her eyes as his scent seemed to envelop her in a warm cocoon. It wasn't that she was tired. No, this was something else, and she didn't have a name for it. He smelled male, spicy, and... safe.

"What about the girls?"

"I always think about the girls. We have to keep Daphne safe. Who better to be with on that task than you?"

"Ben." She opened her eyes. "You just met me. You may not like me tomorrow. Are you sure you want to risk everything on me?"

"Seven, I met my wife, and within minutes knew I would marry her. I'm built like that. When something is mine, I know it instantly. You're mine. That's all there is to it."

"Even if I say it's a bad idea?"

He sucked in his breath. "At any time, you can say you don't want me. I'll respect that and leave you alone. But you have to mean it, because I can taste a lie. I'll know if you're just saying that out of some sort of need to protect me by making me leave you."

"You can taste it?" She traced his features as she wondered if it was possible to memorize them that way. "Are you sure you're not Conditioned?"

"I might be. Maybe that's where Daphne gets it. I never thought of it as being odd, just something I could do."

She closed her eyes. "Then we'll protect you, too. Here's the thing. If I let myself believe you and something goes wrong, I'm going to be destroyed."

"Whether you believe my feelings for you are real or not, I'm still not going to let you die. That I can promise you."

Just like that, she believed him. He had feelings for her. She was *his*, and he wouldn't let her die. Even if she told him it was a really bad idea.

Already pressed up against him, she launched her arms around his neck. God didn't want the Conditioned. Madame told them all the time that they were the work of the Devil, but perhaps a divine presence of some kind had heard her prayers and sent him to her for trying so hard to be good. Or at the very least, to show her what it felt like to belong somewhere before she died.

His lips met hers, and for a second she couldn't breathe —couldn't think, couldn't do anything but stay precisely still and feel the soft-yet-firm press of his lips on hers. Then, as if guided by desire alone, she kissed him back. And—oh yes— it felt like coming home.

They kissed in silence, neither of them moving. She opened her mouth slightly to invite more of his exploration.

He raised his hand to cup the side of her face as a slight moan left his lips. Finally, he pulled back to regard her. He breathed hard, his eyes no longer sleepy but laden with heat.

"Okay, we have to stop." His voice sounded husky. "Or I'm going to lose all my good intentions of treating you with respect."

"I don't want respect."

He laughed, a smile dancing on his face. "Sure you do." He leaned over to kiss her nose. "But I'm glad to know you want me as much as I want you."

Seven might not have known everything she wished she did about the world around her, but she knew one thing— she wanted Ben, and as far as she was concerned, there was no time to waste. "Please, don't stop. Not tonight. I need to feel like I'm yours."

That must have been the right thing to say, because he pulled her into his arms again and drove his tongue into her mouth. She lost herself in the moment. He was rougher this time, and that was fine by her. This was Ben, and he wanted her with staggering intensity.

"God." He sat up, pulling her into his lap. "I want you

so bad. I'm actually nervous about how hot you make me. I'm trying to treat you gently, and all I want to do is drive into you like a maniac."

"Ben." She couldn't believe how breathy her voice sounded. "I'm not a virgin. They sterilized us all a year ago after something happened. I'm not sure what. Anyway, now everyone tries to get away from the guards so they can fuck."

His eyes widened at her choice of words.

She rushed to continue. "I'm not doing that. I've only ever done it once. I found it to be sort of awkward and uninteresting. But I can't get pregnant, and you don't need to treat me like I'm totally inexperienced."

"Honey, you are so incredible. I'm not concerned with your level of experience. I'm worried about my reaction to you. I'm not a violent person, but I have this real need to possess you that makes me nervous. I'm trying to go slowly, to control it."

"No." She rose on her knees before she pressed down on his lap. "No control between us. None of us can know how long we have on this planet. I don't want to screw up a minute of it by holding back from what we both want."

Ben made a sound that resembled a growl. He pushed her down on the bed, looming above her. She reached up to stroke his chest. He was so well-defined, he could have been chiseled out of stone.

"I've never seen a man who looks like you before."

And she wanted to look her fill. A hard bulge, that hadn't been there earlier, pressed out of his dark pajama pants. She reached out to touch the top of it through the fabric.

He hissed out a breath. "Don't do that. It feels unbelievable, honey, but I won't last. I want you too much."

She had never really wanted sex before. She'd tried it

and then never wished to do so again. What was the point when it was so... blah? But now she was hot and bothered inside.

To have him touching her, she would be willing to endure the pain from sex that came next. She wouldn't mind. It might even be nice to be that close.

"You're thinking too hard." He straddled her waist. "What are you thinking about?"

"Nothing important."

He leaned down to kiss the side of her neck. "I'll be the judge of that." He bit down lightly on her skin, and she couldn't believe the breathy sigh that escaped her mouth.

"Ah, I see. My girl likes to be bitten." He grinned. "That's very exciting to me."

"I want to be." She ran her fingers down his chest, loving the feel of goosebumps that popped up on his skin as she did. "I want to be exciting to you."

"You are, Seven, just by being you. I want to know your body. I need to learn all the places that you like to be touched, to be stroked, to be loved."

Did he want her to tell him? She wasn't even sure herself. "I'm not really certain if I have spots."

"You have them. I just bit one of them, and you practically purred."

She felt her cheeks heat up. "Oh, I'm sorry."

"Sorry?" He shook his head. "No, honey, it was so damn sexy. Everything about you is so incredibly hot. I love it, and I'm honored to be the one who gets to seek out all of those places and to hear all of your incredible noises."

"Ben, I'm so embarrassed right now." And she couldn't remember the last time she had been this uncomfortable.

"None of that between us." He helped her up until their faces were so close, they touched nose to nose. "You're mine, and I'm yours. There is no embarrassment between us."

Then they were kissing again, only this time she almost could not keep up with the pressure that was Ben's mouth against hers. He controlled their pace, he set the tone, and she was fine with that. Because she was *his,* and she'd never been anyone's before.

He stopped to tug at her nightgown. "You look like sin personified in that thing. It should be illegal for them to sell clothing like this."

She looked down at what she was wearing. "It's just cotton." Even though it was more risqué than the floor-length white one she wore usually, she didn't think there was anything inherently sexy in her nightgown. It was basically an oversized blue T-shirt.

"Cotton has never looked so good on anyone."

He slid his hand up her leg, and she thought she might have stopped breathing. His fingers found her panties. For a brief second, he touched the outside of her pussy through her underwear. She let out a long breath, trying to keep her head in place. What was happening to her? She wasn't even naked and already she was so unbelievably wet.

"Your heat calls to me like I'm a man possessed." Ben's voice had gotten very low; his eyes bored into hers. "Scoot back."

With one hand, he helped guide her until her head was on the pillow, pressed up against the headboard.

"Should I brace myself?" She wasn't entirely certain why he wanted her where he'd put her, but if he was just going to go and plunge right inside her, she wanted to know ahead of time. The last thing she needed was a goose-egg on her head because she wasn't warned.

"No." He shook his head. "Are you serious, or are you kidding?"

"I'm serious." Although now she was confused.

"I promise you, if you ever need to 'brace' yourself during sex, I will give you a heads-up. Although the idea is really repugnant to me."

"Then why did I need to be up against the headboard?"

He kissed the top of her knee. "Before I'm done with you, lady, you will have a sense of adventure and know you should never be afraid of me. Ever. Someday, when you're an old lady, you'll look back on this and laugh."

His finger pressed deeper into her underpants and she gasped. No one had ever touched her so intimately, not even herself. There was no privacy in Crescent. They slept on beds that were about ten inches from each other. It didn't lend itself to a lot of self-exploration. Fucking took place in hidden spots that didn't stay secret for very long.

"I'm going to take your panties off now."

"Okay." Was that her voice sounding so sultry? Seven felt like a much more adventurous woman had taken over her mind and body. No matter—she liked what was happening to this one much better than the things that took place in her regular life.

He slid the scrap of cotton off with one finger. "Spread your legs open for me, honey. Or better yet, let's take your nightie off first."

She gulped. Ben was going to see her completely naked. She'd been all for this, but what if he didn't like what he saw?

As she sat up, she pulled her nightgown over her head.

"Okay."

"Seven."

"Yes, Ben?" She couldn't look at him. She looked everywhere else she could.

The ceiling... the side of the bed... yes, that was completely interesting.

"You are the most beautiful woman I've ever seen."

Her eyes glazed as he reached out to cup both her breasts. "I feel like I've just been given such a gift, and just so you know, I intend to worship your body all night."

A response formed in her mouth but could she say it? Was she brave?

"Then I think we should get you out of your pants, Ben. Turnabout is fair play, right?"

NINE

Ben hadn't anticipated this when he'd gone to bed, but now that Seven had woken him and crawled into bed with him, he was as happy as he could remember being. Now he was getting to ravish her hot body to his heart's content.

If she wanted his pants off, he'd take them off. If only his arms and legs would obey his commands. Basically, his whole body had gone into "Seven Shock."

He smiled at her, knowing he probably looked sheepish. "Can you help me?"

"It would be my pleasure." The low, sultry tone of her voice made him think it really might be.

She tugged at his pants until they came down far enough that he could shove them off using his feet. The hardness of his erection strained against his briefs. Seven did things to his libido that should have been illegal. The fact that she was Conditioned meant everything about their connection actually might be...

"I want to touch you. I want to be inside you. Stroke you until your sweet juices drip all over my fingers."

"Ben."

Her eyes were huge, and he was sure if he could see her more clearly in the dark, her cheeks would be red. He loved that she could be so easily shocked.

"Do my words make you uncomfortable?" If they did, he would stop. He wanted to say all kinds of dirty, hot things to her, but he wanted her comfortable more than anything else.

"They make me feel... hot inside." She looked down as if that were somehow shameful.

He cupped her face and forced her to look him in the eyes. His cock ached to be stroked, or better yet to find release inside the folds of her hot pussy, but he was a man with tremendous patience—he exerted some now. "That's a good thing. You know that, right?"

"I know that I want you in a way I have never wanted anyone else. Sex was kind of... blah... for me." Her pale shoulders went up and down in a shrug. Seven had a way of saying things that was unique to her.

"Well, we'll endeavor to do better than *blah*." He had a feeling the next few minutes might actually make him feel the Earth move beneath them.

"It's already better than anything I've ever done before, and we haven't done anything yet."

He brushed the hair out of her face. "Just look what kissing you and thinking about sex with you has done to me." He grabbed her hand and placed it on his hard cock.

She smiled as she squeezed the end of it. Pleasure shot through his body at her inexperienced but incredible touch. He closed his eyes, willing himself not to lose it right at that second. He'd wanted her to feel him, to know what was going to happen between them. She wasn't a virgin, but how experienced could she be if she thought of sex as "blah"?

He hadn't counted on almost losing control himself.

"Does that feel good?"

As he leaned down to kiss her, he grinned. "Too good. So stop doing it before I embarrass myself all over your hand."

Her eyes got huge. "Oh."

"Roll over, honey. I want to see you from behind."

"Why?"

She was really too cute for words. "Because I want to see your pretty little ass. Now, roll over, please."

Seven did as he'd asked. Looking at her round, tight ass in front of him made a growl start in his throat. "Maybe someday—not today—you'll trust me enough that we'll do it this way, too."

"It can be done that way?"

The wonder in her voice amused him. She wasn't scared, his Seven, not at all. He squeezed her behind, and she gasped. Using his tongue, he gave in to the urge that drove him, and he licked all the way up her back. She was so thin—too thin, really—and he could see the outline of her spine very clearly in the bumps and ridges on her back.

"I'm going to make it my mission to feed you. A lot."

Her skin felt soft against his lips. And the slightly salty taste on his tongue—he loved it. Taking a deep breath, he inhaled her coffee scent.

He reached the back of her neck and rubbed it gently. She moaned under his ministrations.

"Does that feel good, honey?"

She squirmed. "You have magical hands, Ben."

"Flip over."

"Had enough of my backside?"

He pinched her butt cheek, and she yelped before

losing it in a fit of giggles. "I just wanted to admire your whole body. I've been worshiping it silently."

She flipped over, and, in an instant, he had his hands on her glorious breasts. If there was a God, he'd really known what he was doing when he'd made Seven's parts. Everything was round and supple in the right places. He had a feeling that once he got her fed to a proper level, they'd be even more spectacular.

He bent over, kissing the place where her neck met her collarbone. "Seven, you are your own person. When I say you belong to me what I mean is that you are in my heart, the way the people I love are. Do you understand?"

"I do." She nodded. "Please do that again."

"That's a good spot for you?" He licked it, wanting to memorize her taste. "I'm going to love finding your special places."

Beneath him, she squirmed. "What's happening to me? I feel like I'm going to burst into flames from the inside out."

"That's a good thing." He kissed her again. "I feel the same way."

Reaching down, he stroked her core. He needed his boxers off, now. Never before had the need to be inside another person practically overwhelmed him. Ben didn't know what would happen if he didn't get sheathed inside her soon, but it felt as if he might actually implode.

She moaned, her hands moving up to grab at her face. Her eyes were closed. Her body arched restlessly. Yes, he could make her come. He wanted to more than anything else. First, he would bring her pleasure this way, and then he would do it again from deep inside her.

He adjusted his hand until he found the small bundle of nerves he was searching for. As he stroked it, her eyes flew open, gazing up at him. They were filled with pleasure and confusion.

"Never touched yourself there?"

She shook her head. "No privacy."

"Then I get to be the first to introduce you to how hot that can be? Amazing."

And it really was. He felt so... lucky. Even amongst the horror that would try to take over their lives, he was damned lucky to have her. He got to touch her, hold her, make love to her. The rest of the world could go to hell for not seeing her as the dream she really was.

Her body clenched around his fingers, and she gasped. Yes, this was what he wanted for her. This was what he'd dreamed about. Warmth pooled on his hand as Seven came. She cried out his name in what he hoped was ecstasy as tears slid down her cheeks.

After a few seconds, he needed to say something. "Are you okay?"

She nodded, sort of. "That was..."

"Watching you find pleasure was like a religious experience for me."

Her voice sounded breathless. "Really?"

"And now, sweetheart, I really want to be inside you." He kissed her nose, wondering if she noticed that he was shaking from his need. "Is that what you want?"

"Yes—a million times yes."

He supposed that was enough reassurance, even for him. As he removed his boxers, he felt a huge amount of relief. He was as hard as a rock for Seven, and every brush of the cotton material against his erection had been a little piece of Hell. Still, it had kept him from coming before he'd gotten anywhere near her, which, in this case, was a very good thing because of how fast he knew he would come otherwise.

Seven stared wide-eyed at his cock. She didn't say a word, and after a moment, Ben worried. "Everything still okay?"

"Yes." She looked up, meeting his gaze. "I've never seen one so big."

He had to admit, that did great things for his ego. After all, he was a man. He'd think about the fact that she'd said that all the time now. Still, his "big" cock wanted inside her tight pussy, and that was where he was headed. That very instant.

He laid gentle kisses on her belly as he moved to her entrance. She sighed and pulled his head up to kiss him. The warm heat from her pussy pressed against his hard length, and he shuddered.

The last thing he wanted was to hurt her.

"It's okay, Ben."

Her sweet eyes stared up at him with so much trust. It humbled him.

"I don't want to hurt you."

She nodded, her eyes alight with happiness. "I know. I won't break. Trust me. And you can't get me pregnant. Also, they blood-test us all the time, so if I was sick, I would have been put down earlier."

The fact that she didn't know how fragile she was—or maybe worse that she hadn't been treated as a precious jewel—broke his heart. Still, he pushed inside her an inch at a time. Her gasp as he entered told him his suspicions had been right. He had to handle this with finesse.

For him, it was exquisite torture. Her pussy wrapped around him as though they'd been made to be together. With each inch, he made his way farther inside her heat.

Ultimately, he knew they'd be perfect. He just had to get her there.

Finally, he was fully sheathed. "Wow." He could hardly breathe. This was Heaven. This was what loving another person should feel like—the joining and completing of two souls.

Seven's eyes filled with tears. "Ben, you're completely embracing me like this. I never knew it could feel this way. It wasn't..."

"Shh." He really didn't want to hear about her other experience. Not now. As far as he was concerned, the only moment that mattered was this one. "This is just about us."

She laid her hands on his cheeks. Slowly, he began to move within her.

It was hard not to let himself completely lose all sense in the movements. Plunging in and out of Seven would have been such a release. But she was new to this. He was determined not to hurt her.

"Ben." Her voice was like a caress on his soul. "Let go."

How had she known he was holding back? He smiled down at her. It didn't matter how she knew. He shouldn't be surprised. This was Seven. She *knew* things. He took her words as permission.

He moved fast. One second in, then out again. Back in. She groaned and arched her back. "You like that, sweet girl?" "God, yes." Seven closed her eyes.

He reached between them to squeeze her clit, and she arched off the bed beneath him. "You like that even more."

"It's torture. This amount of pleasure is *torture*."

Her words resonated with him. He knew exactly what she meant. They moved together toward completion, and he could tell it was going to rock his world off its axis. This was monumental.

Seven's passion overtook her like a firecracker exploding. As long as he lived, he'd never forget the sight. Biting his lip, he held back his own release, wanting to make sure hers went on as long as it could.

Finally, in one moment of pure bliss, life altered for Ben. A combination of pleasure and pain overtook him until he lost his vision. Spilling his seed inside Seven was the most visceral experience of his entire life. He couldn't breathe, couldn't think, couldn't make sense of anything.

Forcing himself not to fall on top of Seven too hard, he slumped down gently on her made-for-him-only body. Blackness overtook him, but if he died that very second, he would leave the planet a happy man.

BEN OPENED HIS EYES. How long had he been nearly comatose? An hour? A minute? He stared down at the warm body beneath him and cursed himself, because despite his best intentions he had to be crushing her.

He lifted himself. With a groan, he pulled his amazingly still hard cock out of her pussy. If life were perfect, he would spend the rest of his life inside her and never have to do anything else.

She moaned and put her arms around his neck. Not opening her eyes, she spoke. "No. I like it. You make me feel warm and safe underneath you. Don't go." She was so adorable.

"I'm rolling over next to you but not leaving the bed. Here." He pulled her into the crook of his arms. "Sleep here."

She sighed and shuddered. "I can't go back, Ben. Before tonight, I would have found a way to survive the hours until my death, but now... I can't. I won't even make it through the car ride. I can't ever leave you and the girls."

She was so unlike everyone else he knew. She spoke the truth, always.

"No one is taking you from me. If we have to, we'll go on the run. But I don't think it will come to that."

Seven opened her blue depths and looked at him. "How can it not?"

"If I have to, I'll get an injunction to stop your execution. I'll challenge the constitutionality of the whole thing."

Her fingers stroked his chest, and his cock jumped. He had to control himself. She would be sore. She didn't need another slamming round for a while, as much as he might have wished he could hop right on and go for it.

"I don't know what most of what you just said means."

"It's legalese. The point is that I can make it impossible for them to execute you by claiming that it isn't legal for them to do it in the first place."

She sighed. "Ben..."

"Don't doubt me yet, Seven. For a few minutes, let's pretend I can do this as easily as I said I could. Tomorrow is soon enough for us to play the 'what if' game."

"I don't doubt you. I just know Madame. I know that she can do whatever she wants, whenever she wants." She kissed his chest. "But I believe in you."

"That's all I ask." His head spun. "I think we should try to get some sleep."

"Do you think it's okay for me to stay in here? Would it upset the girls to find me with you?"

"It's highly unlikely they would ever know you were in here."

She paused. "What if they come in to wake you in the morning?"

"They don't do that. When they wake up, they sneak downstairs to watch cartoons because they know I'll make them turn them off when I come down." He could feel his eyes getting heavier. She just felt right in his arms. "Even if they found you here, they'd not really understand what went on. They'd probably think you had a sleepover or something. They love you."

"I love them."

He was enormously glad about that. She hadn't said she loved him, even though she'd admitted to being *his*. It would come—he hoped. He thought she loved him.

"Go to sleep."

She snuggled closer. "At home, in the Institution, there are so many people jammed together, sometimes I can't sleep because people snore so loudly. I sometimes prefer my nights on the floor of clients' homes, because at least it's quiet."

"That's not your home. That's just where you were wrongly imprisoned for so long."

"I'd like to have a home."

His eyes no longer felt heavy. Now he was wide awake. "This can be your home, or wherever we end up. As long as we're together, that will be home."

"Okay." She sniffed. "Do you snore?"

"If I do, are you going to go back to your room? Should I be prepared to sleep alone?"

"To answer your question, no. I would sleep badly the rest of my life to be here with you. And can I take your answer to mean that you do? You cut logs in your sleep?"

He cracked up. Life with Seven would never be boring, not even when the crisis he knew they were going to face was over. "I'm teasing you. I don't think I snore, and if I do, please feel free to kick me or elbow me in the ribs."

"I couldn't do that."

Her words slurred together now. She had to be exhausted. He'd slept a little bit before she'd come into the room, but she had not.

Within moments, her breathing had become deep and even. He stared out into the darkness. There was a lot to do. Seven needed to keep clearing the ghost energy out of his neighbors' homes. He didn't want her to do that too quickly, but she did have to show that she was doing her job to keep Roman or any other member of the Fury from reporting to Madame that she wasn't working.

He needed to speak to his friend Dodie in Georgia. She was the best lawyer he knew at navigating federal statutes. If she wouldn't take on Seven's case, maybe she could at least advise him on the best way to go. He needed to work so he could pay for all of this.

A thought dawned on Ben. All that was important, but there was something he desperately wanted to do that had nothing to do with any of it. He wanted to take Seven and his girls out on his boat. Yes, they would spend part of the day out on his boat.

The world would have to wait a few hours while they did that.

TEN

Seven had never been on a boat before, and she found the experience to be soothing. The movements of the water relaxed her, making her sleepy. She leaned against the side and closed her eyes. Had she ever had a morning like this before? Other than climbing aboard the boat and letting Ben put her in a life jacket, she'd done nothing. *Nothing*.

"Daddy and Uncle Gene rode their boat across the world once."

Seven opened her eyes and regarded Ella. The little girl sat across from her, wearing a red lifejacket. Her dark hair was woven into two braids that fell just below her shoulders. Daphne wore an identical outfit, her hair in one long braid down her back.

"Across the world?" Seven didn't know about a lot of stuff, but she could actually tell certain landmasses on the globe. If someone spoke them aloud, she could remember where everything was located.

Ben laughed from where he captained the sailboat. "Not exactly across the world." His black hair blew in the wind while his eyes were alight with happiness. "Your

Uncle Gene was twenty-two, and I was twenty-one years old. We wanted to have one last hoorah before I went off to law school and Uncle Gene—ahem—went to study English literature."

Suddenly afraid she'd missed some kind of cultural reference,

Seven scratched her head. "Did he not study it?"

"Maybe he did for five minutes before he gave in and let his darker side guide his life."

Ella stood up and slid next to Seven until they sat side by side. "Uncle Gene is a hooligan."

"That's a good way to put it, Ella-bella." Ben leveled his gaze at Seven. "Gene is responsible for you coming to work with us."

"Ah. So he's an important person."

Ben shrugged. "In a manner of speaking, yes. I'll always be grateful he was able to use his connections to find you."

She would, too. If she ever had the chance to do something for Gene Lavelle, she would. "Go on."

Ben laughed. "Right, so our dad had a sailboat. A little bit smaller than this one, actually." Ben looked around the sailboat, and Seven guessed he was remembering the size of the other boat. He really had an amazing mind. Everything he said transfixed her. "Somehow—and now all these years later I can't imagine how—we managed to convince him to let us take the boat and sail it, by ourselves, down to the Caribbean."

Seven stood, nearly falling forward. She hadn't found what Ben called her sea-legs yet. "I like to look at globes. One of the guards would show us where places were. That's quite a ride."

Ben laughed. "Yeah, you could say that. Gene wanted us to make it all the way down to an island called St. Lucia.

We were going to sail down there and then hang out for several weeks before we sailed back."

She couldn't imagine such a trip. Seven had spent days in the back of a van with no idea where she was. What would it be like to be on the water with the horizon gone and only herself to rely on?

"Did you make it?"

He shook his head, his eyes wistful. "No. We had to be rescued off the coast of Florida. It was one giant mess after another. I'm better on this lake than I am in the open water. But my brother did take the trip again. By himself. And he made it, which officially gives him the right to blame all our sailing troubles on me."

As she stared at Ben, a funny feeling started in the pit of her stomach. He was such an incredible man. She had no doubt she loved him, the kind she'd heard the guards talk about and the way the other Conditioned whispered about at night, and that was a gift she'd never thought to have. What was life without love in it? She'd thought her life would end without ever experiencing the emotion.

It was warm outside, but goosebumps appeared on her exposed arms. She rubbed them absently. *Dread.* She swallowed. Yes, that was the emotion taking hold of her insides. Sheer and utter dread. She blinked a few times, trying to clear it from her system. She wanted to be with Ben more than anything. If someone wanted to hurt her, all they would have to do now was to harm Ben in even the smallest of ways.

"What's wrong? You just turned three shades paler." Ben extended his hand to her. "Come here. Are you feeling seasick?"

"No. I'm okay." Still, she walked to his outstretched hands. In the background, Ella and Daphne laughed. The girls seemed always capable of entertaining themselves. She'd never known children so adept at finding amusing games they made up out of their own imaginations. Maybe it was a twin thing.

Ben brushed her hair out of her eyes. They stood in silence as the wind pushed the hair Ben had just moved away back into her line of sight. She blinked a few times, trying to will away her need to start crying.

"What's going on, honey?"

She shivered at the sound of his voice. All she wanted in the world was to crawl into his arms and believe he could make everything better. But that was impossible, and she should have considered the risk he and the girls would be under before she'd gotten into bed with him and let him capture her heart.

"I think, if you love me as I believe you do, then you and the girls should go away and never think of me again."

Ben grimaced. "You can't be serious."

"I am. Dead serious."

"What's brought this on?" He stroked the side of her face and, like an idiot, she stood there and let him do it. Ben was like a drug to her. Already, in such a short time, she was addicted to his touches, consumed by his embrace.

"If something happened to you and the girls, it would kill me."

Ben pulled his gaze from hers to stare out at the horizon. She had no idea what he was thinking, and she wondered if he had decided to listen to her and leave her alone. Part of her was thrilled—she really couldn't abide the idea of his getting hurt. But the other part of her wanted to vomit at the thought that he would give her up.

"When Dana died, I just couldn't believe it." He sighed and looked back at her. "She'd been sick. We knew it was coming. I'm Mr. Prepared, so we had all her affairs in order. She'd read all kinds of books on handling death with young children and had practically written me a dissertation."

Seven wasn't exactly sure what all of what he said meant. She didn't recognize the word "dissertation" or know how one got one's affairs in order. Still, she understood enough to grasp that they had prepared a great deal for her passing.

These couldn't be easy memories for him to discuss.

"Ben..."

He kept talking. "But then she was gone and there really isn't any *preparing* for losing the woman you love and the mother of your children." He sighed. "So all worry about losing you, or any concern you have about losing me aside, I'm not going to go away or leave you because we're both worried about what could happen. We're all going to die someday. There's no point obsessing about it to the point that we can't live our lives. You're part of my life now."

"I just have this bad feeling."

"Seven—"

"Daddy!" Daphne's terrified voice carried over the breeze. She'd jumped to her feet.

"What is it, sweetheart? Seven, hold this." He pointed to the wheel, and before she could object, he crossed the boat to get to his daughter.

Seven gulped as she grasped the steering device. What could he possibly be thinking letting her be in charge of this?

"Just hold tight to it, sweetheart." Ben turned to Daphne.

"What is it, baby?"

"Dark things, Daddy. Dark things."

He kneeled down. Seven turned away from the scene. It

was only going to get worse for Daphne, and Seven didn't want to look at Ben right at that second. He'd see it written all over her face. There was nothing to be done about it. The least she could do was let Ben comfort his daughter and not let him know that his reassurances would mean nothing.

Seven had seen this occurrence many times. Children all started out the same. No one showed Conditioned symptoms at birth. After that, it was anyone's guess when the deviant abilities would begin. She'd been two years old. Daphne's precognition abilities would have seemed pretty innocuous, so meaningless in the beginning that Seven could believe that until she had personally stood in his living room and forced him to face it, Ben had managed to hide the truth even from himself.

He'd probably forced denial down his throat on a daily basis.

Seven gripped the wheel so tightly her fingers turned white from the strain. She took a deep breath and tried not to obsess.

The next step, after the children's abilities began, was what Madame called the Illumination Phase. Seven could remember her own very well. As a child, it had been virtually impossible for her not to shift to the dark light whenever an energy moved in or out of the room. She couldn't stop it. In and out—she'd been terrified. It had felt as if she was out of control of her own body.

But control came eventually. Even the most out-of-it Conditioned learned not to enact their not-from-God abilities unless they wanted to. Daphne was lucky. She had no physical manifestations of her Condition. If Ben could hide her, could keep her from being seen while she went through the Illumination, she would grow up, learn to control it and manage to hide herself in society.

Daphne was Madame's least favorite type of Conditioned.

She might actually not get caught. Unless she got too close to the Fury. They could smell a Condition even if there was no physical demonstration. They would blood-test her, and then it would all be over.

Ben basically needed to go into hiding now. She turned around to look at Ben.

"Sweetheart."

He didn't hear her. The wind had picked up. Seven shivered. Was this abrupt weather change a usual occurrence out on the lake?

"Honey, I'm sure you just imagined it."

He shouted to be heard by Daphne. Didn't he notice how loud it had suddenly gotten? She'd have to speak to him when they could talk. It wouldn't do to tell Daphne that she didn't know what she knew. Nothing would stop it. Denial would only make her feel as if she were crazy.

The boat shook beneath her hands. She could hardly hold it.

"Ben."

He looked up. "Just a second. I'm trying to make Daphne feel better. She keeps thinking she sees blackness on the wind."

That sounded daunting. "Ben, I can't hold the boat. Is it normal to have the wind blowing this hard?"

He stood up. "Come to think of it, no. Daphne, we'll talk about this later. Take your sister and go below."

Ella spoke up. "Daddy..."

"Ella, go."

His daughters nodded before turning to run below deck. In two swift strides, he was by her side. His presence made her feel calmer, but not by much. Something had gone amiss with the weather and that couldn't be good news.

"This was not supposed to happen." Ben took the wheel from her. She'd never been so relieved to let go of something in her life. "Go below with the girls."

"I take it this isn't normal?"

He shook his head. "We had no forecast of this. None. It was supposed to be beautiful all day. Look up there." Seven followed his gaze as dread traveled through her stomach. The clouds above them seemed very, very black.

"Are we going to be okay? Can you handle this?"

"I can. Just go below."

Thunder cracked above them. That couldn't be good. Seven had never been confronted with weather. That was one thing about living in the Institution. You were always inside if it rained. No one wanted to clean up any mud.

She moved, stumbling forward as the boat rocked sharply to the right.

"Seven!" Ben shouted.

She looked up to grin at him. "I'm okay. Just can't walk, apparently."

"No, the boat. It's rocking violently. Can you make it?"

"Sure." She pushed up. The rain pounded hard on her back. She officially hated this weather.

She'd barely stood up when she felt herself wrenched into the air. Ben's shout behind her was the last thing she heard as she was forcibly pulled upward. She yelled, terror overtaking her. Had she been sucked up in some kind of weird weather-thing? What was happening?

She swirled into the air. It felt as though someone held her in their hand. She cried, certain that at any second she'd fall back down into the water. The higher she got, the less likely it was that she would survive her fall.

Still she rose. Realization dawned on her as panic fled. This was weird. She might not know everything, but she knew this wasn't normal. People didn't get sucked upward off a boat to keep going farther and farther skyward. Unless they were, in fact, being picked up and moved.

There was a weather Conditioned at Crescent. He didn't communicate much with anyone else. Mostly he kept to himself, but Madame loved him. Rumors abounded that Madame made a lot of money under the table selling his powers to high bidders. If you were rich enough, you didn't have to endure rain on your daughter's wedding day. You could pay to make sure it didn't happen.

What was his number? Seven bit down on her lip as the wind whipped her hair against her face. Five-Thirty-Two. That was right. Five-Thirty-Two, it appeared, had another talent beyond weather control. He could move things, and this time it was Seven he had plucked up from the boat.

The question was, why? Why did Madame want her back so badly that she'd risked exposure by moving her from a boat where someone could see?

Ben. Oh god, Ben. He'd seen it. He was at risk.

She struggled against the wind, knowing it was futile. Even if she got away, she'd only plummet back down to the water or—who knew—maybe by now the land.

If she made it back to Crescent, she'd be dead upon arrival. But why? The sad truth was that she would find out the answer probably moments before she perished.

What kind of sick joke did fate feel the need to play on her? Introduce her to Ben only to rip him away or have him hurt? Show her love so she could know just what she'd missed out on right before her death?

No. None of it was fair. Seven screamed at the top of her lungs. This was too much. It was too unfair. Tears sprang from her eyes as her hands fisted at her sides. Her head thrashed from side to side. So many conflicting emotions threatened to overwhelm her.

That was when she felt it. Energy. It had formed around her. How was it possible, and where had it come from? Her gift pushed at her mind, wanting to shift phases so she could see what only she could.

What the hell? She might as well give in to it. Maybe it would be more bright-orange light sent to explode like a fire-cracker around her. Then she'd never even get any answers. She'd just fade away to nothing.

At least she might be able to go out with a fight.

She let the energy pull at her. With no worry about anyone looking, she let her eyes change fast. No one would be screaming in horror. Ben hadn't minded her devil-black eyes. Pushing all thoughts of him from her mind, she let herself enter the dark space.

Quickly, she looked around. There was no light. Nothing.

How was that possible?

"Would you like out of this situation?"

Seven gasped. "Who said that?"

"You can't see me? Damn it. I was pretty sure I'd figured all this out."

"No, I can't see anything." Seven shook her head. Was she losing her mind?

Had she been pushed into some kind of delirium?

A shadow formed in front of her. It looked like a man, but it had no form—it was only shadow. "Now? Can you see me now?"

Seven's hands flew to her neck. "Are you the Devil?"

"What? No. Sheesh. I'm just having a little trouble projecting my full form. Yeah, she just asked me if I was the Devil."

Okay, now I'm really confused. "Who are you and who are you speaking with?"

"I'm sorry, I should have said. My name is Spencer, and my brother Roman contacted me about getting you out of the trouble you're currently in."

Seven blinked a few times to try to clear her head. "Roman the Fury?"

"That's the one. I'm talking to the group of people I'm with. We're all working together to make this little interaction between us possible."

"Okay." Seven scratched her head. "It felt like there was energy."

"There was—or is, rather. Anyway, it's complicated. Once you're with us—if you choose to come—we can teach you what it is that you really do."

"What I really do?"

"That's right. You have only a mediocre understanding of it. No Conditioned in captivity really understands what they are capable of. But I can't take you from where you are without your permission. It's part of the rules we've set up for ourselves to keep our location a secret. It keeps all of us safe."

"I would love to be taken from here. If you don't, they're going to kill me."

Spencer, the black shadow, nodded. "I know. Madame wants you dead very badly. We're not sure why, but we're going to find out."

"Could you bring Ben and the girls, too? They're going to be in terrible trouble." And thinking about it made her feel ill.

"We can't."

"Then I can't come." She wouldn't leave Ben. There had to be a way to get herself freed and get back to Ben.

"You'll die if you don't, Seven. You'll never make it back to him, and let's face it, he's safer without you."

"Why can't he come?"

Spencer sighed. "He's too connected to the outside. If we take him while he's still so wrapped up in the world there, his disappearance will be noted. People will ask questions we can't handle. Maybe there will come a time when we can take him. I'm not sure. But we can do our best to make sure he's safe. Come with us, Seven. The rest of this, we can work it out."

Seven realized she really didn't have a choice. If she stayed, she was dead, and then there would never be any chance to get back to Ben. If she went, she would find a way. He'd be terribly worried. She would have to find a way to contact him, to make sure he knew she was alive.

For the first time in her life, she didn't believe her destiny had to end at the hands of one of Madame's executioners. Yes, she would go. She would go and find a way to make a life for her, Ben, and his girls.

Wherever she went, it had to be better than here. "Take me with you."

ELEVEN

FIVE YEARS LATER

He was going to have to file more paperwork. Ben threw his pen down on his desk. There was always more goddamn paperwork. File one injunction, hit another wall.

"Got a minute?"

Ben jumped. He hadn't even heard Gene come in. But that was standard these days. His head was always somewhere else.

"Of course." He cleared his throat as he gestured around the room. "You can sit if you can find a place."

"I don't dare. The last time I tried, I moved something pivotal, remember?"

Gene grinned at him as he walked slowly toward the desk. His brother wanted something. Too bad Ben had nothing left to give to anyone.

He'd failed. That was all there was to it.

"What do you need, Gene?"

His brother sighed. "This is about Daphne."

Now that would get his attention. "Has she been discovered?"

"No, of course not. If I've told you once, I've told you a

thousand times, Daphne is safe and protected. As long as we keep doing what we've been doing the last two years, nothing bad is going to happen to that baby."

He knew that, of course. Taking Gene into his confidence after the nightmare of the boat trip had been a risk, but one that had proven to be a blessing. Gene loved those girls, and if anyone had the ability to break the law without worrying about the consequences, it was his big brother.

"So what's going on?" Ben looked at the clock. "She should be with the tutor now."

"She is."

He raised an eyebrow. "Then what?"

"Ella tells me that Daphne is dreaming about the girl again."

Ben wanted to throw something across the room. Instead, he sat back in his chair and counted to ten. That didn't thaw his temper. It didn't help that Gene stood there silently, as if he was completely patient to do nothing but wait.

"We all think about her, Gene. She was ripped from my boat in the middle of the day by a strange—I don't know —*thing*, and we never saw her again."

His brother crossed his arms across his chest. "One of these days, you'll have to come across a better word for what took her than *thing*."

"Yes, well, according to the media, I'm probably crazy. Now, back to Daphne. She's going to dream about Seven for the rest of her life." They all were. Ben saw her regularly in his sleep. It was one of the reasons he spent so little time in the nightly activity. "Unless my daughter has suddenly picked up another ability to speak with the dead, then she's just dreaming about Seven like any person does when they've been through a trauma."

"The trauma was five years ago. You don't think it might be a good idea to speak to your very talented daughter and see if maybe she might have something useful to say to you?"

He shook his head right before he pounded the desk. "No. I think the best thing Daphne can do is to never talk about any of this. Ever. For the rest of her life, she is going to have to pretend she sees nothing. She might as well start getting used to it now." As he jumped up, his chair fell backward. "So if that's all..."

"It's not." Gene shook his head, a small grin forming on his face. "Talking about that Conditioned woman is the only thing that gets a reaction out of you, ever. Other than that, you've become so resigned."

"Yeah, well, life is shit. What can I say?"

Outside his daughters, there wasn't anything he looked forward to. The need to punish those who had taken Seven fueled him, but he was wise enough to know that when he met his goals—and despite his failure, he knew he would never stop until he did—he would find a cold reward of nothing waiting for him.

"She died. You didn't."

Ben stalked forward, getting in Gene's face. "I'm aware of that."

"You didn't get this worked up over Dana."

"I can't do anything about incurable cancer except give money to research that may or may not actually be getting done. I *can* stop bullies who imprison, abuse, and eventually kill a portion of our population for no good reason other than that they can, and I might remind you that if they knew about her, Daphne would—"

Gene held up his hand. "I know. I don't know why I'm

baiting you." His brother scratched his head. "That's not true. I do know."

No one could get him more upset than Gene, and no one could defuse him faster. Ben suspected he sometimes did it just to prove he still could. Their relationship had changed over the last five years. Truth was, Ben would never have imagined Gene could be so good to all of them. So helpful. So familial. But he'd stepped up when Ben had needed him. He'd taken care of the girls when Ben had managed to look like a lunatic in the press. Gene had protected all of them.

"If you know, then why don't you just tell me what has gotten you all pissed off instead of making me nuts?"

"You got another file."

Ben's heart sped up. "Another file? Where is it?"

Gene sighed. "I left it on the desk in the reception area."

Turning on his heel, Ben ran the small distance between his office and the desk that would belong to his secretary if he actually had one. "Why would you leave such an important thing out where anyone could get it?"

"Who would get it, Benedicte?" His brother followed him.

"Anyone could." He reached the desk and snatched up the manila folder.

As had happened every time, Ben turned over a large manila envelope with a typed address. It held no return mailing information, and like always, it arrived on the same date as it had the previous month and every month before that. It stated Ben's name with the words "Care of Eugene Lavelle" below and then the address of Gene's office. Ben's office was listed publicly, but each time the envelope came through Gene.

In the beginning, Ben had been convinced that Gene

actually knew the person who sent them, but he no longer was. Gene probably disliked the secrecy even more than he did.

He ripped open the seal. It was funny, but receiving the letter that came with the money and information every month had become one of his favorite things. He'd never met the woman—if she was a woman and not a man using a fake woman's name—but the way she wrote to him always lifted his spirits.

"It's just too weird. If I can't find out who this person is, then no one can. And everyone can be found. I don't trust it." Gene sniffed.

"It doesn't matter." What Ben really wanted was to have Gene leave, or at least go into the other room so he could read his letter alone. "Every small advancement I've made has come from information from this woman. Whoever she is, she's helping. End of story."

Gene nodded. "I knew you'd say that. Go on. Read your damn letter. I'll wait for you in your office. I'll be sitting in *your* chair." Ben waited for Gene to leave the room. It was stupid; it wasn't as if Gene was going to read over his shoulder. Still, it felt better to read her notes alone.

Dear Ben.

He smiled. The letters used to come addressed to Mr. Lavelle, but about a year ago she had started calling him Ben. He wasn't sure why it had changed, he was just glad it had. She felt like a friend to him, even if he'd never gotten to write back to her. Somehow, it was as if they communicated.

Ben sat on the reception desk as he continued reading.

I trust this letter finds you well, and that the information I provided you helped in the tour you took of the Crescent facility a few weeks ago. I was beyond relieved to see that the information you gave to the authorities about the state of things inside the medical center there was actually acted upon. What a change!

Your hard work and selfless pursuits on behalf of the Conditioned warm my heart. Although I worry that perhaps you are spending too much time on it. Do you ever do anything just for fun? Not that I'm much better. I think it's been five years since I spent a day simply doing nothing at all. Maybe I should take my own advice for a change.

I've never spoken to you about my organization, the group I am affiliated with that helps me in my endeavors. We, like you, find the treatment of the Conditioned within the Institutions to be horrifying, and we are determined to find a way to eventually release all the Conditioned from their unfair captivity. We cannot thank you enough for all you have done. I know that numerous Conditioned have had their lives spared at Crescent due to your unwavering efforts on their behalf. The last injunction you filed to stop the executions still holds fast there, but Madame Joan is, I understand, quickly losing patience.

I fear for your wellbeing. That is why this is the last letter I will be sending you.

Ben's heart sped up. No. That was unacceptable. He wouldn't be able to continue without her.

But fear not. I believe the time when we can all see each other is coming. I believe this with all my being.

Gratefully,

Shiri Roberts

Ben kicked the desk hard. "God damn it." He didn't need Shiri fearing for him. He could take care of himself, and his girls were well protected. He needed vengeance. It was all that drove him.

Seven deserved vengeance. Despite what society said,

she had mattered. Madame had even claimed that Seven had never existed and, as far as the law was concerned, she hadn't. Even though they'd had such a short time together, he had loved her deeply. He wouldn't—couldn't—rest until he'd made sure that what had happened could never happen again.

Ben closed his eyes. If only he wasn't so tired. He rubbed his forehead.

"Good note? Bad note?"

Gene's voice made him snap out of it. He opened his lids. "Bad note. It will, evidently, be the last one. Although she did still send a check."

He pulled it out of the envelope. "Now I'm apparently being paid for doing nothing for her."

"You've done a lot. More than anyone else could. The Institutions are impossible to bring down. I've told you a million times. I'd rather go in guns blazing, but you found ways to use the law. Ben, it's not a small thing. Your lady would have been proud."

He shook his head. "It could never be enough. I failed her."

"They pulled her out of the boat using some kind of specialized tornado. How could you have prepared for that?"

Ben could barely answer. Fatigue drained him. "I shouldn't have taken her out on the boat. I had this idea that we could spend a normal morning together. I should have packed her away and run. She knew. She understood how dangerous it was."

"How dangerous it still is. If Madame Joan gets her way, they're never going to find your body."

"I know." He nodded his head in agreement. It weighed on him. The girls needed him, but how could he look at himself—or them—if he let this go? Daphne might need someone to fight for her someday.

"If you had gone on the run, they would have found you eventually. They would have gotten to her. That's what they do. Trust me, I understand. I'm exactly the same as they are. You don't get to be powerful by turning back and not getting what you want."

For the first time in his life, Ben felt he could really relate to his brother, because he would never stop. Ever.

The door banged open, and they both whirled around. For a second, he couldn't believe his eyes. Standing in front of him was a person he'd thought never to see again. Five years had aged him, as it had all of them, but there was no mistaking Roman Lewis, the Fury who had showed up during his time with Seven.

"Roman Lewis?"

Gene looked at Ben. "You know this person?"

Ben didn't miss the way Gene's hand had reached into his blazer, ready to grip the revolver Ben knew to be hidden there.

"I met him once. He's a Fury."

Gene shook his head. "That doesn't fill me with confidence." Roman put his hands out in front of him. "Relax, both of you. If I was here to hurt you, you'd never see or hear me coming."

That was probably true. Ben nodded to his brother, and Gene took his hand out of his coat. It used to bother him that Gene had most likely killed people. Now... well, there were lots of people in the world who deserved killing. It bothered him less, and if feeling that way made Ben a bad person, then so be it.

"So what are you doing here, Roman?" As casually as he

could, he slipped the letter from Shiri underneath the organizer on the desk. He really didn't want Roman finding it.

"I came because a mutual friend of ours asked me to make sure you were both all right."

Ben shook his head. "We don't have mutual friends, Roman. I'm devoted to bringing down the people who keep you in those expensive clothes. I don't want anything from you."

Roman smirked. "You're going to eat those words someday. Trust me on that."

"If that's it, you can leave as you came in."

Gene cleared his throat. "Don't you want to hear what the man has to say?"

"No." Ben didn't know where his hostility toward Roman came from. Maybe he somehow blamed him for not saving Seven. It was irrational, but Ben didn't really give a shit.

Roman looked at his watch. "Turn on the television."

"What?"

Roman nodded at the set that hung on the wall. "Do it, or I'll turn it on myself."

Gene turned around as he picked up the remote to turn on the screen. Ben couldn't remember the last time they'd used the thing. He wasn't even sure why he had it. Maybe Gene had insisted five years ago. The whole time was a blur.

A newscaster was shouting into her microphone. Behind her, a building burned brightly. Ben narrowed his eyes. He knew that place.

"That's right, Penelope, I'm standing in front of the Crescent holding facility that houses and controls the Conditioned population for the southeast sector of the

United States, where, just minutes ago, we are told, at least ten bombs exploded simultaneously."

A female voice spoke. "Can you tell us what the damage is, Sabine, and if any of the Conditioned escaped the facility?"

"We aren't sure. As you can see, things are in upheaval here, but we are being told that at least some of the Conditioned did make it out of the facility before the fires rapidly spread. Madame Joan Martin, the proprietress of Crescent, seems to have escaped the blasts."

Behind him, Ben heard Roman swear. He stared at the Fury. Joy and horror mixed inside Ben. Joy that somehow someone had managed to blow the place to smithereens. Horror that Madame had still managed to get away.

"Shouldn't you be off helping to collect everyone, Fury?"

Gene sighed. "Ben—"

Roman interrupted. "Listen to me, Ben. It would make my life a great deal better if you were dead. You have to trust me on this. Something I have wanted badly for many years could actually be mine if only you died. And yet—"

"I don't know what game you're playing, Roman, but—"

He never got to finish, as Roman shouted over him. "Here I am to save your ass because, as it turns out, you are actually a worthy person. In about ten minutes, the police are going to be here. You've made quite a name for yourself as a Conditioned advocate. They are going to want to question you."

Gene stepped forward. "How do you—"

"Because I do. That's all you need to know. I have to disappear. You need to know nothing."

"I don't know anything about this."

"Ah, but you do." Roman took a step in their direction. "Both of you do. Or at least you know a name you can no longer remember—temporarily at least. Shiri Roberts."

Rage threatened to overtake Ben. "What do you know about her? If you've hurt her, Fury, I'll—"

"You'll what?" Roman laughed, a cold sound. "It's because of Shiri that I'm even bothering with you. The police will have mind readers with them. Fury who can know your deepest secrets."

Gene cursed. "Then how do you expect him to handle this?"

"You're both going to forget. Temporarily."

Ben finally understood. "You're going to take the memory of her from us."

"And all correspondence that you've kept from her, including the letter you just put underneath the organizer on that desk."

He swallowed. It made sense. "How do I know you aren't going to take other memories, and that you'll give me her memory back when this is over?"

Roman looked at his watch. "You don't. But think of it this way. I could have taken your memories and you never would have known. I did you the courtesy of telling you. That must mean something."

"But—"

A noise on the screen got his attention. He turned to look. A man sat in a chair, his face and body concealed by shadows that made it impossible to see him clearly. He began to address the television audience. Ben glanced at Gene. He rubbed his head. What was going on? Oh yes, there had been explosions at Crescent. What else had happened? A slight feeling of confusion assaulted him, but he didn't really care. He felt remarkably calm, and he couldn't shake the song *Tomorrow* from the musical Annie from his mind.

The man on television spoke. "My name is Guy McKidd."

Ben turned to regard his office. Something was missing, but he had no idea what it was. Other than Gene and himself, no one was there. *Weird*.

The door to his office banged open as five armed police officers rushed in. He should have been surprised to see them, but he wasn't, and he had no idea why.

Calmly, he raised his arms to show he was unarmed.

Gene reached for his gun even as Ben called out for him not to. He pulled his hand out without his weapon. "Ben," he whispered. "What the fuck happened to my revolver?"

TWELVE

"It's done."

Shiri exhaled. "Thank you."

She hit the end button on her cell phone and tried to concentrate on what was happening. Guy needed her total focus. If any of the Fury were able to get through their wards to send damaging energy to harm Guy, she would need to defuse it. Gone were the days when she'd just let the energy manipulation happen. Now, she could actually sense it coming and control it. It was pivotal that she not lose all her hard-won control.

But she couldn't help but feel utter and complete relief after Roman's phone call. Ben knew nothing that could get him in trouble, although the Fury and the Institutions would still try.

Her phone vibrated. She looked down as she walked quietly away from the room where they were filming Guy's announcement. It was a message from Addison Lewis, her beautiful friend who had started the Conditioned movement's recent momentum when she'd run off with Spencer Lewis, the man who was now her husband. Before that, she'd been the formidable Addison Wade. Shiri shivered to remember that she hadn't known about any of that when she'd been locked up in Crescent.

As her hands shook, she read the message twice, a skill she'd quickly learned in the last five years. They had confirmation.

Madame Joan had lived. The bombs that should have taken her out hadn't gone off. They'd brought down Crescent, but not Madame and her sick ministrations. The woman was still around to cause hell to those who didn't deserve it.

She looked up as Tara walked into the room. Tara Finley had befriended her the moment she'd stepped foot into Guy McKidd's compound. The woman had once been in the Safe Dawn Institution before Addison and Spencer Lewis had broken her out. She was a very powerful fire-starter.

Tara could also be a mega-bitch, which meant it was a really good thing that she liked Shiri as much as she did. "Did the Fury manage to protect your friend?"

Shiri nodded. "The Fury has helped us tremendously over the years. He's Spencer's brother. He has a name and you know it."

"Roman has his own agenda and you *know* it." Tara rolled her eyes as one of their people operating the camera shushed her. She took Shiri's arm and moved her farther out of the room. "He's in love with you."

"We're friends."

Tara shrugged. "Maybe. But he's in love with you."

"It's not important today. None of the personal stuff matters today. Today is about freedom. Our brothers and sisters are gaining freedom. As soon as the bombs go off in Ashes, they'll know they have to release the others."

Tara pulled her into a hug. Her voice was barely a whisper. "Even our Seers can't predict what will happen. Shiri, they're never going to just let them go. Ever."

She shook in Tara's arms. Amongst themselves—the group of Conditioned who had managed either by luck or with help to get to the safety that was Guy McKidd's private island—they were split almost straight down the middle about what the future would bring. As Tara had said, even their very gifted Seers didn't know.

Tara, Guy and some of the others thought outright war was inevitable. Ultimately, they'd won on the bombing vote. But Shiri believed in her heart of hearts that there were peaceful ways to win the day. Ben Lavelle had found methods to keep the Institutions partially in check, and over time things could get better.

Tara shook her head as if she'd read her mind, even though that wasn't one of Tara's talents. "Too many people would die in the meantime. I can always read your thoughts right on your face."

"I know." She pulled Tara tighter before she let her go.

Touch was hugely important to all of them. Other than meaningless sex, most of the Conditioned had never gotten to touch just for the sake of it. Everyone was always embracing each other.

"So how did I do?"

They both turned to look at Guy. With his bald head and the gold hoops he always wore in his pierced ears, he looked like a pirate. The first time Shiri had seen him, she'd wanted to run away and hide. But he was kind, most of the time, and when she'd finally gotten over her panic, she'd remembered hearing his name. It had been his mother who had bought her clothes at the mall, the first nice clothes she ever remembered wearing. Guy had loved that story when she'd told it to him. Or at least she thought he had. Guy didn't share his feelings all that often.

She stared at him blankly, knowing Tara was doing the same thing.

"You ladies didn't watch me, did you?" He rolled his eyes.

Tara laughed. "We watched you do it a million times."

Guy held Tara's eye contact a moment longer than was appropriate. He always did, and the only one who didn't seem to notice was Tara. Shiri tried not to grin and almost didn't. She managed to make it last only a fleeting second, but it was long enough that Guy noticed and glared at her.

No one could blame Guy for his infatuation. Tara was gorgeous. Even though most of the Conditioned had no idea where their heritage lay, Shiri thought that Tara's family had been Armenian. She had high cheekbones, black hair and brown eyes that men seemed to fall into.

Shiri sighed. Roman might or might not have been in love with Shiri. It didn't matter.

"Did Roman take care of your friend?"

Shiri smirked. "Reading my mind, McKidd?"

"Am I touching you, Shiri? No, I'm not reading your mind."

She stared down at his covered hands. She'd never seen Guy without gloves and probably never would. Even with the blockage, he could pick up thoughts and memories.

"Yes, Roman took care of it."

"Shiri."

She knew what he was going to say and stopped him. "I know. Not yet. He can't meet me yet."

For years, she'd maintained her patience on this subject simply because she didn't want to put Ben and his family in danger by associating with her.

"Come on. I'm tired of being inside." Guy gestured for them to walk in front of him.

She smiled. Being able to determine when she did and didn't want to go outside was one of the treats of getting to live a self-determined life. They stepped out together into the sunlight, which felt different here than it had back in Louisiana.

The Caribbean sun warmed her pale skin.

"Don't get burned, sweetie." Tara laughed as she strolled down toward the water. Guy stood still, watching Tara's movements.

"Your first week here, you got scorched. I thought we were going to have to fly you to a hospital somewhere for sun poisoning."

Shiri smiled at Guy. "Yes, I remember. I was the one living through it, if you'll recall. You're all sorts of sentimental today. I don't think I've ever seen you like this before."

"If we've made a mistake, a terrible mistake, then this place we've built will all come to an end."

"Guy." She touched his shoulder, making sure to keep her hand on the cloth of his shirt. Still, he flinched. She'd long ago learned to disregard the way he reacted upon initial contact. He still needed to be touched, maybe even more so than anyone else. "We'd follow you to Hell. You know that."

"I do and that's why it's so hard." He cleared his throat as he looked down at his watch. "It's almost time for Ash. We should hear from Spencer any moment, Shiri."

She smiled. "What is it?"

"I hate that you couldn't bring them."

Her grin fell, and she fought the tears that wanted to spill. "It made sense. You didn't know him. He was an unresearched person, too connected to vanish. There's so much here that's more important than my silly heart."

"No, there isn't. I think we made a mistake. What is any of this if we can't be happy?"

Her mouth fell open. "Guy..."

His cell phone chirped loudly, and he grabbed it to look down at the number.

Quickly, he answered it. "Talk to me, Spence."

"Good." Guy gave her the thumbs-up. "Did we get the warden? Yeah. Good. We didn't at Crescent. She's still at large. We think the Fury has her." Guy paused, listening to whatever Spencer Lewis was saying on the other end of the phone. "Addison has started pick-up. She thinks about thirty percent of the Conditioned are in the wind. The other seventy percent we have. So compete with your wife, see if you can do better. The other two islands are all set up."

Shiri had heard enough. She moved fast, away from Guy. His confession had rocked her. She ached for Ben and his girls. The only thing that had kept her going was the absolute belief that it had been the right thing to do to keep herself hidden from him, and that someday they could be reunited.

Tears fell from her eyes, and she wiped them away as she ran toward her bungalow. When was the last time she'd cried? She sniffled at the thought. Five years. The first night she had been here.

Spencer had moved her through dark space—an experience she hoped never to have to repeat—and after being introduced to everyone on the island she'd been left alone in her new home to find her footing. It hadn't taken her any time to start bawling. Two days later, Tara had dragged her cried-out self outside to face life.

She wasn't that girl anymore. The girl with no name. The Conditioned victim who had spent her life being used by a maniacal woman who had wanted her put to death before her time. If she was sometimes sad that the one bright part of her miserable life before she'd arrived couldn't know she was alive, then it was her problem to handle.

But now Guy said that decision had been wrong? *Ah, hell.*

She flung open the door and threw herself down on her bed. Her face down on the pillow, she took a shallow breath. It smelled like home in here, and she could think. She could somehow make sense of this.

As she closed her eyes, she called the energy that existed in all living things. Within a few seconds, she'd created a barrier that would keep all but the most gifted dark-space travelers from entering her space. That trick was one of the first Spencer had taught her. Shiri wasn't a passive participant in her gift: she got to control it.

A whisper traveled on the wind. *Seven...*

Shiri sat up. Who had said that? No one used that name, no one. It was one of Guy's rules. Every person on the island had a name, and if they didn't have one, they came up with one for themselves. It had taken her weeks to come up with hers, and she still wasn't sure if it had been the right choice.

Seven, help us.

She got off the bed. "Hello, is someone there?" She sent her talent out to check the energy she'd strung around the bungalow. There was no break. No one had approached.

Please, Seven, come out of hiding. They've taken my dad and my uncle. Everyone has left. They're all scared. We don't know what to do. If you're there like I think you're there, please come back for us.

Daphne. Shiri fell to her knees. Oh God, Daphne was also a Telepath. That wasn't such an easy power to hide. Most Telepaths changed slightly when they used their physical power. How had Ben handled it? She'd had no idea. A dual power? Very rare. Like Guy and Addison.

Shiri bit her thumbnail. Ben and Gene had been taken. Both of them. And they weren't back yet? But they didn't know anything. Roman had taken care of it.

They should have been released when the Fury saw they had no information.

Oh, damn it.

Shiri stood. She wasn't a Telepath. She couldn't speak back to Daphne, but someone could. Lesley could answer her.

"Lesley!" She ran in the direction of the main house. "Lesley!" Over and over she screamed the other woman's name until she was just about to the house.

Her friend rushed through the front door. They nearly collided before Lesley grabbed Shiri's arms to steady her. "What is it? What's happened?"

"Ben, my friend. You remember him?"

Lesley raised an eyebrow. "Friend?"

"Okay, whatever. His daughter, Daphne. You remember, I told you about his daughters and that one of them—"

"Is Conditioned. Yes."

"She just spoke to me telepathically."

Her friend fell silent. "She's telepathic? I thought she was a Seer."

"It seems she's both."

"Damn." Lesley fell silent, chewing on her bottom lip.

"Can you answer her for me? They've taken Ben and Gene and haven't returned them yet."

"I can't answer until I speak to Guy."

"Right." The adrenaline surging through Shiri's veins made her hands shake.

"Let's go."

Lesley grabbed her hand. "Come on."

They ran together through the paths their group had carved out for themselves. When Guy had come to the island, there had been nothing. By the time Shiri had gotten there, most of the work had been done, but she had done her part digging and paving when necessary.

The paths had never seemed so long as now. Daphne needed her, and Ben was missing. Oh, and Ella must be suffering greatly watching all this happen to her family. It was hard for Shiri not to imagine them as the little girls they'd been when last she'd seen them. Five years had passed. They'd be eleven years old. Not little anymore, and she'd missed them as much as she'd missed Ben. Oh, how she wanted Guy to say yes. There was no way Lesley would break any rules.

Well, that was too bad. If she couldn't speak to Daphne telepathically, she'd go to her personally. She wasn't a prisoner. They couldn't make her stay if she insisted on going. *Could they?*

Together, they nearly slammed into Guy. He was still on the phone, but that was his standard pose these days. She couldn't imagine that organizing an uprising was an easy task, even if you had been planning it for it most of your life.

He held out his hand to them as he hung up the phone. "What's going on?" He looked directly at Shiri. "Why did you run off like that?"

Shiri shook her head. "I've been contacted telepathically by Daphne, Ben Lavelle's daughter."

Guy whistled through his teeth. "I didn't know she could do that. I thought she was a Seer."

If Shiri had to answer that question one more time, she was going to pull out her hair. "Apparently, she can do both. I haven't been in contact with her for five years. I didn't know. That's not important. I need Lesley to answer her."

"Hold on a second." Guy held up his hands. "I know you haven't seen her in five years. I'm not an idiot. There was a purpose to my question."

Shiri clasped her hands together in a gesture she hoped would show her frustration without being outright rude. "I'm sorry, Guy. Please go ahead."

"Don't you think it's ironic that this new power we knew nothing about, despite Roman watching them so closely for us for so many years, shows up on the day we blow up not one, but two Institutions?"

"No." Shiri heard his words, but the doubt that should have presented itself with them didn't. "It's not weird. Her father is missing. Why would she have reached out before now? They've apparently taken her uncle, too. The girls have to be terrified."

"If Roman is correct, the girls have the strongest wing of the New Orleans Mafia watching their every move. They're safe."

"No, Guy. They're not. I know the timing sucks. I get it. This is the last thing you need, but either you let Lesley answer her, or I'm going to see her myself."

Guy leaned back against the closest palm tree. "You would do that, Shiri? You would go to this child even if I said that by doing so you wouldn't be able to come back?"

She sighed. "Guy, you just told me that keeping him away had been a mistake. Let's rectify it."

He nodded. "I think you just answered my question, didn't you? If I don't agree to this, then you'll go. You'll leave us."

Even though it killed a part of her to have to admit it to the man who had taken her in, clothed her, taught her, and protected her for five years, she nodded slowly. "Yes, I would go and not come back."

He smiled, showing the dimple in his left cheek. "Now there's the backbone I like to see in you. Five years ago, you were broken. But you fixed yourself. Go get your man and your girls."

"How can I get Ben? He's in the custody of the Fury."

"Go see Addison. She'll help you. I'm sorry, I can't let Lesley contact her. It's too risky. We don't know what they're monitoring, even if Daphne doesn't mean for it to happen."

Shiri sighed. It wasn't what she'd wanted, but it was better than nothing.

Guy grabbed her arm. "Just remember this. If they have her father, the girls will do anything to get him back. That's how these things work."

"I'm just one little Conditioned woman. As far as they were concerned, I was pretty weak. Why would they care that much about getting me back?"

"Why did they want you dead so badly in the first place? We don't know. Watch yourself. Be careful getting back. I'm going to need you to help me with all the folks who're going to be coming. They'll be wounded, like you were. Maybe worse."

"I'll hurry."

As she turned to run away, a slight fear settled into her stomach. What if Ben didn't want to come with her? What if he didn't care about her anymore or he couldn't understand what she'd done?

"Shiri."

She turned around to Lesley's call.

"Yes?"

"We'll miss you. Hurry back home."

Shiri loved that word. *Home.* But it never had been, because Ben hadn't been with her. If she could bring him back, then it would be home, for the first time in her life.

THIRTEEN

Ben hadn't smoked a cigarette since he was in college—he'd sworn to himself that he never would again—but he was ready to make an exception to his personal rule. If only someone would offer him one. He leaned back in his uncomfortable chair and drummed his hands on the table in front of him. The fluorescent light that illuminated the interview room buzzed above him, and he knew that at any second he would acquire a migraine headache.

He rubbed his forehead. No one had been in to see him for an hour at least. They'd taken his watch and his cell phone, so he couldn't be exactly sure that was how much time had passed. But it felt like at least that long. Of course, it might only have been ten minutes, with the buzzing fluorescents making it seem so much longer.

Somewhere off in the distance he could smell coffee brewing, but like the cigarette, no one asked him if he wanted any. He sniffed the air again. That scent. Coffee. It reminded him of someone but he couldn't place who. He rubbed his head again. Something just felt... off.

The police had dragged him in here and left him in this chair. How on Earth they thought he could have had anything to do with the bombings at the Crescent, he didn't know. Sure, he fought against injustice like anyone with a moral sense would, but bomb an Institution? He wouldn't have the slightest idea how to go about doing that.

He'd been separated from Gene, which didn't surprise him at all. If they really thought he had planted a bomb, then they would want to divide him from his support system and try to get the truth from someone else.

Two men had arrived shortly after that. They hadn't uttered a word, just kind of stared at him weirdly and then looked at each other with frightened eyes. He'd asked for a lawyer, and they had left.

That had been it. That had been the last time he'd seen another human being. He leaned back in his chair. In a minute he would throw it against what he assumed was the two-way mirror he faced.

The door swung open and an older woman marched in. She held her back straight as if she had a board attached to it. Short white hair stopped at the nape of her neck except for where it curled slightly under her ears. Silver cat earrings adorned her earlobes and a tight expression graced her lips.

Ben would have known her anywhere. He'd been fighting the good fight against her for years. She was Madame Joan, the proprietress of Crescent—the Institution that had burned to the ground just that morning.

He looked up at her, surprised by the smile that wanted to cross his lips. She must have been in deep trouble if she was stooping to speak with him. In the five years since he'd picked up his cause, she'd never taken one meeting with him. Not one. Yet here she was now. It was almost too bad that he couldn't take credit for the problems she was facing.

"Mr. Lavelle."

Her voice had a slight French accent that he imagined she thought made her sound sophisticated. The woman hadn't lived in France since she'd been three years old. There was no way she still had such a thick intonation. No, that was as put-on as the rest of her. Ben knew a lot of her secrets, much more than he should have known. He rubbed his forehead. Why did he know so much about her? How had he acquired that information? God, he must be losing his mind. Or had lost it already. Who the hell knew?

"You have been tampered with." Madame spoke her words with such a sneer that he thought she should give lessons on the act to those who wanted to learn it.

"I'm not sure what that means. As far as I know, I haven't been 'tampered' with." He sat forward, determined to overcome his fatigue and not let her have the upper hand in this conversation. "If I'm being accused of something, I want a lawyer. If I'm not, I want to be released. And for the record, I'm pretty sure that no law in this land would give you the right to question me about anything. I am not Conditioned, and you have no jurisdiction over me."

Her eyes lit up with anger. "The whole country is in an uproar. We are under attack by a madman who wants to let loose the most dangerous monsters ever born. Some of them are already causing havoc. I assure you, Mr. Lavelle, no one in the world cares about your *rights* at the moment."

He shrugged. "Maybe not at this moment, but in a few weeks when I bring a lawsuit against you, this police department, and the entire state of Louisiana for violating my rights, then you will care very deeply."

As a rule, Ben didn't make threats he didn't intend to keep. He felt giddy at the idea of filling out the paperwork to take them all down. Forms and legal precedents had never excited him as much as they did right at that moment.

"Who says you're going to live through this experience, Mr. Lavelle? If I have my way—and I always do—you won't be walking out of this room alive. Or maybe I can let you live... as a vegetable. I'm sure your daughters will love having to care for you for the rest of their lives."

Now the woman had gone too far. "You may be able to kill me. I don't doubt it. You are a sick bitch. But you'll never stop what has happened. Those 'monsters' are going to come down on you. They'll redefine the word nightmare."

"Do you know what amuses me about this? You don't even know why you feel this way. My boys tell me that your memory has been so tampered with that you don't even know who Seven was."

He blinked. It was as if she were speaking gibberish. "I'm sorry, did you say something about the number seven? I'm usually pretty good at following conversations but my mental prowess clearly doesn't apply to you."

Madame sat down on the table and leaned over until she was inches from his face. He could smell her sour breath, and it made him want to gag. He forced himself not to give in to the urge. It was a small inner victory, but he would take it just the same.

"Do you know what amazes me about you at the moment? I'll repeat this again. You don't even know why."

"Once again, you might want to work on your conversation skills. I have no idea what you're talking about."

She shook her head. "For the last five years, you have

been a thorn in my side. The Council didn't want you touched. Oliver Wade said you were to be left alone, that you would fade away into obscurity, remembered only for being a rabble-rouser at best and a lunatic at worst. I was willing to put up with your craziness because I understood where it came from. You loved the girl."

He had no idea what she was talking about. "I've loved one woman in my life, and her name was Dana Lavelle. She was my wife, until she died of cancer when my girls were two years old."

"No. You loved again." She laughed. "You've had your mind erased, although who is capable of this level of manipulation, I cannot imagine. As far as I knew, there weren't any Conditioned Mind-Erasers left alive. In general, we put them to death as soon as we find them."

"That's disgusting." Anger surged through his veins. The woman had no right to put to death people's loved ones. She had to be stopped. It had to end before anyone else...

He blinked a few times. Before anyone else what? Before what happened to whom?

"Ah, yes. You're finding you have blank spots, aren't you?" She stood and walked to the two-way mirror. "There are places in your head where one plus one is not adding up to two. Something you can't seem to remember."

She was remarkably accurate in her description, but he wasn't going to let her know that. He didn't like—at all—that they were playing around in his head, and he didn't trust Madame Joan any further than he could throw her. Just because she said something odd was happening in his head, didn't mean she hadn't planted the sensation there just to fool with him.

This whole thing was fucking bullshit.

"I want my lawyer. If you want to charge me with something, charge me. If you're going to kill me, I can assure you there will be consequences and not necessarily of the legal kind. My brother—whom you'd better let out of here unharmed—is a powerful guy. His employer will seek vengeance for this."

There had been a time when Ben would have hated the idea of having anything to do with the people Gene worked with. Now he owed them for taking care of his girls. It was amazing how many shades of gray Ben had become comfortable living with over the last five years.

"She was picked up off your boat. I took her away from you like you were a meaningless, powerless being who couldn't protect what was yours. You were nothing. You were smaller than a maggot in the world."

He rolled his eyes. "Lady, I have no idea what you're talking about."

"You went on the news. You made a fool of yourself. No one would have anything to do with you."

"I promise you, if that had happened, I would remember it."

"Ben." He hated the way she said his name. It made his skin crawl. "Why did you decide to take on the Conditioned? Of all the things you could have done with your life, why would you risk yourself and your family for them?"

"Anyone who saw the atrocities would."

"No." She slammed her hand down on the table. "They've butchered you."

Madame placed a hand on his forehead. Ben tried to jump backward but felt frozen in his seat. He couldn't move. His heart pounded hard as his body instantly became paralyzed. What was happening? He couldn't panic. That was the most important thing.

"Damn." She shut her eyes as she sighed dramatically. "You're ruined. Ruined."

She stood, and Ben could move again. He narrowed his eyes as he surged to his feet. "What the fuck did you just do?"

He almost never cursed, but this crazy woman clearly did bad things to him.

"I gave it one last try."

Realization dawned on Ben like a bomb going off. "You're *Conditioned*."

She waved her hand as if what he'd said was of minimal importance. "All the leaders of the Institutions are. How else do you control a monster other than by using one? And I am, you know, the worst kind of monster."

Her face lit up when she delivered that last piece of information, as though she'd practiced it a million times.

"Been trying that out in the mirror, have you? Very well done. Brava." Ben clapped his hands. "Now, where is my lawyer?"

"You have no rights here." She laughed. "I may not get the answers I need from you, but by God I will finally get rid of the one person who has been driving me crazy for five years."

She raised her arm. Ben had one second to wonder what other sick abilities the woman possessed, would use to harm him, before the first gunshot went off.

As his heart practically ripped from his chest, Ben dove for the floor.

Madame whirled around as the door burst open.

"Who are you?"

Only the slightest hint of a tremor indicated what Ben

knew must be abject terror. He poked his head out from under the table and tried to hide his grin. His brother had some very powerful friends.

"You have two people here who belong to me." The man's name was Paul Mendoza and, like Gene, he had spent most of his life doing illegal things to earn his place in the Mob world that ran certain areas of Louisiana. "I've come to get them back." Paul's gaze traveled up and down Madame's figure. "I don't much care for shooting old women."

"I could bring you down in two seconds. You'd never get to pull the trigger."

Paul snickered. "That's true, I'm sure. But then you'd never see him coming."

Ben jumped to his feet, grabbing the chair he'd sat in before his feet ever touched the floor. Using muscles he hadn't flexed since his days playing high school baseball, he whacked Madame over the head with the chair. She crumpled to the floor.

He stared down at the woman he'd just struck. She was evil personified to Ben.

"She's not dead." Paul stepped forward. "So whatever guilt trip you were about to give yourself, get over it."

"Sad truth is that I wasn't all that concerned about it."

He wanted her dead. But her words strung out in his mind. Had he been "altered" somehow? Were there memories, life experiences he'd had that he now couldn't remember?

Still, it wasn't the time for self-indulgent moralistic questions.

"Where's Gene?"

"We dragged him out of here a few minutes ago. They beat him up pretty badly. I guess they were going to use his pain to get to you. He's pissed as hell. We're pretty sure he's going to be fine."

"That's good." He needed to see his brother, to make sure he was all right.

Also, maybe Gene could shed some light on what Ben couldn't remember.

Not to mention, if he didn't get to see his girls fast, he was going to freak out.

He wasn't an anxious man, but even he could be pushed too far.

"Let's go." Paul shrugged. "Don't mind the dead bodies on the way out."

Now that was something Ben had never thought to hear in his whole life. Maybe he was a little sick in the head, because it made him smile. "You guys are amazing, did you know that? What are we going to do with her?"

"Leave her. The boss said to try to avoid killing her if we could. She's got friends in high places he'd rather not piss off if he doesn't have to."

Ben stepped over her body. Maybe she would get a brain bleed and spare them all the trouble of having to deal with her again.

"You should see your face. Gene said you had a hidden bloodthirsty side, but I didn't believe it. I've always thought of you as being Mr. Strait-Laced."

Ben nodded, following Paul out the door. "Up until five years ago, I was."

The question of why he had changed was one he was going to have to figure out. Eventually. He ran out of the building after Paul.

Life had certainly gotten really, really strange.

BEN STRODE into his house behind Gene, who was being supported by two of his underlings. "Put him on the couch."

"I'm awake, Benedicte. I can certainly decide where I want to be placed," Gene snarled. "Plus, my legs do work, so all of this carting me around like an invalid is a waste of time."

"All right, where would you like to be?"

Eugene fell silent for a moment. "The couch."

"Uh-huh." Ben shook his head. "You always were a surly bastard when you were hurt or sick."

"Jerk."

Ben looked at the guard—Raul—who stood by the stairs.

"Are the girls upstairs?"

"Yep. They've been quiet tonight."

They were probably freaked out. For all that Gene's group kept them protected from the outside world, the men were a bunch of gossiping old women amongst themselves. There was no way the girls didn't know he and Gene had been taken.

Ben took the stairs two steps at a time.

"Daph? Ella?" he called out as he approached their bedroom. Pretty soon they wouldn't want to share anymore.

It dawned on him suddenly that they might not be able to stay in the house. When Madame woke up, she was going to come after him again. There was no way she'd let the fact he'd whacked her over the head go unpunished. He might need to take the girls on the run for a while.

They didn't answer him, and he knocked loudly on their door. They were eleven now, and as Ella always told him, "in need of privacy."

"Ladies?"

No response. Screw their personal space. He flung open the door.

Their room was empty. The only movement came from the wind that floated through the open window, blowing their green-and-white curtains gently as it flitted through the room.

Sheer and utter dread invaded Ben's soul. He couldn't hear anything except the sound of his own breath coming in and out of his lungs. This was his terror; this was what had kept him up at night. The girls. Someone had taken the girls.

He didn't realize he'd shouted until he heard the sound of pounding footsteps trampling up the stairs. Raul pushed past him into the bedroom.

"What the fuck?" Raul cursed. "No one got in here tonight. No one, boss."

Ben wasn't their boss, but he wasn't going to correct him. Not now. "Obviously, someone did. They got them from right under your nose."

He didn't want to imagine what Madame was having done to them right at that moment. Red filled his vision. This was rage. He would murder whoever touched his babies. Kill them—torture—maim.

"Hold on." Gene's panting breaths came from behind him. Ben watched his brother stumble into the room and sit down on Ella's unmade bed. "Let's look at this."

"Look at it?" Ben hollered at Gene. "You can't even walk up the stairs. You want to pretend you're some kind of CSI unit?"

"Fuck off for a second, Benedicte." His brother rolled his eyes at him. "There's no signs of struggle in here, nothing to indicate that anything went awry at all. I promise you, one of the girls would have yelled. Ella has no problem screaming like a banshee anytime she feels threatened."

Ben stared blankly at Gene, trying to make sense of his words through the haze of anger, fear and guilt that threatened to overtake him. What was his brother saying? If they hadn't been taken, then what? Had they left?

He stormed over to the window and looked down. It wasn't that far up but they would have hurt themselves if they'd tried to jump. Beneath them were Ella and Daphne's top bed sheets, tied together in a heap on the grass in the backyard.

"Hell."

Gene spoke over Raul. "Ben?"

"They climbed down."

Ben whirled around to look at Gene. His brother lay back on Ella's bed, his eyes, which were practically swollen shut from his beating, closed in pain. "I knew it."

A million possibilities flew through his mind, including the very real need to get his older brother to a hospital. "Where would they go, and why would they do this?"

Gene's eyes cracked open. "They've probably had a contingency plan for years. An idea of what they would do if we both vanished. I bet you it was Ella's plan. The girl is so much like me."

That might have been true, but Ben had no clue where they'd gone or who they'd go to for help. He sank down on the floor. How could he protect them if his mind was missing all sorts of information he needed?

Ben had never felt so ineffective in his life.

"We'll start a search pattern, boss. We'll get them."

Raul sounded desperate. He probably didn't want Gene to kill him for losing his nieces.

"Sounds good."

He'd already lost... who? Who had he lost that made him know he could never stand to lose someone again? Not Dana. Yes, he'd lost her, but this was different. Madame's words resonated deeply with him. He knew in his gut that the Institutions had already taken someone from him. No way, no how were they getting anyone else. Not while there was breath in his body.

FOURTEEN

Shiri stepped off the plane in the New Orleans airport feeling very proud of herself. She had successfully used her fake identification to travel all the way to New Orleans without setting off anyone's radar as to her true identity. Guy was really, really good at hiding them. If she hadn't been so terrified the entire trip, she might have enjoyed her first couple of airplane rides. Instead, she'd wanted to puke the whole time.

Her good mood lasted only until she'd stepped out into the humidity of a New Orleans summer. She lived in the Caribbean; it was ridiculous that the heat of Louisiana could affect her so deeply. Maybe it was a sense-memory thing.

A car pulled up in front of her by the curb, beeping its horn to get her attention. She bent over to regard the driver, and after a moment of staring blankly at the person inside, she couldn't help her grin. Addison Wade Lewis, fully disguised so even her grandfather might not recognize her, smiled back. If she hadn't known Addison would meet her at the airport, she'd have had no idea who the woman was. Shiri opened the car door and got in.

"Addy, look at you with dark-brown hair! What does Spence think?"

Addison's blue eyes, covered now with brown contacts, danced with laughter.

"He only saw me like this for about ten minutes before we separated. He's in Arizona."

"And what did he think?"

"He liked it even less than I liked seeing him with red hair." She scratched her head. "I guess we both like each other as we are."

Shiri stared at Addison. "And the baby? Are you still sick?"

"Frankly, it's amazing either Spencer or Guy let me come on this mission. Don't you start, either. I haven't been sick in weeks. I feel good. The baby is growing just fine, and all I've been doing is watching and reporting. As soon as I get you set up, I'm going back home, and then I'll put my feet up and pretend I'm a lady of leisure."

Shiri laughed. She loved Addison Lewis like a sister. "Yeah, right, I'll believe that when I see it. You'll be all over Jeremy and worrying yourself sick until Spencer comes home." Addison loved Jeremy, her nephew, like a son.

"Come on now, Shiri. Let me live in my own fantastical delusions of doing nothing for a while, won't you?"

Shiri sighed and leaned back in her seat. "Only if you let me pretend I can actually get this done successfully." *Only if you let me pretend Ben will be at all glad to see me and not hate me forever for hiding for five years...*

"Of course, you can." Addison patted her on the leg as she pulled the car into traffic. "The girl called out to you, right? Guy's message was, I believe, deliberately vague. That means she needs you. You'll take care of this."

"I hope so. I've never lived out in the open. I don't really know how to handle myself in the real world."

"Sure you do. You just took two airplanes to get here. There's nothing more intimidating than an airport. If you can do that, you can do anything. You have cash—which will open a ton of doors if need be—and a whole support system of hidden people to help you."

Shiri wished she had Addison's optimistic nature. Somewhere on the flight from Puerto Rico to Miami, Shiri had started to doubt everything she hoped would happen. Maybe Ben would want nothing to do with her.

"I've got some news on Benedicte Lavelle."

Shiri had almost never heard his full name used. She hadn't even known it until she'd started writing to him. When the guard had first taken her to him, she had simply thought of him as a client even though she was sure someone had said his full name. He'd called himself Ben. He was listed in the Louisiana Bar Association using his full name, which was how she'd discovered it. "Oh yes? Did we find out where he's being held?"

By nature, Shiri wasn't a violent person. Not at all. But she would hurt anyone who'd harmed Ben. She knew that as intrinsically as she knew anything.

"He's out. Roman texted me an hour ago. Apparently, Ben's brother's people shot up the place and got him out."

"Oh, thank goodness." Tears spilled from her eyes, and she wiped them away, not caring if she looked snotty in front of Addison. Besides, they'd been through a lot together and the other woman wouldn't care.

"It's good. Yes."

Shiri could hear the hesitation in her voice. "But?"

"Are you ready to see him?"

She had been ready to see him for five years. She'd never wanted to stop seeing him. But she didn't want to lie to Addison. "I'm anxious."

"That's natural."

"What if he hates me?"

Addison shook her head. "He's devoted himself for five years to taking on causes for you. I don't think a person who hated you could do such a thing."

"He thinks I'm dead. That's why he did that stuff. Trying to tell the world about what happened all but destroyed him. For that, he might hate me."

Her friend exhaled a loud breath. "He might be a little... mad. But once you explain that you weren't allowed to contact him, I think he'll just be relieved you didn't die."

Shiri hoped that was all he felt. She could handle *mad*. She hoped.

Seven.

She gasped. Daphne hadn't tried to contact her telepathically since the first attempt. Shiri turned to Addison to explain what was happening.

Are you coming for us, Seven?

"Are the girls not with their father?"

Addison turned the car down the next street. Shiri had no idea where they were and was glad she didn't need to drive the car. She had enough going on.

"Apparently not. I've never been so frustrated in my entire life *not* to have a particular power before."

We've gone into hiding. Can you hear me? Sometimes I think I'm crazy that I think this actually works. Maybe it just works with Ella. I don't know. We've gone to the boat, Seven. Please come find us there. Please.

Daphne sounded so forlorn, even telepathically, that Shiri could hardly stand it.

"Addison, I need you to take me to Ben's boat."

Her friend shook her head. "I don't know where that is."

"I bet Roman does. He knows everything." It was always a little bit scary just how much her friend was capable of doing. Shiri pulled out her phone and texted Roman for the address of the boat dock.

She could remember everything about the boat—she could even remember what the place where Ben kept the boat looked like—but she had no idea how to get there. A sense of direction had never been her strongest ability. She could get lost walking around the island, and she had been there every day for the last five years.

Her phone beeped. She looked down. "That's not what I asked."

"What?" Addison stared out at the road in front of her.

"According to Roman, Ben moved the boat a few years ago to some place called the Bonnabel Boat Launch."

"Still doesn't help me." Addison swore. "Roman can never be easy. Obviously, we need an address. I swear, he might be Spencer's brother, but they're like night and day in terms of handling them. Spencer always shares too much."

Shiri had always found Roman to be really easy going and nice. But everyone else either ran from him or complained about him the few times he showed up on the island. Either way, they weren't in a position to criticize him right now.

"I'll ask him for an address."

"No. Don't. If he's being deliberately obtuse, he'll only continue to act that way for his own reasons." Addison's hands had turned white on the steering wheel.

"Do you know how to use the internet function on your phone?"

"Yes." Shiri tried to hide her smile. She'd been clueless about almost everything five years ago and had to be taught things that were second nature to some of the other Conditioned on the island. Addison still sometimes treated her as if she didn't know how to tie her shoes. "I'll use that to look up the address. Good idea."

She pulled out her phone and Googled the location. "It looks like it's right at the end of Bonnabel Boulevard in Metairie. Does that help?"

"It's better than nothing, I suppose. We're going to have to turn around."

Shiri gripped her seat. She'd never driven with Addison before, but if Spencer was to be believed, she acted crazy behind the wheel. Her friend maneuvered the car into what Shiri suspected was not a legal U-turn until they were driving in the opposite direction. Tires screeched and horns blared.

"Do I need to remind you that it would be very, very bad for us to get pulled over?"

Addison rolled her eyes. "Do you or do you not want to get to that girl before someone else does?"

"Still..."

"Oh, that reminds me." Addison drummed her hands on the center console.

"Right behind you in the back seat is a bag. Get it, will you?"

She obliged, glad to have something to do to occupy her mind so as not to obsess about Daphne and Ella. How had the girls gotten to where they were? Why had they thought they needed to? She bit down on her lip as she pulled Addy's bag onto her lap.

"What's in it?"

"The new you."

Shiri shook her head. "Pardon?"

"You sounded just like Guy right then." Addison snickered.

"Pardon."

"Would you prefer I said *huh?*" Pregnancy had given Addison Lewis a strange sense of humor. Or maybe Shiri just didn't get what was funny.

"Inside that bag is the new you while we're here."

"What?" Shiri pulled open the black bag, and it didn't help the confusion. All she saw inside was a plastic container.

"Open it."

Shiri did and suddenly she understood. Inside the contraption was a black wig. She swallowed. It was stupid that she was getting emotional about this. For God's sake, it was a wig. It didn't mean anything. Why was she getting worked up?

"Shiri? I get it, okay. It was hard for me to put my wig on, too."

"Why?" She sniffled as she wiped away one of her tears. "It's just a wig."

"Because it means hiding. And on the island, none of us have to do that. We all just get to be who we are, period." Addison sighed. "When we come back here, it's all about disguises. I spent my whole life acting a part until I met Spencer. You had to live behind walls, treated like some kind of a prisoner."

Shiri felt her hands shake. "And putting on this wig does *not* mean that I'm going back behind those walls. It means that I'm refusing to stay behind them, right?"

Addy's eyes were filled with tears. "We can't be seen in

public. We can forget that when we're not here, but not when we are." She indicated her fake brown hair. "It's impossible to forget that we didn't really get away, we just found a good hiding place. Someday, someone might find us."

"No. They won't, because we're coming out of hiding whether they like it or not."

Addison laughed. "Now you sound like Guy."

"We all spend way too much time together."

They fell silent as Addison made a left turn. Someone honked, and Shiri suspected her friend had done something else wrong. She wasn't in the mood to correct her anymore.

"Do I just slip it over my own hair?" She'd never put one on before.

"Your own hair is probably too long."

Since she had come to the island, she had refused to cut her hair. It had been her own form of rebellion against her past life. Madame had made her keep it a certain length: just below her shoulders. Long enough, according to Madame, for it to be pulled back but short enough that she looked unassuming and nonthreatening to their clients. Now it fell almost to her rear end.

Even she had to admit it was a little ridiculous. In her fantasies, she'd seen Ben again with her hair waving in the wind and he'd been drawn to her like a man possessed by the sight. She rolled her eyes at her own silliness.

"I'll pull it up and then put the wig on top of it."

Addison nodded. "It's not like you have to fool the FBI. You just have to be able to walk around in public without attracting too much attention. Of course, you could probably leave it off, and Guy would never know."

"It's not Guy that worries me." His temper might have been loud, but he was a gentle soul trapped in the body of a powerful man. If some were afraid of him, that served his purposes. Shiri just wasn't one of those people who found him particularly intimidating—at least not anymore.

Now, the thought of Madame finding her was enough to make Shiri shiver. If she got caught, she'd be back in an Institution and probably tortured before she was put down.

No, the wig was going on. Right now. She flipped her head over and fiddled with her hair until it was restrained on the top of her head. With only the tiny visor mirror to help her, she had to do most of it by touch alone. After a few tries, she managed it. Next, she maneuvered her now-black hair onto her head. Her hair was really long, and it didn't feel like there was even a bump under the wig. Guy must have had it specifically made to fit her head.

"How does it look?"

Addison eyed her sideways as she drove. "Amazingly, you got it straight the first time. It's real hair, you know. Just like mine. I'm not going to ask where he gets the stuff."

"One of his sources." Guy seemed endlessly able to acquire whatever they needed.

"Spence probably knows, but I'm not going to question him about it either. Some things are better left unknown." Addison pointed forward. "Oh, there it is. The Bonnabel Boat Launch."

Shiri squinted to see the boat dock ahead. "This isn't where it was last time. This isn't the same dock."

"Roman did say they'd moved it."

"Yes." Dread filled her stomach. Were the girls there alone?

"Pull up over there. I'm going to see if I can find the slip."

"Shiri, I'm not sure they're just going to let you run

about the dock staring at everyone's boats on a private marina. Someone might question it."

"Then you're going to do your best to distract whoever it is that monitors this place."

Addison's eyebrows shot up. "I am?"

"You're Addison Wade, remember? I'm sure you can keep a couple of boat managers busy for an hour or so."

"I'm sure I could. If you think you want to handle getting to the girls without me."

"Addison, if I can't do that, I might as well never leave the island again for the rest of my life."

"All right." Addison pulled the car into a space. "I'll just go in there," she said, pointing at a building that read *Dock Manager*, "and see if I can waste everyone's time."

Shiri opened the door and jumped out of the car. Her black wig bounced on her shoulders. It felt heavy on her head and it itched. She might not make it five minutes with this thing on her head. Plus, she was certain she looked pretty severe with black hair. Maybe that was why Guy had sent her that particular color.

He had a warped sense of humor. She just hoped she didn't terrify the girls.

She ran out onto the dock. The boat had to be there somewhere with the girls on it. Neither of them could be left alone like that, and the longer they were unprotected, the more likely they would get caught.

She shuddered to think about it. Ben's boat had been called *The Twins*. Hopefully he hadn't changed the name of it. If he had, she might never find them. Now would be a really wonderful time for Daphne to start speaking telepathically with more details than she'd been dishing out.

Shiri had to work fast. Despite her statements to Addison, she wasn't one hundred percent convinced Addy could keep people busy for a full hour. It wasn't as if she could announce herself to be Addison Wade. They'd haul her off to an Institution as fast as they would Shiri.

She spotted a familiar boat, and for a second, she stopped breathing. There it was: *The Twins*. A grin broke out on her face. The boat still existed and the girls were on it. Rushing forward, she tried to keep her excitement at bay. It was possible the girls weren't in there. It was possible this whole thing was a setup.

Nothing good had happened yet. She needed to maintain her cool.

It wasn't as easy getting onto the boat as she'd thought it would be. The last time she'd done this, she'd had Ben to help haul her onboard. She looked down at her shoes. The sandals she had on did nothing to help her balance. She slipped them off her feet, hoping beyond hope she could manage this without killing herself.

Shiri grabbed the side of the boat to steady it, only that didn't work. It moved, and her torso and arms went with it as her legs stayed on the dock. For a second, she stayed precariously both on the side of the boat and the wooden landing. Her heart rate picked up as she realized what was about to happen right before it did.

The boat, guided by the current, pushed farther from the dock. It couldn't go out into the lake—no, the rope holding it tied to a piling prevented it from doing that. But it could—and did—sway too far out for Shiri to keep her feet on the dock and hold on to *The Twins* at the same time.

Seconds felt like hours, and yet they went by too fast for her to get herself firmly back on the dock. She had no choice. Wherever the boat went, she was going with it.

As she wrapped her arms around the top rail, she prayed she wouldn't fall into the water. At best, she was a lousy swimmer. She'd only done it a half a dozen times, and only because Guy insisted that living on an island required they all have a rudimentary understanding of how to swim. Shiri had not taken to it naturally.

"Oh, shit." She never cursed. Her early training on how to speak and what to say still controlled most of her word use. But this seemed like a good time to let loose. "Shit, shit, shit."

Her feet kicked as she tried to use her lower body to leverage herself to the top of the boat. At her third attempt to pull herself up, it started to move back toward the dock. Two heads popped up above the side of the boat and stared down at her. For a second, they looked confused. Utter joy filled Shiri's soul. Daphne and Ella looked so grown up and so beautiful.

"Girls." Her voice was a mixture of terror and relief. "I'm going to fall in the water."

They were both silent. Then Daphne's face swirled with emotion. When she spoke, her voice was choked. "Seven, it's you."

"Well... sort of. No one calls me that anymore. I'll explain. Could you help me by pulling me up?"

If she didn't end up in the water, it would be a good day.

FIFTEEN

Ben tapped his foot on the accelerator, making the car go even faster. He dared any police officer to pull him over in the mood he was in. An Institution had blown up that morning. Shouldn't they have better things to do?

The girls were at the boat. He just knew it. When he'd finally given himself permission to calm down enough to think, he'd figured it out. They loved the boat. They were after him all the time to go back out on it. If it were up to him, he'd sell the damn thing. He ground his teeth together. And why was that? Why did he want to sell *The Twins*?

He had no idea. It was as though the answer was on the edge of his mind. He could feel it, but he couldn't access it.

Ben knew for certain that the girls were there and maybe, assuming their minds hadn't been messed with, they could tell him what the hell was going on or what he'd fucking forgotten.

He pulled into the parking space too fast, slamming on his brakes. They screeched as he stopped. As fast as he ever had, he got the door open and got out of the car.

A brown-haired woman passed right by him, banging into his arm.

"Oh, I'm so sorry." She smiled.

He nodded. She looked familiar... somehow. He didn't have time to care how. His babies—even at eleven they were still his babies—had run away and put themselves in danger. He needed them. Now. And then he could holler at them for what they'd done. But first he had to hug them and assure himself that they were completely unharmed.

He grabbed his boat key out of his pocket. Leave it to the girls. He'd have bet almost anything they'd made a copy of the goddamn key. Sneaky. There was no doubt they were capable of such a feat.

Running down the dock, he saw a black-haired woman standing on his boat with his daughters. His eyes got huge. Who the hell was she, and what the fuck was she doing there with them?

"Hey!" he shouted as he ran toward the scene. His hand reached into his jacket, and he felt what he knew lay there. Gene had insisted he take the gun, and now he was glad he had. If that woman meant his daughters harm, he would shoot her in the head with no remorse.

"Get away from them!" He pulled the gun out and aimed it at the woman's chest, surprised by just how steady his hand felt.

"Dad!" Daphne shouted, her smile getting wider as he ran toward the boat.

"Is that a gun?" Ella sounded horrified.

"It is, baby girl, and I'd rather not have to use it. So step away from the stranger while I figure this out."

"Girls, do what your father says."

He didn't know who this bitch with the black hair was,

but he'd had enough. In no way did he want the girls to listen to her over him.

Daphne and Ella scrambled away from the woman. He grabbed the hook that hung near the pole where his boat was tied. He pulled the boat toward him and boarded with ease.

He stared at his girls for a moment, drinking in the sight of them, unhurt. If they had been alone, he would have grabbed them until they begged him not to hug them so hard. But he had this stranger to deal with, and he didn't like unknown people near his girls. He blinked. Especially Daphne. Why was that?

Hell, this was getting annoying. He wanted to kick the ass of whatever Conditioned person had done this to him. "Girls, get behind me."

They responded quickly, running to do as they were told. That was a change. Usually he got an argument over everything. Even their tween brains must have recognized the gravity of the situation.

"Who are you?"

He stared at the woman even as he asked the question. She was tall, his own height, with striking green eyes he thought a man could get lost in. But that didn't mean they weren't full of deceit, lies, and evil agendas. Once upon a time, he might have romanticized a beautiful woman, but these days he knew better than to trust his softer side.

Her hair was the darkest shade of black he'd ever seen on a purely Caucasian woman. He suspected it wasn't real, and that made him trust her even less. Unless she was ill, she had no business wearing that wig. It spoke of hidden agendas.

"That's Seven, Dad." Daphne's voice sounded higher than usual. She was afraid. Good—the girls needed to understand just how dangerous things were. He couldn't protect them from this forever.

The woman spoke. "He's not going to know me, Daph." She didn't seem afraid, although when she met his gaze, it was with a wariness that showed him she wasn't stupid. She knew how much trouble she was in.

"Don't talk to them."

She nodded even as she sighed. "All right, Ben, if that's what you want."

"Shut up. Don't act like you know me."

She crossed her arms over her chest. "I'm not sure I do. The Ben Lavelle I knew would have at least let a woman explain things before he pointed a firearm at her chest."

Her words burned him a bit, but he ignored the sensation. Madame and the Institutions had kidnapped him. No way, no how would he make the mistake of thinking any of them were safe. Psychopaths wanted to hurt him, and what better way than to go after his family?

"I'll ask questions. You'll answer them. That's how this is going to work."

She nodded. "For the moment."

"I have a gun pointed at your chest. I'll ask as many questions as I want to for as long as I want to."

The woman had the nerve to simply raise an eyebrow. Her guts impressed him, begrudgingly. Of course, it could simply mean she was crazy. Either way, he didn't have time to indulge in any musings on the stranger with his kids.

"You can put the gun down. You don't want to shoot me. If you did, you would feel terrible about it. I promise you, I am not any risk to your kids or to you. I won't try to go anywhere."

"We'll see." He motioned with his gun. "Move over there."

It was important that he put some space between this woman and the girls. The farther the better, while he figured out what to do.

She complied by walking backward, not taking her eyes off him. Keeping his aim with the gun, he watched as she chewed on her lower lip.

"You really don't know me at all, Ben?"

He shook his head. "Why should I?"

"Because we were... friends."

This was such bullshit. "I assure you, I remember my *friends*."

"Not necessarily. I'm a little bit concerned that Roman took more of your memory than he was supposed to."

"I don't doubt that someone has messed with my mind. If you know anything about that, you'll be lucky if I don't shove you over the side of this boat."

She sighed. He could feel wariness coming off her. Not fear, he noted, which he found odd.

"Who are you?"

"My name is Shiri Roberts."

He digested that. Did he know that name? *No.* "My daughter called you something else. A number. Seven. Why would she call you that?"

"That is the name she knew me by. It's the name you called me, too. It was the name I was given when I lived in Crescent."

Now that he could believe. Rage surged through his veins.

"You work for Crescent, and you dared to come near my children?"

"No, I don't work for Crescent. You couldn't be more off in that assessment."

"Dad," Ella's voice called from behind him. "What are you doing?"

He raised his free hand to hush her. "I will speak to the two of you when I'm ready. Until then, do not say a word."

"Five years ago, you helped me when I needed it. To save you now, we made a decision to remove some information from your mind. That information could have been used to hurt you."

"You and your Institution buddies have been trying to get to me for five years. Now I find out you've messed with my mind, and you want me to believe you did it for my benefit? This is nonsense." He stalked forward and grabbed her arm.

She gasped, her eyes large, as she regarded him. Good, she should be nervous. "Let's go. Girls, follow me."

He wasn't going to get any real answers here. But his brother could, and the longer he wasted time, the longer those people could be out there causing havoc to his life.

Ben wasn't satisfied sitting around and letting things happen to him anymore.

He was going to take action against anyone who wanted to harm his family.

"Girls, climb over the edge of the boat, use the ladder and walk to the car. I'm right behind you."

He squeezed Shiri's, or Seven's—whoever the hell she was—arm tightly. "You will walk with me."

"That's fine." Her voice sounded strained. "I've told you. I want to cooperate with whatever you need."

"We'll see."

Ben tugged, and she followed him. He could feel the softness of her skin beneath his fingertips. As he forced himself to take a deep breath, he caught the scent of coffee in the air. That aroma always made him smile. It was like being caught in a good memory he couldn't quite enter, but which made him feel good regardless.

In this case, the scent seemed to be coming from the girl he held. All right. He shook his head. So what? She smelled nice? It didn't mean anything. It didn't mean that what she said about helping him was actually true.

"You said we were friends?"

She looked at him sideways. "Yes, we were... friends."

"Why did you hesitate like that when you answered? I know you're holding something back."

Shiri nodded. "Of course you do. You could always smell a lie."

He jerked to a stop. That was absolutely true and, in fact, that was the exact phrase he used to describe what it felt like to him to know when someone spoke an untruth.

"How do you know that?"

She sighed. "You told me. Look, I can make all of this better. Would it be okay with you if I used my cell phone for a minute?"

Now he really thought the woman was out of her head. "No." He extended his hand. "Give me your phone."

"I can't do that."

He raised an eyebrow. This was more in line with the behavior he expected from her. Still, it made his gut ache. "Why not? I thought you weren't here to harm me."

"I can't give it to you because I don't have it on me. I meant that I could go and get it." Her eyes fumed. "But even if I did, I wouldn't give it to you, because I won't let you risk anyone else. If you want to doubt me, that's your prerogative. I can't even blame you, since apparently you've had your brain really, really messed with. But I won't tolerate anything happening to anyone else."

So the lady had spunk. That was fine. Gene's people

would know how to deal with her. He swallowed away the lump in his throat that formed as he thought that. What was wrong with him that a gorgeous woman could make him go soft and gooey when he needed to be hard and tough?

He pulled her forward toward the parking lot, where the girls now waited for them in the car.

"Let me ask you something, Ben."

"I told you, I'm going to be doing all the questioning."

She was silent for a moment, but he didn't dare hope she'd actually listened.

The woman was infuriating. What part of "don't talk" didn't she understand?

"What happened to you, Ben? What happened in the last five years? Is this just frustration at not having your mind intact, or is something else going on here?"

"Don't act like you know me, Shiri."

He said her name, and it didn't feel right on his tongue. If he'd known her before—and that was a big if—then he hadn't called her Shiri. He must have used his daughter's name for her. Seven. Had Madame been talking about her? Had she been the reason that he'd started his vendetta against the Institutions?

They walked together past the other cars in the lot. Shiri looked over at one. For a second, he thought he saw her shake her head "no" to someone, but when he looked over, no one was there. This wasn't the time to let his imagination go crazy. He had to keep it together.

"You're hurting me, Ben."

He looked down, startled to see that he was gripping her thin arm so tightly. As he took a forced deep breath, he released his grip slightly. In his life, he'd never harmed a woman, and he didn't intend to now—unless he had to the way Madame had forced him.

"I'm sorry."

"It's okay." Her eyes shone up at him with tears unshed. "I'm so sorry this happened to you. It's all my fault."

"Now *that* I believe."

Even as he forced himself to stay angry at her—she had been with his children, and he had no idea who she was or if she was a potential threat—he could feel the adrenaline leaving his body a little bit. They were okay. The girls were seated in the car, buckled in and looking fairly chagrined. Whatever they'd been through, they'd clearly come out the other side unscathed.

He pushed her into the car, keeping the gun aimed at her the whole time. If she didn't do something truly bad, he would probably not be able to fire it at her anymore. But she didn't need to know that.

As quickly as he could manage, he made his way into the driver's seat and started the car. It would be impossible to drive and hold the gun. He sat for a second and contemplated his options. Clearly his career as a criminal would be a short one. How the hell did Gene manage all these eventualities all the time?

"I'm not going to hurt you or the girls. You can put it away until you get me wherever we're going."

"Do you read minds? Is that your talent? Is that what the Institutions pay you to do?"

She sighed, folding her hands in her lap. "You weren't this obstinate before."

"Deal with it."

He put the gun back into the holster hidden by his coat as he tried to concentrate on operating the car.

"No, I can't read minds. It's not my talent. My gift is being able to track, eliminate, and occasionally use ghost energy. It was why I was brought to you five years ago, although you won't remember that." She looked out the window. "The Institutions don't pay me. In fact, if they knew I was alive, they'd kill me."

Now that was information he needed. "So according to you, the Institutions consider you their enemy?"

"Correct." She turned to regard him, but he couldn't make headway with her expression. She was either hugely relieved or incredibly annoyed. Either way, he had to remind himself, he didn't care. "We have that in common, then. I've been a thorn in their side for years."

"They consider me more of a problem than they consider you."

Remembering Madame's crazy scene earlier, Ben highly doubted that.

But he wasn't going to reveal too much about that to Shiri. He didn't trust her.

"Why is that?"

"Because I'm an escaped Conditioned. That makes me a fugitive. You're a regular human they can't quite figure out."

"Dad." Daphne's voice pled with him to look at her, so he glanced up through his rearview mirror.

"What's wrong, honey?"

"Seven came because I called her."

He tried to swallow his temper. How had his girls gotten themselves into so much danger? "You called her on the phone?" He turned his head briefly to stare at Shiri. "My daughters have your phone number?"

"No," Shiri and Daphne answered at the same time.

Ella sighed. "Daphne spoke to Seven telepathically."

He tried to digest this even as he tasted blood in his mouth from where he'd clearly bitten down on his tongue upon hearing Ella's words.

"She did what?"

"I spoke to her telepathically." Daphne squirmed in her seat. "At least I think I did. We were just discussing it when you showed up with that *gun*."

Okay. He was going to have to explain that to his daughters in a way they could understand. They were young girls, not quite teenagers, but not little either. Sometimes, it was hard to know what to explain and what to leave alone. This was not going to be something he could or should avoid discussing.

"I heard you, sweetheart. I'm just not a Telepath myself. I can't answer. It's kind of like speaking into a monitor. I could hear what you said, but I couldn't respond to you. Another Telepath could answer, but given the circumstances, we thought it safer to send me to you rather than answer you directly."

His daughter was Conditioned? His heart felt as if it might explode from his chest. "How long have you known you could do that, Daph?" They were going to have to hide her. He'd need a plan...

Shiri touched him on the arm. "You already knew, Ben."

"I did?" No, he couldn't have forgotten that.

"Roman must have thought it was one of the things that shouldn't be available for inspection in your head."

"Roman?"

She let go of his arm. "The guy who did this to you, upon my request. He thought he was helping. I can see why he wouldn't want anyone in the Institutions to find out about Daphne."

"So just to be clear that I'm not missing any of this lunacy, you're saying that I know you? I knew about Daphne? And I've had my memory erased?"

"That about sums it up."

"Except for the fact that we all thought she was dead, Dad. She got ripped right off our boat. She floated up in the sky and disappeared. We haven't seen her in five years."

Ben eyed the woman next to him. "You're going to start from the beginning and not stop until I'm satisfied that I know who you are and what you want from my family."

SIXTEEN

What did she want from his family? Shiri closed her eyes and leaned against the headboard of her bed. Not that she had much choice. She was handcuffed to the headboard and couldn't go anywhere. The feeling made her want to rage to the universe. But it was either lean back and stay still or break her arm. She closed her eyes; the entire situation made her heartsick.

What she wanted from his family she couldn't have—not while Ben didn't know who she was. He refused to believe she was entirely trustworthy, and she couldn't blame him. Truth was, Shiri was *not* entirely trustworthy. She'd abandoned him. He might not remember it now, but he would whenever Roman got around to fixing his neurotransmitters so he could have his own life memories back in his head.

Finally, she opened her eyes to look at the scene in front of her. Ben didn't live in the same house. How had she not known that? With every bit of information she'd managed to garner about him over the years, how had she not known that important detail? She hadn't seen much of the place, but it seemed as if he now lived with Gene, surrounded by the Mob. Five years had altered his life in ways she'd never anticipated.

On dark nights on the island, it had filled her with happiness to think of him going through his days the way she imagined he used to. Instead, he was practically living in self-made seclusion, fearful for the life of his family. She kicked the mattress beneath her. Somehow, some way, she should have made Guy bring Ben and his girls to her.

Not that anyone ever made Guy do anything he didn't want to do.

A little thread of concern filled her mind, one she couldn't seem to push away. Had Roman done this on purpose? Everyone was always telling her that he was in love with her. He'd never told her he was, and it didn't matter anyway, since she was irrevocably in love with Ben and would be for the rest of her natural life. And maybe beyond, if such a place existed...

She shook her head. Now was not the time for existential musings. Had Roman done this to Ben to make it so they couldn't be together anymore? She couldn't believe he would do such a thing, not when he had been responsible for saving her life five years earlier. He'd risked everything for her. He wouldn't want to ruin her happiness now. No way would she believe that.

The door opened quietly. Ben entered the room, shutting the door just as silently as he'd opened it. The last rays of sunshine filtered through the cracks in the shade, casting him in a twilight haze. It made him look both beautiful and scary at the same time. The gentle man who hadn't let her sit on the floor didn't seem to live within him anymore. Her sweet Ben had left five years earlier.

A tear slipped from her eye. It would have been better if he'd never met her.

"My daughters are hysterical messes." His voice sounded hoarse. "They're not liars, so I've decided to believe them, that the story they tell me is true."

Shiri nodded. The only problem she could see with that fact was that his daughters had been so young when everything had happened. Shiri doubted Ben had told his six-year-old girls much of his personal relationship with the woman they'd called Seven. He'd probably just left it that they had been close friends.

How much had they understood on their own?

Not that it mattered. Without his memories, he didn't love her, and you couldn't make someone feel that way simply by telling them they once did.

He walked closer, his stride slow and steady. "They tell me you were pulled off the top of my boat, in front of my eyes, into the sky."

"Yes. Madame used one of her goons to capture me that way."

"Why would she do that if she could have just come and gotten you from my house?"

Ben's words, his questioning of her, the way he still looked at her as though she were nothing to him—it all added up to make her feel dead inside. She wanted, needed really, his arms around her. Her body craved his scent, his taste, his essence. This close to him and unable to curl up in his warmth. It was torture.

"I don't know. I never saw Madame again after that, thank God," she sniffled.

Perhaps she should have been embarrassed that he knew she was upset, but he still looked like *her* Ben. Shiri would never be humiliated to let *her* Ben know anything she thought or felt. "Maybe she somehow knew you would never turn me over to her."

He didn't comment on her remark, and she wondered if he was thinking he would have, in fact, handed her over if asked. She was glad she didn't know what he actually thought.

"Why did she want you back that badly? According to the girls, you're a Ghost-Reader. From my research, I know that's profitable for the Institutions, but certainly not worth risking that level of trouble to retrieve one who hadn't even gone rogue."

"I can't answer that either."

He rubbed his face. "I need answers to my own life. I need to know what's going on here."

"Ben, I can get your memories back any time. I need to make a phone call."

Or maybe she didn't. It was highly likely that Addison had already called in help even though she'd tried in the parking lot, without giving herself away to Ben, to tell the other woman no.

"Shiri." Ben sat down next to her on the bed. "It doesn't help your case here that you keep admitting to having something to do with the fact that my head is messed up."

It was weird to hear him call her Shiri. She'd given up Seven the day she'd finally named herself. But it still sounded strange on his lips. If she tried, she could hear him saying her name—*Seven*—in passion the night they'd made love.

"I could lie but, in addition to the fact that I prefer to tell the truth, we both know you'd know if I did."

"Try to put yourself in my position." He scooted closer to her as he lowered his voice. "I'm aware that I do know you. We definitely communicated for a period of time five years ago. I have no memory of any of it."

"But the girls told you." It was important that she stay positive, keep him in a good place.

"Yes. They did. But they were six years old. At that age, I'm not sure what they did or didn't understand about how I felt. Maybe I pretended to be your friend to set them at ease. I have no idea."

She'd wondered about how he would see the girls' perspective. Opening her mouth, she tried to think of something to say, but there was really nothing, so she closed it. It was better to remain mute than to perhaps make things worse.

He continued. "I have had portions of my memory erased. I have spent the last five years working to get Conditioned people rights, and now I have been violated."

"Ben..."

He held up his hand, so she let him continue. "I don't know if what got taken out of my head is actually because I discovered something you don't want me to know."

"No." She struggled against her restraints. More than anything, she wanted to touch him. "Please, Ben, you have to believe me."

"Don't pull. You'll only hurt yourself." He touched her arm as she leaned back against the headboard again. She swallowed. For a second—a split second—she thought she had seen heat in his eyes when he looked at her. As if he saw her as a woman and not as just a person whose motives were questionable.

"What are you proposing to do, Ben?" She didn't want him to take his hand off her arm, but he did. "You can't keep me locked up in here forever. Or maybe you can, but I don't believe you'll do that. Are you going to have your brother's people torture me?"

Shiri hadn't met Gene yet. But she knew who he was. She'd sent all her correspondence to Ben through him for five years.

"No." He shook his head. "I won't do that to a woman. But I am going to figure out what's going on. Gene and I have put our heads together and come up with a plan. I'm not going to tell you what it is, but you are going to feature in it."

"I see." Her heart beat hard. "Ben, I just got very nervous."

"Good. You should be."

Without warning, he reached out and roughly pulled the wig off her hair. It caught on her head for a second, and she gasped. Her head itched and had long ago become covered in sweat from the heat of the wig.

"I'm sorry. I didn't mean to hurt you." He flung the wig across the room. "That thing was driving me crazy."

"It's okay." But it wasn't. Nothing was okay. Even in her worst nightmare about reacquainting with Ben, she hadn't conceived of matters going this badly.

She couldn't even begin to imagine what she looked like. Her hair must be an utter wreck on top of her head, still pulled back like some deranged librarian but now covered in sweat as well. Just minutes earlier she'd been crying, so her face had to be streaked and disgusting.

"You're a redhead."

That seemed sort of nonsensical. "I am."

"Usually I don't find redheads attractive."

Her heart fell into her stomach. She tried to speak through the lump that seemed to have found a home in her throat. "I'm sorry to hear that."

Before she could blink, he'd leaned forward and pressed his mouth to hers. She closed her eyes, stunned by the suddenness but thrilled at the same time. What the hell was going on? But then she didn't care because this was Ben —*Ben*—and he was kissing her.

His lips were strong but also soft as they met hers. She moaned, loving the feel of it, and he slipped his tongue into her mouth. His kisses were intense and demanding. With his mouth, he forced her attention, her surrender. She was happy to give him what he wanted. Surely some part of his brain must have remembered this. She broke their kiss so she could stare into his brown eyes. There must be some place inside him that Roman hadn't been able to reach. What had been between them had been so complete—even if his mind couldn't remember her, perhaps his body could.

"Untie me so I can touch you."

He shook his head. "No."

Ben kissed her again, this time biting down gently on her lower lip. She sucked in her breath. What was going on here?

"You can't touch me."

"Why not?"

He didn't answer her, instead feasting on her mouth again. The answer seemed pretty clear to Shiri. Ben didn't want them to have a real connection. He was attracted to her, despite his rude redhead comment, but he didn't really want to open up to her.

The real question was why she was going along with this.

Maybe it was because Ben kissed so damn well.

"You're thinking too hard."

She raised an eyebrow. "If I don't get to touch you, you don't get to analyze my internal musings."

"Did we do this before? Or were we really just friends?" His gaze met hers, but she couldn't read his emotions. This Ben was so closed off from her.

He couldn't remember. She'd known that. So why did it still hurt? She blinked away her tears. "Once. We did this once. The day before I got taken."

"Oh yes, the day you got swept off my boat that I can't remember." He nodded his head.

He kissed her again. She couldn't deny that she liked the kissing, especially if that was what it took for Ben to get through whatever was going on inside him. He moved until one of his hands braced him above her on the headboard. The other stroked her cheek gently.

"You really are beautiful, which fucking sucks."

"I thought you didn't like redheads." She couldn't help her snide comment. He'd burned her a little bit with that remark. "Why does it suck?"

A half-smile formed on his lips. "Because women who may or may not be setting you up for some kind of destruction shouldn't be gorgeous."

"I'm not here to harm you, Ben. I came to help the girls. I'd like to assist you, but you have to tell me what you're planning."

"No." He sniffed at her neck. "You smell like coffee. It's driving me bananas."

He'd told her that same thing five years earlier. She smelled like coffee? No one else had ever mentioned it, and she had no idea why that would be. But if he liked it, she'd gladly take that on as her scent. Why not?

"You still smell more like sandalwood. Did you buy more soap from a fundraiser?"

He pulled back, putting some distance between them. "You couldn't know about that unless I told you."

So he was finally catching on. "You told me."

"I... ah... I bought more. But online. The girls are home-schooled. It was the only way we could guarantee safety."

"Makes sense." Ben would always know how to take care of his girls.

"Yes, I know."

Something about the way he spoke had changed. The quality of his voice sounded different.

She had one second to dwell on that before he grabbed the handcuffs that had kept her restrained to the headboard and unlocked them with a key he pulled out of his pocket.

"You're untying me?"

"Yes."

"What made you change your mind?" Why was she even asking? Why couldn't she just keep quiet and be glad she was going to finally get untied?

"It's complicated." He removed the final binding off her other wrist, and she raised her hands to rub them.

He eyed her motions. "Were they too tight?"

"No, it's just painful to be tied up in any position for hours." If it bothered him that he'd left her like that, then that was fine. He shouldn't have done it.

Ben hopped off the bed and extended his hand. She scooted forward and took it. His hand was so much bigger than hers. They were relatively the same height, but he was larger than her was in so many ways. If he wanted to, he could hurt her.

Shiri stared at him as she contemplated whether or not she felt fear toward Ben. He'd certainly been trying to act threatening. Yet she didn't. Maybe she was a fool, but Ben seemed like a wounded animal. Someone had harmed him —in his mind that was Roman, Madame, and possibly Shiri

—and someone had potentially threatened his children's wellbeing.

There was no way he'd be able to remain calm about all of that. If only she could make him understand that she could bring him back his memories and straighten out this entire mess.

They walked out of the room. Ben led her down the hallway to a long staircase.

She vaguely remembered the route from when she'd been dragged upstairs by one of Gene's associates.

This time she could focus on the details. It looked similar to the inside of the home Ben had lived in previously. The same pictures lined the walls, with some additional new ones. Mostly they looked like they were of the girls and their uncle. Where had Ben been and what had he been doing? There was no way he could possibly have worked on the Institution stuff all the time. This was exactly the scenario she'd wanted him to avoid.

"I guess the kids have been spending a lot of time with Gene?"

Ben made a non-committal noise that didn't confirm or deny what she'd said. Frustration was rapidly becoming her new best friend. How much more could she take? She couldn't talk to him and act as if she didn't know about his life. Where the hell was Roman with Ben's memories?

Together, they walked into the living room. Gene, whom she knew from his pictures, sat surrounded by other people she didn't know. Shiri took one more glance around the room. That wasn't true. The goon, Raul, who had dragged her into that upstairs bedroom, sat facing the television. As soon as he saw them, he shut it off and rose. Within seconds, everyone except Gene had stood.

Ben moved forward slightly, blocking her from the

others. She swallowed as nerves tightened up her stomach. What was going on?

"I've changed my mind. We can't do it."

They couldn't do what? Shiri looked at all eight men in the room for answers and found none. Blank stares and hidden expressions were all that answered her silent query.

Gene cleared his throat. He looked so much like Ben, only more fatigued if that were even possible, considering how exhausted Ben seemed. "I have good news and bad news, little brother."

Shiri could feel tension radiating off Ben. "What's that?"

"The good news is I agree with you. Our plan was flawed." Gene struggled to his feet. Why was he so weak? Had he been hurt?

"And the bad news?"

Yes, what was the bad news? Shiri didn't like any of this. She'd changed her mind. Things had been better when she'd been locked in the bedroom. Cowardice wasn't one of her traits, but right now she'd have loved to be able to run and hide.

"I changed the plan, and it's too late to do anything about it."

Ben stalked forward. He grabbed his brother's shirt. Gene faltered as though he might fall over, but Ben's strong grip kept him upright. If she wanted to, she could probably run from the room now. Instead, she stayed put, feeling as if someone had driven a nail into her coffin. Intuition had never failed her.

Whatever was going on here would not be good news for her.

"This is my life. You change plans without even discussing it with me?"

Gene narrowed his eyes, looking more frightening than he had earlier. This was the man Shiri had read about. He'd worked his way up the ladder until he was second in command of the Giallani Mafia family. Gene wasn't to be trifled with, and yet Ben didn't look the least bit afraid of him.

"You weren't thinking straight. We can't bust back into the building we already got out of and kidnap Madame. Trust me, I'm good at these kinds of things. We'd never get out of there alive."

"I agree." Ben shook Gene. "What did you do?"

"I called the eight-hundred number for the Institutions and told them who we had, but we'd only give her up to Madame herself. She's on her way."

Shiri took a step backward one second before her knees gave out. She hit the ground hard and was up again quickly. Oh God, yes, this was panic. Gene had called and turned her in to Madame. She was a dead woman. Where were they?

Any second, they could burst through the door.

This had been a mistake, a terrible error in judgment. Ben didn't love her anymore. He couldn't even remember her. And now her life would be over.

SEVENTEEN

Ben's ears rang at Gene's announcement. His brother had *called* the Institutions and told them to come here? He shook Gene, not caring about his brother's injuries.

"Are you out of your fucking mind? You sent them here? They'll take her. She'll never get away. And the girls, Gene. The girls. They could discover Daphne."

Gene shook his head. "Discover what about Daphne?"

Realization dawned on Ben in a whoosh of understanding. Gene didn't remember that Daphne was Conditioned. Ben only knew because he'd rediscovered it in the car. He'd never told Gene. *Oh, hell.* His brother also didn't know about the past history between Ben and Shiri.

Ben might not have been able to remember it, but he knew he had loved kissing her. If he hadn't found some self-control, he would have taken her while she was still cuffed to his bed. Their shared history didn't seem important where his libido was concerned.

"Daphne is Conditioned." He spoke through clenched teeth, knowing that all ears in the room could hear him.

Had Raul and the others always known about Daphne, or had the reason for their protection been kept from them? It didn't matter. The girls wouldn't be staying here, not for another second.

He dropped Gene even as his brother sputtered out nonsensical remarks. There was no use blaming Gene. It was too late for that, and his brother hadn't known. That fact didn't make it better. It was simply the truth.

"Ben." Shiri's voice sounded strangled.

He whirled around to look at her. She'd collapsed to the ground, and her face was as pale as snow. As he bent over her, his mind moved at a thousand miles a minute.

"We're getting out of here. You, me, the girls—"

Gene called from behind him. "I'll help."

Ben ignored him. He was grateful to his brother, had a feeling that the things he couldn't remember would make him even more so, but this wasn't about his brother anymore.

"Come on, we're getting out of here." He pulled on her arm.

"It's too late." Her eyes met his. They were dry and calm when they should have been filled with tears and hysterics. "Can't you feel them?"

Ben couldn't feel a damn thing except anxiety to get Shiri and his girls out of the house. "They're not here yet. There's still time."

"No, Ben, there's not." She jumped to her feet. "Not for me. They're here; they're surrounding the house. But it's not too late for the girls." She grabbed his arms, shaking him hard. "You can still get your girls out. They don't know about them. There's still a chance to save Daphne."

"Shiri, no one—"

She shook him again. Ben closed his mouth at the intensity in her eyes.

"Move."

One second Ben was moving toward the door and the next second he was blocked. The room filled with the Conditioned. Or at least he assumed that was who they were, because they'd appeared out of nowhere.

He did a quick headcount. There were eight very large, very pissed off men surrounding the doors and windows, blocking all his potential exits. Gene's men raised their guns. Ben braced himself. If there was going to be a battle, he would push Shiri to the floor. He'd gotten her into so much trouble without ever meaning to. Guilt warred with anger inside him, and he fisted his hands, wishing he too held a gun.

One silent, tense second passed and all the guns that Gene's men held disappeared. Gasps and curses filled the room as one of the newly arrived Conditioned stepped forward.

"We are the Fury."

This was the second time in as many days that Ben had had to put up with the Fury. For a supposedly secret organization, they were certainly parading themselves around.

Gene spoke from behind him. "There's been a mistake."

"Oh no, there has not." Madame Joan sauntered into the room as if she owned the place.

Ben took a small amount of pleasure at the protruding, purple bruise on her head from where he had whomped her with the chair. He swallowed. There was no way any of them were getting out of there unscathed.

"You got the drop on me earlier, Mr. Lavelle." She looked at Ben, and he wanted to punch her, hard. As he watched, she turned on her heel to regard Gene. "Imagine my surprise when you were so helpful as to call and tell me you had some of my reported-dead property here at your house." The bitch smiled. "I bet you didn't expect it to go like this, did you?"

"Madame," the Fury standing the closest to the woman said. "I'm sensing more than one Conditioned in the house."

Madame raised her eyebrow as Ben's heart sped up. He turned his gaze to Shiri, begging her silently to understand his internal question. Was it possible? Could they actually just sense Daphne's Condition?

"Don't be stupid," Shiri scoffed. "It's just me."

"Madame..."

"If your Fury are so impeccable, how did I get away in the past? How did we manage to blow up your precious Institution in the first place?"

Madame gasped, turning three shades redder. "You? You were involved in blowing up Crescent?"

Shiri shrugged, and Ben grabbed her, pulling her into his arms. He knew what she was doing. He wouldn't—couldn't—let her. In an impressive maneuver, she managed to wiggle out of his hold.

"Don't touch me, Ben. You betrayed me. As far as I'm concerned, you're as bad as she was."

Somewhere inside him, Ben's soul screamed. He didn't know this woman. As far as his memory went, he'd only known her for a few hours. But her words wounded him as though she's shot him in the gut.

"Shiri..."

She ignored him as she continued her tirade at Madame. "I arranged the whole thing. I blew up your Institution all by myself. Boom. Your safe haven is gone."

The Fury next to Madame lunged forward. Ben moved to intercept him, but not before Shiri kicked him in the groin. His eyes got huge as she pushed the man forward. Behind him, Gene's men pounced. If they couldn't fire weapons, it looked as if they would fight one-on-one.

Ben followed Shiri as she darted around the corner toward the staircase in the front hall. Good. He was sure she was heading out the front door, which was why he gasped when he saw her climbing the stairs instead.

"Shiri, what are you doing?"

She didn't answer him as she took the stairs two at a time. He followed in her wake as the shouts behind him increased. "Where are you going?"

Damn it, she needed to answer him. It felt as though his heart would escape from his chest, it beat so fast.

"The girls," she called over her shoulder. "Second door on the right."

She skidded to a halt in front of the door. Ben nearly collided with her.

"It's locked." Shiri struggled with the handle. "Shit, it's locked."

He could hear the frantic edge in her voice and it matched his anxiety. They were out of time. Why couldn't they get a break? He reached behind her to pound on the door.

"Girls, open this door immediately. It's life or death."

Ben didn't usually want to frighten them, but today he had no choice. The door flew open, revealing Ella on the other side.

"Dad."

He looked over her shoulder. A tall, blond man stood holding Daphne by the arm.

"He just appeared."

Daphne visibly shook. "Daddy."

Ben held out his hands. He wanted to rush the man, to pound him into the ground, but he didn't dare risk Daphne in the hands of a Conditioned man whose powers Ben didn't know.

"Let her go. We can work something out." He had to. This wasn't an option.

His daughters were his whole life. He'd kill, maim and slaughter for Daphne.

"Roman." Shiri scooted in behind him. "It's okay, Ben. He's a friend."

"Then why does he have his hand on my little girl?"

"I'm saving her life." Roman stared at Ella. "Coming? Or am I taking your sister without you?"

"No one is taking anyone anywhere."

Roman narrowed his eyes. "Listen, I appreciate that you're a good dad even if you're a total imbecile when it comes to Shiri. But you have two seconds before Madame and her crew bust in here. They're not here now only because I put up a force field around the room that stops them from being able to enter. But it won't hold, and I'm not going down for you."

"You can trust him, Ben."

Shiri's words implored him to believe. It had been so long since he'd let anyone do anything for him, since he'd actually felt that someone else could take care of his girls' needs.

"I guess I don't have any choice." He spoke through gritted teeth. "When will I see them again?"

"Ella." Roman ignored his question. "You don't have to come. You can stay here and someone will come and take you. That's just the truth. But you can do as you please."

Ella wore a guarded expression. He could see himself in

her so clearly. Ella was capable and strong. "Wherever Daphne goes, I go."

"Okay."

Ella rushed to his side as Roman spoke. "Shiri, I'm taking them to the spot. I'm going to have Addison transport them." Roman visibly swallowed. "I'm not strong enough to take you too."

"I know." Shiri nodded. "This is the way I want it."

"This isn't the way any of us wants it, kid."

Just that fast, his girls vanished, taking his heart with them. He tried to speak but couldn't. Instead he whirled around to regard Shiri. "He's safe?"

"He is." She nodded and stepped forward, touching his arm. The sounds of chaos in the hall downstairs increased. "But you're not if you stay here. They're coming for me now."

"We can still—"

"No," she interrupted. "We can't."

Three men rushed into the room. "How were you keeping us out?"

One of the Fury grabbed Shiri and pulled her up against him. Ben watched her wince, and he tried to lunge for her. Three other Fury restrained him.

Ben fought with every ounce of energy he had, and still he felt powerless against them. They were holding him back not just with their bodies but with something that felt like a brick wall that formed around him. He roared with anger.

"Let her go."

She didn't turn to look at him. Instead, she answered the Fury who held her so tightly Ben could see fingerprints on her arms.

"I have all kinds of talents." Shiri's voice had gone blank. "Erecting shields to keep you out is just one of them."

"That was never one of your talents before." The man said as he tugged on her hair. She gasped and closed her eyes.

Still, when she responded, her voice sounded strong and alert. Ben was overcome with pride for Shiri. How did she stay so brave in the face of so much danger?

"I guess you boys don't know everything you think you know."

That earned her a slap across the cheek. Ben reared back as he tried to drive himself forward to get to her. His movements didn't do him any good. He couldn't budge, but damn it, he wanted to kill someone. No one touched what was *his*.

Ben's eyes widened at the thought. *His.* Yes, she was, but why? Was he finally starting to remember what she insisted was the truth? Had they been together?

Madame walked into the room. She took a quick glance around as if she didn't care one way or another what she found. He knew that wasn't true. The woman was all smoke and mirrors. It was all about the show with her.

"I've been trying to decide what punishment to lavish on you, Mr. Lavelle." Her eyes gleamed with satisfaction. If he got free, after he rescued Shiri, he was going to whack Madame over the head again—this time making sure she died. "But before we get to all that..." She turned to regard the Fury who held Shiri. "What happened to the other Conditioned person? Did you lose them?"

"Whoever it was had left by the time I got up here." The man paled.

"Unacceptable, Fury. You know your job." The woman enunciated every word as though everything she said was somehow akin to gospel and wasn't possibly to be misheard by whoever listened.

"Yes, Madame."

She walked a step closer. "You wouldn't want to have to go live in an Institution, would you? Because that is what happens to Fury who fail. Your nice, cushy life outside the walls disappears."

He nodded, and the telltale tremor of a man on the edge started in his hands. Maybe Shiri could maneuver an escape while he was distracted.

"You have my deepest apologies, Madame."

"Isn't this sweet?" Shiri's voice dripped with sarcasm. Ben felt torn between laughing and telling her to shut the hell up so she didn't end up in more trouble.

"He's very, very sorry."

Madame rolled her eyes. "Take her to the holding cells. You see, little girl, it doesn't matter that you blew up the Institution. We've just relocated, and we're rounding up all the escapees now. They can't survive without our help. They can't even feed or clothe themselves."

"Liar." Shiri spat out the word.

Ben couldn't take it anymore. "Shiri..."

She didn't listen. "They can be taught, as anyone can be. And you don't have them back. You're *lying*."

"Get her out of here, Fury."

"No! Damn it." Ben tried to throw himself forward, this time earning an elbow to his nose for his efforts. It didn't matter. He'd take a thousand hits to the face if it meant he could stop what he knew was about to happen.

He refused to close his eyes from the pain. As if keeping his gaze fully focused on Shiri could somehow keep her in the room with him, as if it could prevent them from taking her, he steadily held her gaze.

"Shiri..."

She shook her head, and he watched her blink away tears. "It's okay, Ben. I had five extra years to live a life I could never have imagined for myself. It was such a gift. Remember that when you think of me."

She sucked in a breath, and he realized that tears were streaming down his cheeks. When was the last time he'd cried? How could he feel this acutely for a woman he couldn't remember?

"Ben, I love you."

Just like that, she was gone. Ripped from his life. It felt as though they'd opened a wound inside him that he couldn't close. Anger poured out of him, and he raged against his invisible restraints. This couldn't be happening.

Madame grinned. "I don't think I need to punish you. I think the fact that you can live a long, miserable life without her, knowing that I killed her, will be enough torture for you." She sighed, elongating the sound as if even breathing was an important event. "Or maybe I'll come back to kill you. You'll never know."

Just as the Fury had vanished with Shiri, the room cleared out immediately. Ben fell to the floor, his body slamming into the ground as though he had no muscles to hold him up. He didn't mind the pain; in fact, he relished it. His daughters were gone, taken by a man he didn't know, though Shiri said he was trustworthy. Madame had Shiri. He would never see her again.

No.

Everything inside him railed against that thought. It was unacceptable.

Somehow, he would have to find a way to get her back. Gene rushed into the room, followed by his men.

"Ben." Gene kneeled next to him. "Are you okay?"

His brother's frantic tone was what made him look up. "No, I'm not fucking okay."

Two guys grabbed him by the arms and pulled him into a sitting position. They should have left him on the ground.

"I'm so sorry, Ben. The guys beat her so easily last time. I thought it would be the same deal. They'd come in, we'd overwhelm them, and we'd get some answers."

Ben could see the genuine remorse radiating from his older brother's eyes. He wanted to forgive him even as he wasn't sure he could. "It was a stupid fucking plan. They had time to prepare for us. This isn't like one of your operations. We can't just smash things until we get what we want."

"I know that." Gene visibly swallowed. "Now."

"Hindsight is twenty-twenty, is that what you're saying?" Ben tried really hard not to hit his brother. His whole life was a giant shit-hole, and he had no idea what to do about it.

"I screwed up."

"Ya think? The girls are gone. One of Shiri's friends got them out, but I have no idea where they are or if I'll ever see them again." He closed his eyes. "Shiri has been taken by the devil herself, and she's going to be killed. I can't even be mad at you, because you were just doing what you always do in the way that you do it."

His brother fell silent for a moment. "What are you going to do, Ben?"

"I have no clue." He pounded on the ground, not caring if he broke every bone in his hand.

Gene grabbed him. "Ben!"

"Well, isn't this touching?"

Ben almost didn't hear the person speaking over the roaring in his head. He panted as he looked up to see the man who had taken his daughters, leaning casually against Ella's dresser.

Ben shot to his feet. "Where are the girls? Are they fine?"

"They're with friends. They're worried about you and Shiri, but they're fine. In a few hours, they'll be taken to a safe place where no one will hurt them or find them."

"I can't let you do that. They're my daughters. You can't just take them away permanently without me knowing where they are."

Roman nodded. "I agree."

He did? Ben hadn't expected that response. "You do?"

"Yes. You're a very good dad, you're just a piece-of-shit man."

Gene shouted from behind him. "Hey."

Roman took two steps closer to Ben. "I *love* her, you asshole. I've loved her most of her life. I saved her life. I brought her to safety, and she doesn't even look at me. She never even thinks of me that way. No, for five years all she could do was dream about getting back to you. And what happens when she does? She gets taken while saving your worthless ass."

Ben wanted to punch Roman in the face. He *loved* Shiri. Ben had no right to be jealous—the woman had just told him she loved him—but he was. This was all so fucked up. Still, he tried to find a reasonable argument even as his gut burned with the truth of Roman's words.

"I can't remember her. Someone took my memories. I'm operating with no information here. I don't know who to trust."

Roman raised his eyebrows. "I thought you were braver than that." He shrugged. "Guess I was wrong."

"What does that mean?"

"Want your memories back?" Roman snapped his fingers.

"Here, take them back."

Flashes of light passed before his eyes. He heard someone screaming and realized it was his own voice. He fell to the floor, feeling as if his head might explode.

EIGHTEEN

Shiri awoke to consciousness slowly. Awareness came to her in stages. First, she realized she was lying on a cold, hard floor. That eliminated the possibility that she was at home in her beach cabin, safe and secure with only the absence of Ben and the girls to plague her. Then the pounding at the base of her skull, where the Fury bastard had struck her, stole all her attention.

It really, really hurt. She groaned, wishing she *were* back at home, where Laurel could heal her. But that wasn't going to happen, and where she currently resided—wherever it might be—wasn't a place where wishes came true. In fact, the absence of hope helped to define the Institutions. Those facilities were where dreams went to die.

And now she resided in one again. She supposed she'd had a good run on the other side and, hell, she'd aged five years since she'd vanished, which meant she was that much closer to forty, the age when she should have been marked for death. At least Madame would get her closer to the legal date.

Shiri made herself concentrate on other noises besides

her pounding head. Somewhere not too far away, water dripped. A slow, steady but constant sound was the only thing she could make out.

Tentatively, she attempted opening her eyes, first the left one and then the right. The room swayed for a moment before it righted itself. There were no dark circles or streaming colors blurring her vision. She'd learned basic first aid from Laurel, enough to know she was probably not concussed, even though her head hurt like hell.

She pushed up until she was sitting with her legs crossed in a pretzel position. What had happened to Ben when she'd left? Her demands to know about him had been what had gotten her whomped on the head. Apparently, he was a sore subject for Madame and her men. *Good*. Shiri exhaled.

Ben.

Nothing had gone with him the way she'd wanted it to. If only there had been time to get him his memories back before Roman had escaped with the girls. She would have loved to have seen him look at her with recognition one more time before her life ended.

The door to her cell swung open, and Madame entered. She crossed her arms over her chest and stared down at Shiri with disdain evident in her gaze.

"Seven-Two-Four, are you done causing trouble, or should I have the Fury here hit you again?"

Shiri stared up at Madame Joan. The five years she'd been gone had not been kind to the other woman. Her once platinum blonde hair had faded until it looked like a shell of its former glory. Lines that had not been on her face darted out from the sides of her eyes and her mouth. Laugh lines, people called them. Shiri knew Madame never engaged in such a frivolous activity as humor, so they'd appeared on her for other reasons. She didn't want to imagine what those *activities* had entailed.

"Answer me, Seven-Two-Four."

All at once, Shiri understood why Guy had insisted that they all take names upon arriving on his Island. Seven-Two-Four. She was someone different than Shiri. Even when she'd lived in Crescent, she'd been called Seven, not Seven-Two-Four. Madame could shriek all she wanted about Seven-Two-Four, she could threaten her, she could even kill her if she wanted to. But her actions would never really touch Shiri's soul. That wasn't who she was, or even who she had ever been.

Shiri smiled, and Madame took a step back as if she'd been struck.

"You look deranged."

She did? Well, that was fine. It was better than appearing pathetic. Maybe she was a little bit nuts.

"Answer my question, you ungrateful heathen. Are you prepared to be cooperative now?"

"The real question is why do you need my cooperation?" Shiri tapped her hand on the floor of her cell.

"That is none of your business. Your only role is to obey me and hope that I don't kill you immediately for your disobedience."

"Then I guess you're out of luck, because my days of listening to you have long passed. Feel free to kill me if that's a problem."

Shiri wasn't going to play games with this woman. No way, no how. Madame had brought her here to end her life. She wasn't going to make it any easier on the woman or delude herself into thinking that if she helped her, she might somehow survive.

It was all bullshit.

Too many people had lived and died trying to give the Conditioned freedom to live their lives. Shiri wouldn't be doing anything to damage that effort, ever.

"I could take the information from your head without your permission."

Shiri laughed, a cold, hard sound that she couldn't believe she'd made herself. "If you could do that, you would have already. What is it about me that has you so worked up? You went to a tremendous amount of effort to try to retrieve me five years ago when I would have disembarked the boat an hour later, and you're very upset by my presence now. What is it, Joan? What's put a bug up your ass?"

Shiri deliberately used one of Guy's most coarse expressions on Madame Joan. She'd dropped the Madame on purpose, too. She was tired of kowtowing to the people who abused her. She'd had five years to discover her worth, and she wasn't going to lose her gumption in just five minutes with these sick people.

"How dare you."

Despite her throbbing head, Shiri stood up on wobbly legs. It had to have been apparent to Madame Joan that she was unsteady, but Shiri didn't care. For her, it would be considered a personal triumph.

"How dare I? Well, I guess I'm suddenly starting to realize that for some reason you find me threatening. Why is that, Joan? Why do I scare you so badly?"

"You?" Madame advanced two steps, but Shiri didn't budge from where she stood. She'd hold her ground until the end. "You're nothing. You're a Conditioned maggot whom I've had the misfortune to have to feed and clothe since the time you were two. For twenty-five years."

Shiri swallowed. "I thought no one knew how old I was." Silence filled the room. "I'm assuming it was twenty-five years. Who cares to keep track of how old any of you are?"

"I care. Lots of people care. More and more, you're going to see things change because we will force them to." Now she was completely spitting out Guy's rhetoric but that was fine. If it worked, she'd take it.

"You're talking about your petty revolution? It's already being squashed. The leaders have all been captured. We are the Institutions. Even the government doesn't control us."

No. She was sure she would have known if that had happened. Somehow, she would have felt it. It might have been stupid—or naïve—but Shiri believed in her fellow Conditioned who were out there fighting for everyone. They were so connected, had spent so much time together, she had to believe she would know if they were all gone.

Not to mention, Madame was a notorious liar. Believing anything she said seemed like a really bad idea.

"I've had enough." Madame stormed up to her and grabbed her by the shoulders. Shiri fought against her hold, but Madame was freakishly strong. For a woman who was significantly smaller than Shiri, she had a strong grip Shiri couldn't break. But the huge bruise she sported proved she could be bested.

"I'm taking your knowledge. I'm taking it. All of it belongs to me."

Madame squeezed her cranium. It hurt, and Shiri wildly flung her head to try to dislodge her. Her efforts didn't work. This couldn't be happening. Anger fueled her energy, and Shiri struck back with the only weapon she possessed: her power.

Spencer Lewis had told her time and again that while she felt as if her power were defensive at best, some day she would find a way to manipulate her energy so that it could be offensive, too.

Right now, she wanted Madame to hurt—to burn for all the things she'd done. Shiri sent her energy outward until it surrounded Madame. The other woman seemed so consumed with her quest to invade Shiri's mind, something she was apparently having trouble with, that she didn't notice how Shiri had stopped struggling.

Why should she bother? For the first time in her life she knew exactly what would happen. Shiri was going to burn Madame.

As if she'd willed it, Madame dropped her hands. Feeling no need to move, Shiri stayed where she was to watch what she was sure was about to happen. Madame grabbed the exposed parts of her arms.

Her eyes got huge as she stared at Shiri. "You. You did this to me? I always knew you were a dangerous bitch. I should have put you down when you first came to me."

"Maybe you should have." Shiri threw some more energy in Madame's direction and the woman screamed. "This was why you were afraid of me, right?"

"I have never been afraid of anything in my life." She scoffed even as she started to double over in pain.

"Yes, you have." Shiri took a step forward. "I think you go through every day absolutely terrified."

Madame fell to her knees. "Make the burning stop."

"I can't." Shiri found she just couldn't feel sorry about that. "You have all the ghost energy I could internalize from the city of New Orleans flowing into your veins right now. The energy signatures of all the dearly departed from God knows how long ago."

"You could stop it if you wanted to."

"Maybe I could."

Shiri kneeled down to look at her. Truth was, Shiri didn't know if she actually possessed the power to stop it. She'd never done this before. It had been so easy to make the decision to torture Madame. The woman had tormented her with threats of death her entire life.

"You're not like this. You're soft and easy, forgiving." Madame's eyes implored her. "Please, I'll let you go. You have my word. I'll leave you alone if only you stop this."

Shiri sighed. She didn't believe for one second that Madame would keep that promise. Even if *she* left Shiri alone, she would simply have someone else come after her. That was the problem with liars and manipulators—you could never believe a word they said.

But Madame had hit her target correctly. This wasn't in Shiri's nature, and as much as it felt good to see Madame start to turn red in pain, she couldn't let her die this way. In her heart of hearts, even though she no longer believed she'd been damned at birth, she still wanted to go to Heaven. It might be the only place she'd ever see Ben again.

Assuming he'd even want to see her.

Shiri sighed. If she'd sent it into Madame, she could probably take it back. Centering herself, she let her mind move into the other space, the place where she could see energy acutely. Numerous shades of red, blue and pink flowed inside Madame, as they did to Shiri whenever she ingested them. But unlike Shiri, Madame's body rejected the onslaught. She wasn't an energy container, as Shiri was. It was as though she had poisoned the other woman by forcing her to ingest it, and now it was burning her from the inside out.

With a tilt of her mind, she called the energy back into herself—a little at a time. She didn't want Madame to become aware all at once that it was happening. Shiri might not have wanted to be a murderer, but she didn't mind tormenting her tormentor for a little while longer.

After a few seconds, Madame must have felt the difference.

Her shoulders relaxed, and her pained, dilated eyes eased.

"You're so easy. I would have left you to die."

Shiri nodded. She already knew that. "I'm aware. It's why you've run one of the most horrendous Institutions for the last thirty years, and why I could never do anything like that."

Madame struggled to her feet. "You might be surprised. I was born Conditioned but no one ever locked me away. No, I was too strong for that. Too powerful. I rule all of you. I'm a billionaire. I could be even more so if Susan hadn't gotten caught and had managed to kill you."

"Susan? You thought she could kill me?" Finally, that made sense to Shiri. "And don't pretend you weren't as burdened by the Institutions as we all were." Shiri could have laughed if it wasn't so sad. "You've spent your life in that box they called Crescent, and they gave you the illusion of power. You're still just a pawn, but so much worse than that, too, because you abused those who could have used your help."

Madame slapped her across the face. It burned, and Shiri tasted blood from where she'd bitten down on her tongue during the attack.

"I may not be able to get into your head, but someone can. I'll bring the entire Fury down on you."

Shiri fisted her hands at her sides and restrained herself from responding to Madame's physical attack. No way would she give the woman the satisfaction of seeing how badly that had hurt. "Why did you come for me when I was with Ben and his family? What had happened?"

"I didn't want you to end up like this." Madame snarled. "There is no saving you now. God will have nothing to do with you."

As she rolled her eyes, Shiri knew beyond a shadow of a doubt that Madame did not believe a word she said. She might not have Ben's ability to taste a lie, but Madame had lost her cool, and her perfect façade had disappeared.

"Don't give me the God-talk. You don't believe that any more than I do. The Institutions have been speaking the 'devil' talk for over three decades to terrify the Conditioned." She shook her head. "No, tell me the truth. Why did you want me dead?"

Madame straightened, pulling at her clothes as though dislodging a few wrinkles could somehow make her orderly again. "You destroyed my plans. I had a network of people helping me all over the place. They'd infest places with ghost energy. Eventually people would move. We'd sweep in and buy the real estate."

Shiri's mouth fell open, and she could do nothing to stop it. Finally, when she could find her voice, she spoke. "But you sent me out to clear those places."

"Yes." Madame raised an eyebrow. "It was a perfect storm for me. I got paid for your services, and ultimately I got the property I wanted."

"Money? This whole thing was about money?" Shiri wanted to scream, to rail against how the people who had controlled her life had so easily decided when she could live or die based on a profit margin.

"You were never supposed to live through the encounter with Lavelle's neighbors. It should have been too much for you. Half that amount nearly killed you when you were a child."

"But I got too strong."

It was all so clear to her. She'd been useful, profitable, for the Institutions, but Madame had known she'd eventually get too powerful to be fooled. She was supposed to be ended before that happened.

But they'd saved her—Guy, Spencer, Roman, and the others had saved her life before Madame could make it so Shiri never gained her full power range. Even before that, Ben had saved her soul. If he hadn't shown her love—shown her what love was supposed to be—she never could have embraced the idea that she could be more than she'd ever been.

"And now my abilities are so formed, so tight, that you can't even get in my head anymore." Shiri smiled at her. "It must be making you crazy to have your plans screwed up. And now Crescent is gone. Things are going askew all over the place."

"I have ten Fury outside this door, and they will do whatever I tell them to do to you. One way or the other, I will get the news of these terrorists from you."

Shiri had no doubt the Fury could abuse her. She'd seen it done often enough. But she needed to believe that she could withstand their ministrations. She would not break.

"I told you. I blew up the Institution. I arranged it. There is no one else involved. I've been hiding out for years, waiting for the opportunity to do it."

Madame spoke a string of words in French that Shiri strongly suspected were curse words. "You blew up two Institutions within hours of each other on two different coasts of this very large country?"

"Yep." Shiri hadn't actually heard that the one in

Arizona had worked. That was good news. Still, she tried to keep her expression bland. "I set the charges in Arizona to go off, and I was just lucky no one found them."

"Liar. The person whose blurred image spoke to the country about your so-called revolution was a man."

Shiri shrugged. "An actor I hired. He read the words I told him to read."

"You did? You did all of this? Someone like you manipulated this whole thing?"

She put her hands on her hips. "As you pointed out, I am so much more powerful than you ever wanted me to be. I'm evil, right? Why shouldn't I have been able to handle this whole thing on my own?"

Shiri didn't expect Madame to believe her. It would have been absurd to believe that only one person could have done everything by himself or herself. But she had no intention of changing her story.

"I've had enough of this."

Madame walked toward the door and rapped on it three times. It opened, and she stepped out into the hall. The door clanged closed behind her, sealing Shiri back into her fate.

Immediately she started second-guessing herself. Should she not have spoken to Madame like that? Would it have been better to have simply kept quiet and said nothing at all?

She'd wanted to know. For years, she'd obsessed over the way Madame had seemed to pursue her endlessly. Why had she wasted so many resources retrieving one Conditioned girl who could easily have been picked up using less difficult means?

Now it made sense. Madame had been afraid of her. She'd been a variable element whom Madame had needed to eliminate before she got too powerful, too sure of herself.

Shiri sat down on the floor. At least she knew the reasons. Her life sometimes felt like an endless slew of questions without any real answers presented. But now at least she could understand how Madame's sick mind worked.

There was no peace in having the answer, just a kind of numbness that her life had been driven and controlled by so many evil people.

The door burst open and three Fury filed in. Lucky her. Apparently, today's antics weren't finished yet. She sighed as she stood up. If nothing else, she could give the appearance of being on steady ground.

NINETEEN

Ben paced in front of the phone again, staring down at the device as if it held some kind of magic answer to all his problems. Roman was on speakerphone to someone named Guy, whom the Fury hoped could solve some of their problems. So far, his response seemed less than satisfactory.

Guy spoke through the phone. "I'm telling you, it's not as bad as it could be."

Roman snorted. "Bullshit."

Ben tuned out their conversation. This was the same refrain he'd listened to for the last hour. Guy felt that Seven —*no*. He shook his head. *Shiri*. She was called Shiri now— could actually get herself out of trouble. Roman scoffed at this idea, and the debate continued. Ben was basically, on a fundamental level, useless.

His daughters were with Addison Wade—now Lewis— which blew his mind, and he hadn't been allowed to see them since they'd left with Roman earlier. He couldn't blame the others for thinking he shouldn't be involved in anything. It was his fault they were in this predicament.

Worry threatened to overtake him for the millionth

time, and he pushed it away. Shiri was Seven. Seven was Shiri. And no matter which way you added it up, he'd gotten the woman he loved captured and killed. It was his fault for even thinking he could go along with Gene's plan in the first place.

His body had known her. Why hadn't he trusted himself? He closed his eyes. He'd gotten her back from the dead without even knowing it, and lost her again. In his wildest imagination, he couldn't have conceived the amount of pain he was in right now.

If he wasn't careful, he was going to fall into a big, giant pit of it and never return.

"There is a solution."

Ben opened his eyes as Gene spoke from the doorway. He leaned against it as if it might support him in the event that he hit the floor. Ben had never seen him so tired before.

"I'm all ears." Ben would take any solution anyone wanted to present.

"I think it has been pointed out about a dozen times now that we can't storm into the building where they're holding Shiri and bust her out. My men did that to get Ben and me out yesterday. They'll be prepared."

Roman made a loud grunting noise. "Yes, you were lucky. I assume this plan is going to go better than the one you made that got Shiri taken in the first place." The Fury stared at Ben as if he wanted to run him over with a truck.

Ben held the Fury's gaze. He knew his own culpability. If something happened to Shiri, he didn't know if he'd survive it.

Gene took an unsteady step forward. He sported all kinds of new bruises since the fight in the living room with the Fury who'd invaded the house. Ben wasn't sure his older brother could take any more abuse without expiring.

"I take full responsibility for that blunder. Ben had nothing to do with it."

Roman rolled his eyes. "Bullshit. However you altered the plan, Ben was involved in its first inception."

"Roman." Guy sounded as if he gritted his teeth as he spoke. "Not helping."

"As I was saying, the bad plan *I* came up with aside, we can't storm the place with massive power and bust Shiri out."

Ben wished they could. His heart hurt thinking about her being in there. He had so many questions he wanted to ask her, but mostly he wanted to hold her, to press his head up against her chest and listen to her heartbeat, to find a way to make sure they never had to be separated again.

Roman took a step toward Gene. "What, then, do you suggest?"

"Since you've made it clear that you can't do that popping in and out thing you do—"

"I can't. The Fury is all over that place," said Roman. "They'll sense my presence, and I'll never be able to help anyone again. I'll be named an enemy."

"I thought you said you loved her." If Ben's voice sounded harsh, he really didn't give a shit.

Roman put his hands on his hips. "I do."

"No, you don't. Because if you loved her, if you really loved her, you wouldn't give one crap about whether or not you got caught and your days of subterfuge were over." Ben took a step toward Roman. "There's nothing I wouldn't do. I would die for her. I would kill. I would take her place."

"That's good." Gene's voice interrupted their power-play, and Ben took a deep breath. He wanted to pound someone, and Roman seemed a good candidate.

"Because one man has to sneak inside."

"Good. I'm your guy," said Ben.

"You?" Roman threw his hands in the air. "You, Mr. Lawyer? Are you going to break the law?"

"For Seven, I would do anything."

Guy's voice from the phone broke into the conversation. "I think you have to get used to calling her Shiri, Ben."

He'd call her anything she wanted if only he could see her again and assure himself of her safety. But part of him would always think of her as Seven. When she'd become his girl, her name had been Seven.

Gene sighed. "Want the details, Benedicte?"

"I'll do anything, Eugene." Anything at all. No way would Shiri not be coming out of that building alive.

BEN SCRATCHED HIS NECK. Roman's Fury uniform itched like hell. Maybe it was why the other man existed in a perpetual bad mood. With all the money pouring into the Institutions, they couldn't find a better way to dress their Fury?

He approached the door. Roman had told him to look pissed and annoyed. No one would dare question a Fury entering the holding cell areas. The Institutions had taken over a floor of the Orleans Parish Prison on Gravier Street while they were out of their own building.

Ben was ushered quickly through the top floors into the elevator that would take him to the basement without anyone even asking his name. Hell, he'd had a harder time buying a lottery ticket once. No identification? The fake driver's license they'd spent hours working on burned a hole in his pocket.

He stepped into the elevator, and it dinged as it started

its descent. It must only go to that floor, because he hadn't pushed any buttons. This situation called upon him to be basically inconspicuous. Still, he needed to act the part. One way or another, he had to be unnoticeable while also being as assertive and frightening as Roman.

Ben fisted his hands. He wasn't afraid, just anxious to see Shiri and to get her out of there.

The doors opened with a creak. This was New Orleans. Things like public safety in elevators didn't rank very high on the priority list. He smiled thinking about it. There was something about living here that other people didn't understand. If he got Shiri out, they'd have to leave his beloved city. That was fine. Moving and living a life hidden from others would be a small price to pay to know that the people he loved could all finally be safe. But he would miss the little quirks of this place.

He stepped out into the hallway, smelling the dank, musky stink of a place that had seen water invade its perimeter and not been properly cleaned up. Really, they should have knocked the mess down.

Ben walked like a man on a mission. Roman had said she was being held three doors down the hallway. How the Fury knew that, Ben hadn't asked. Roman knew lots of things he shouldn't and he was capable of doing things people, even Conditioned people, shouldn't be able to. Like take away people's memories.

"But does it make you want to lock him up?"

Ben froze where he walked. Slowly and deliberately, he raised his head to look at the person who'd spoken. Down the hall a distance was a man who hadn't been there seconds before. He leaned casually against the wall with a smoking cigarette in his hand.

Okay. This was what everyone had worried about.

Improvisation. Ben had to be able to think on his feet. He'd done it for years in court; he could do it now.

"What?"

"I asked if you thought, Mr. Lavelle, that Roman should be put behind bars for the rest of his life to conduct hard labor because he has the potential to do dangerous things. Is the potential to be trouble enough to keep him locked up?"

Well, Ben was screwed and he knew it. But he didn't feel out of control. This guy knew who he was, but he would still figure out how to get through this.

"Yes, I do know who you are. I can read your mind." The man took a step off the wall toward him. "Do you think he should be locked up?"

"No." Ben shook his head and took a step toward his unknown questioner. "I've spent the last five years working like a lunatic to get the people who *were* locked up let out. I do not feel that just because someone could do something means they will. I think with training, help and early diagnosis, the Conditioned could be taught to control their powers and even use them to help others." He shrugged. "And if that makes me an idiot or naïve, so be it."

"Really? We don't frighten you?" The stranger threw his cigarette on the floor without putting it out. "Not even a little bit?"

"Sure, some of you frighten me, but that doesn't mean that my fear gets to dictate everyone else's life."

"Interesting."

Ben looked the man up and down. The stranger was taller than he was by at least three inches. He had red hair and green eyes. Dressed in his Fury uniform, he would have been the nightmare of every non-Institutionalized Conditioned hiding in the world.

"Yes." The slight smirk plastered on the man's face fell. "I'm the stuff of nightmares."

"You look to me like a man stuck in a bad situation." A thought dawned on him, but he pushed it away. He didn't want the Mind-Reader to know what he thought. "It seems to me that you had two choices. Live in an Institution or have some semblance of freedom with just the occasional job of stalking uncaught Conditioned to bother you. Bet you never thought you'd have to handle anything like this?"

"No. I didn't." The man extended his hand. "Bryan Teege. I've been wanting to shake your hand for some time."

Even as Ben shook his hand, he realized he had no idea what was going on. "Why would that be?"

"It's not every day that one of *you* takes an interest in one of *us* to the point that they're willing to risk their own life."

Ben tried to find his patience. This was all fine and good, but he needed to get to Shiri. Another time, perhaps he might be more interested in discussing how the average American didn't know or understand what was really going on in the Institutions.

"I love her." What else was there to say?

"I know. Which is why you're going to want to get into that room before they kill her." Ben's heart fell into his stomach as Bryan continued to speak. "Let good old Roman know that he's not the only one who does his part to fight back when he can."

"Where is she?" Ben swallowed. If Bryan wanted to help, he'd gladly take all he could get. There was nothing in the universe he wouldn't do for Shiri.

Bryan pointed at the door to his left. "Not much time left."

As quickly as Bryan had arrived, he vanished into thin

air. Ben had no time to dwell on it. He ran toward the door as he pulled the key Roman had promised him would open any door in the Institution out of his pocket.

He stuck the key in the door, and for one second he doubted. Had Roman told him a lie? Did he possess some kind of agenda no one knew about? Would this prove to be all for naught?

Then the handle turned. Ben shoved the door open as he stormed into the room. Shiri lay on the floor, three Fury staring down at her.

"What are you doing to her?" Ben's voice shook, and for a second the whole room seemed bathed in red.

"Who are you?" The tallest Fury turned to regard him.

"Don't worry about it."

Ben might not have been getting any answers, but he was getting Shiri out. He pressed the magnet in his pocket. Roman, whom he would never doubt again now that he stood in Shiri's cell, had told him that it momentarily disabled the Fury. They would have only the same abilities as Ben. It would be three-on-one, but at least it wouldn't be three super-humans against him.

He didn't give them a chance to figure out what was going on. Instead, he pulled out his gun and pointed it at the tallest one's head. Roman said the Fury saw no point in carrying weapons. They could do with their minds what most people couldn't even do with a deadly device. In this case, it would work to Ben's advantage.

"You might be able to subdue me. Maybe. But I'll shoot two of you before you ever get the chance. So ask yourself, are you the one who's going to live or are you one of the two who will die? It's basic statistics."

The one who stood to the right clutched his heart. "Oh God, what are you doing to us?"

The magnet was supposed to disable their powers, but Roman hadn't mentioned anything about causing them pain. Not that their discomfort would have stopped him from doing it. Only Shiri mattered in this scenario. Still, it would have been nice to have been warned. Ben had had enough surprises to last a lifetime.

Maybe several lifetimes.

"You're like me now. You don't have your powers. So what's your choice? Do we fight, or do I get out of here with my lady and you can say I subdued you?"

The tallest man's eyes rolled to the back of his head seconds before he hit the ground. Ben cursed and jumped back, barely able to miss being squished by his dead weight before it slumped to the floor. The other two men looked at each other seconds before they bolted from the room. He dropped his gun to the ground, wanting both hands free and hating the damn thing anyway.

"Nothing like loyalty," Ben muttered to himself as he rushed to Shiri. If they had gone for help, he had seconds at best. He had to get her to the elevator. Once he got into the mechanism, Roman had felt he could successfully whisk them out of the building using teleportation and still not get caught.

Ben bent down and scooped Shiri up in his arms. She weighed nothing. For a woman who reached his own height, he had to have had more than fifty pounds on her, and he wasn't considered overweight. Didn't they feed her on her island? She'd been this skinny when she'd been starved in the Institution.

She was out cold and didn't stir even when he called her name. The device had obviously affected her, too, but he'd expected to be able to wake her. What had they been doing to her? He hoped Roman or one of his cohorts would know. She didn't look as if she'd been physically assaulted.

Ben ran as fast as he could down the empty hall. He didn't hear any alarms going off, but that didn't mean there weren't some going off somewhere he wasn't aware of. And so far he hadn't seen Madame, which was too bad, because he really wished she'd give him an excuse to shoot her in the head.

Shiri's eyes flew open. She groaned, and he squeezed her tighter.

"You're going to be okay, sweetheart."

"No." Her voice sounded hoarse. "Not you."

Ben couldn't blame Shiri for not wanting to see him, not after the way he'd treated her.

"We're almost out of here."

He realized he shouldn't have spoken almost the second he did. It was clearly a challenge to the universe that he'd actually thought he was home free. The elevator doors opened, and Madame sauntered out as though she were strolling through the park instead of into a virtual war zone.

"Hello, Mr. Lavelle. How unpleasant to see you again." She stared at Shiri in his arms. "I hadn't anticipated this. Set her down, unless you want her to die."

He didn't want to do what she said, but he wasn't willing to risk Shiri either. In what he hoped was a smart move, he set her down next to the elevator. She made a sound that was something between a moan and a scream. "Just go, Ben."

He didn't look down at her. Why shouldn't she believe he'd let her down? He'd done nothing to show her he wouldn't. That would change right now.

"Would you like to know, Mr. Lavelle, how I became the Madame of this Institution when so many of my Conditioned brothers and sisters were being locked up like animals?"

"No." Ben wanted to wring the life out of this woman. He couldn't take one more second of her fake French accent. "Didn't you grow up in the United States?"

She narrowed her eyes at him, and he realized he'd startled her. Good, let her be surprised.

"I was born in France."

"Yes, but you were raised here, right? If I'd come into this world in Greece, it wouldn't mean that I spent the rest of my life putting on some pseudo-ridiculous attempt at speaking Greek just to—*what?*—Seem European? Are we all supposed to be impressed?"

"Do you want to see what I can do?" The woman advanced on him, all pretext of being a so-called lady gone. She reminded him of Medusa, her hair full of snakes, ready to turn men into stone with just her gaze.

"No. I want you to get out of my way before I do to you what I did to your Fury seconds ago."

"You're talking about the magnet in your pocket that takes away the power of whoever it is used on. I'm not interested in it. Nothing takes away my power. That's what I tried to explain to you. They are Conditioned. I am a God."

Before he could blink, the woman was on him. Her hands on his head, she knocked him down to the ground, levering her weight on top of him. Ben didn't even have time to gasp.

"I am the stuff of nightmares, Mr. Lavelle." He had heard that phrase when Bryan had uttered it. It was obviously a favorite amongst the Conditioned.

She hadn't lied. Within seconds of her hands colliding with his head, Ben couldn't make out what was real and what wasn't. His eyes filled with visions, and soon they were all he could see; they were all that was real in the world.

His girls were lost at sea. Surrounded by monsters, he couldn't get to them. A giant snake lunged out of the water, aiming for Daphne. He screamed and tried to get to her, but he was powerless to move. His feet were glued to the ground as though they were roots from a strong tree that would never move.

"Daddy!" Daphne cried in anguish, tears in her eyes as the monster dragged her under.

Ella was next. This time the snake swallowed her whole before diving back into the dark depths, where he couldn't follow.

The scene changed. Now he was on the floor of a hospital room. Ben only knew his location because of the smell of antiseptic. He'd never forget the overwhelming stench of chemical cleaning products from the time he'd spent with Dana in the hospital. The scents of the things that were meant to help people get healthy had come to represent death to him. He couldn't do anything but lift his head to watch what happened.

Shiri lay strapped to the bed, restrained by her hands and feet. A man with a black mask approached her with a needle in hand.

"You have been sentenced to death." The masked man's voice sounded nonhuman, like it was part animal. Ben screamed for release. Why couldn't he move? Why couldn't he get to her? "Prepare to be judged by your maker."

TWENTY

Shiri struggled to get to her feet. Madame cackled like a deranged witch as she gripped Ben's writhing body. What was she doing to him? Madame's horrible abilities were infamous in the Institutions. If someone messed with her, she destroyed their mind—infested it with such frightening images that not everyone came back from the abyss where she'd taken them.

For years, Shiri had believed the woman's own bullshit, that somehow she should be thanked for taking basic care of the people whose lives she had been entrusted with.

She had to get Ben away from her before it was too late to get him back. It took her a few seconds to orient herself to being upright before she could move. Her vision narrowed the longer she stared at Madame. No one got to hurt Ben. Too much had happened, too much had been taken from her. Ben would not be one of those things.

It seemed obvious to Shiri what she was supposed to do. Her body knew what to do even as her mind railed against the thought. Almost by its own volition, her hand reached out in Madame's direction.

She took in and expelled ghost energy, played with it. Earlier that day she'd shown Madame that she could push it out onto other people. But the real reason Madame had been afraid of her was because of what Shiri had always known she could do—even as she'd refused to do it.

But not anymore. There were lots of kinds of energy in the world. Shiri could touch all of it. And she was going to take Madame's life energy.

As if thinking it could make it happen, Shiri felt the power move through her fingers. Madame gasped and tried to turn around, but Shiri's energy drain kept her pinned where she was.

"You can't kill me. You're not built to kill." Madame's voice barely registered above a squeak.

"I couldn't have until you harmed him." Shiri sighed. "Now I don't even feel sorry."

She didn't lie, ever. Madame's death might creep up on her later as a regret or a guilt that bothered her, but right now she just wanted it over with.

"What about Heaven? God won't forgive you for this."

"I don't know what God does or does not want from me. But you're going to know what the divine thinks about you sooner than I will."

For years, Hell terrified her. She'd have done anything to avoid it. But now? She was more afraid of living the rest of her life worried about the small woman whose only real accomplishment involved abusing others.

Scenes from Ben's torture filled her mind. Shiri wasn't sure why she was receiving Madame's imagery, but then again, she'd never taken someone's life energy before. She could see what Madame made him see. Visions of herself being executed, his girls dying, his brother being gunned down as he was powerless to do anything about it made her want to gag. Yes, this woman was a cancer to the world. She needed to be cut out of it.

As quickly as it had begun, it ended. Madame slumped down on top of Ben. Shiri could feel the other woman's life-force slip through her like so much dust in the wind. If she left part of herself behind as ghost energy, someone else could deal with it. Shiri had handled enough of Madame's energy to last a lifetime.

Shiri shuddered. She didn't feel regret about what she'd done. By contrast, she felt relieved. But it had taken a tremendous amount out of her. Between taking care of Madame and the mental beating the Fury had been giving her, Shiri wasn't sure she could keep her eyes open for another second.

She kneeled down, wanting to be close to Ben's warmth. Gently, she shook him. "Ben." Her voice was hard to make out even to her own ears.

She tried again.

"Ben. Wake up, please."

For a second, she thought he wasn't going to open his eyes. Maybe she'd been too late. Maybe it had taken her too long and he would be forever lost to Madame's madness, even with his assailant dead. Finally, when she thought she would just close her eyes and let fate take her wherever it wanted, his eyelids opened.

He stared blankly at the ceiling. Was he really there, or were his eyes still unseeing? Using the last of her energy, she reached out to stroke the side of his face.

His head turned, and he blinked several times quickly as he stared at her. She wanted to smile but she didn't have the strength.

"Seven?" His voice sounded like a croak, and he cleared his throat. She wouldn't have corrected him even if she could manage to speak. He could call her whatever he wanted.

He turned his head, and realization spread across his expression that Madame was dead. He pushed her dead body off his own, a feat Shiri hadn't been able to manage herself.

It would have taken too much coordination.

"Did you do this?"

Shiri wasn't sure she managed a nod, but she must have. He grabbed his head.

"You rescued me. I came here to save you and you saved me instead."

That was debatable. She'd been unconscious and he'd rescued her from her captors. That he had even managed to get into this place seemed a miracle. In any case, she didn't care who had rescued whom; she just wanted to sleep.

"We have to get out of here."

Ben staggered to his feet. Sweat creased his brow, and she wondered how he had managed to stand up. Most people took months to recover from one of Madame's assaults. The images Ben had seen would have sidelined her from thinking, let alone moving. Yet Ben still managed to cope. Her love for him surged inside her. Even if he didn't feel the same, she knew she could subsist on how she felt in that moment for the rest of her life if she needed to.

Nothing could happen to him. "Go."

It was a miracle she'd managed that word. Nothing else mattered. He would be safe. Madame was finally gone. She could sleep now.

SHIRI OPENED her eyes and immediately closed them

again. Why was the room moving? She had no idea where she was, but she knew it shouldn't have been rocking the way it was. Had she hit her head?

"Shiri, can you hear me?" She recognized the voice, but it wasn't the one she wanted to hear.

She opened one eye to look out carefully at the world.

"Roman?"

"Good, you know me." His grin looked like one of relief.

His words made little sense to her, and she opened the other eye. If she was going to have to process things she couldn't understand, it was better to do it with both eyes open.

"Why wouldn't I know you? Where am I?"

"One question at a time." He stood, walked to a table, and poured her some water from a pitcher he picked up. When he returned to her side, he handed her the cup.

She took a sip. The cool water quenched the thirst she hadn't yet realized she had.

Roman sat down on the side of the bed. He sighed. "To answer your first question, I was worried your brain had been totally scrambled. You've been completely out of it for the last week. I've been working really hard to bring you back. For the first time ever, I was afraid my healing powers wouldn't be enough. I thought you were gone."

"What happened to me?" Shiri tried to sit up. The room spun, and she paused. Roman grabbed her arm. His support felt nice but he wasn't the person she wanted comforting her.

"You killed Madame. I'm not really sure how you did it, but you did."

Roman's words brought the whole scene back to her. Like a movie in fast forward, the memories since she'd been taken from Ben's safe house flew past her eyes. Yes, a lot had happened. Maybe she should go back to sleep.

"Where is Ben?"

"I have no idea. He's somewhere around. There aren't all that many places he could be."

Shiri bit down on her lip. "What does that mean?"

"We're on a boat headed back to Guy's island."

She had been unconscious and missed getting onto the boat?

"How long have I been out of it?" She thought he might have told her but she couldn't remember. Clearly, her brain wasn't quite right yet.

"You officially slept through half of this hellish ride." The boat jerked violently to the left, and Roman groaned. "It's been like this the whole time. We're not traveling through great weather."

"Who's with us?" Shiri tried to process all the information she was being given. She felt the need to catch up as fast as she could. The idea of being out of it didn't inspire her with a lot of warm feelings. Instead, it made her feel slightly ill.

"Other than you and me, it's the girls, Ben, Gene and Addison." Roman grinned. "My sister-in-law is enjoying this ride less than me. Apparently, being pregnant makes the whole thing even less fun."

"I can't imagine." She shook her head. They were taking Gene to the Island?

Whose idea had that been? More than anything else, she really needed to speak to Ben. Shiri swung her legs over the side of the bed. "I'll go see if I can help."

Guy had instructed all of them in basic sailing. He'd felt that with their isolated situation, they had to know how to get off the island if needs be. Hence the sailing lessons.

"Wait a second. I'm not a doctor, but I can't imagine it's a good idea for you to go running around."

She shook her head. Roman would never understand her need to go check on Ben and the girls. He wouldn't get it.

"I feel fine."

"Then hold off a second so I can speak to you."

That startled her, and she ceased moving. What could Roman want to discuss that was so important?

"Okay." He'd done so much for her. She felt immense gratitude toward him. He really was one of her closest friends. Shiri could somehow find patience in her rush to see Ben to talk to Roman. *Somehow*.

"Shiri, I've always been in love with you."

She knew it made her a terrible person, but as Roman stood in front of her confessing his love—something everyone had always told her, but she'd refused to deal with —she wished she'd run out the door instead.

BEN STOOD in the hallway outside Shiri's room. He shouldn't have been eavesdropping. To his credit, he hadn't known she was awake. This had been his spot for most of the last week. When he wasn't captaining the ship with Gene, he sat here. Being in Shiri's presence was the only thing in the universe that felt right, outside of being with his girls.

He clenched his hands upon hearing Roman's words. No way did he have the right to be jealous. Time and again, he'd proven himself to be useless to Shiri. She needed to be with someone like Roman, someone who could protect her, who could keep her safe, who could have killed Madame for her instead of forcing her to do it herself.

A light illuminated the hall from where the door sat cracked open. He peered in slightly. Roman had taken Shiri's hands in his own. No. Ben shook his head. He couldn't watch any more.

They were so beautiful together, Shiri with her strawberry blonde hair that looked in some lights like spun gold, and Roman, tall and blond like a Greek god come to life, to live amongst the mortals. He could care for her. In Roman's keeping, she would never be hurt again.

Ben hadn't been able to maintain her safety on his boat the first time he'd been gifted with her, and the second time, when she had come back from the grave, he had been responsible for her near-death. For once, he was going to do the right thing for her. He was going to stay away from her and let her be with the person who could make her happiness a reality.

Hoping his footsteps were silent, he crept back up the stairs.

_____

SHIRI PULLED her hands out of Roman's. "Please, stop. I don't need you to list all your good qualities. I know them. You're my friend. I care about you a great deal."

Roman sighed. "You care about me. Like a friend."

She nodded, her heart breaking a little. Really, Shiri never could have gotten through life without Roman. She would have died at Madame's hands twice. But she couldn't make herself feel something for him that wasn't there. Ben held her heart. He always had and always would.

She wasn't sure of Ben's feelings, but she wouldn't

pretend love for Roman because it was simpler. Having spent as many years as she had behind the walls of the Institution, she would not live anything but a life of authenticity.

"I had to tell you. I hope you understand. I couldn't go on wondering what would have happened if you had known."

Shiri nodded. "I get it. And Roman, I know there is someone out there for you. Someone you will love with all your heart and who will love you, too. It's not me. Even if it feels like it is right now."

Roman smiled, a half-smile that made Shiri feel even sadder.

"I don't think so, kiddo."

"Will you leave as soon as you get back to the island?"

He shook his head. "I can't go back. I'm pretty sure I got caught on my way out of the building with you and Ben. It means I'm hidden now—like the rest of you. So much for my grand idea of helping everyone from the shadows until we could all go out in the sun."

"Was it a big deal? All of us getting away? Did we almost get caught?"

Roman shook his head. "Other than three Fury staring straight at me when I pulled you and Ben out of the elevator, we didn't see anyone else. It was a fairly quiet escape. The news is abuzz with stories of Madame's death. They're saying an escaped Conditioned killed her. It's really gotten all the regular humans good and scared."

Shiri felt sorry for all the trouble she was sure she'd caused for the Conditioned in hiding, but she'd do it again if she had to. Madame had needed to go. As far as she was concerned, she'd done the public a service.

Roman shrugged. "Anyway, if Ben is a big idiot, I'll throw him overboard for you."

Shiri smiled. Roman had proved himself to be a gentle-man. He'd taken her turning him down remarkably calmly, and he wasn't doing anything to make her uncomfortable. They'd need to take some time apart, though. Maybe they could be friends still.

"I think, actually, that we'll have to take a little break from spending a lot of time together."

Shiri gasped. "Did you just read my mind?"

"I did." He didn't look even a little bit sorry about it.

"Exactly how many powers do you have?"

"Thousands of them."

"Thousands?" The idea blew her mind.

"At least." He crossed his hands over his chest. "Am I scary now?"

"You've always been a little scary." He nodded. "I know."

THE WIND on the deck of the ship pushed on Shiri as she attempted to make her way across to the other side. Roman had told her the boat was huge, but she hadn't really antici-pated how large it actually was. Guy had tremendous resources at his disposal, and apparently this vessel was one of them. Ben and the girls had been staying on the other side of the ship. Evidently, there had been a real concern that she actually might die, and Ben had been trying to protect the girls. She hoped her arrival alive and well would be a good surprise for everyone.

Especially Ben...

He'd come for her. But had that been solely because of his guilt that she'd gotten caught? At no point in their brief interaction had he said anything about his feelings for her.

Maybe he didn't have them anymore. Maybe five years was too long a separation. Maybe he was angry with her for disappearing. Maybe...

"Careful. If you fall overboard, I'm going to have to go in after you."

Shiri's head darted up as she stared at Gene. He stood by the wheel, staring down at her from his raised spot on the deck. She'd been so consumed with her thoughts that she'd completely missed him.

"Should I feel confident that you're captaining this ship or worried about it?"

"I'm the most competent at it. I'm not sure if that's a good thing or a bad thing. Addison assures me that when she's not throwing up all the time, she's a good captain. I don't believe her."

Shiri nodded. "You should. She never lies. Spent too many years having to pretend every second of every day."

"I can relate."

He could? Shiri knew very little about Gene except that he worked for the Mob, he'd taken care of Ben for five years after Ben had been ridiculed in the media for standing up for the Conditioned, and he'd come up with the plan that had ultimately gotten her kidnapped.

What was he doing there?

"How did they convince you to come along?"

"No convincing necessary. I've made a lot of mistakes. This was not one of them."

A strong gust pushed Shiri up against the rail.

"Whoa," Gene called over the whirl of the wind. "You'd better get down. I'm going to tie myself to the mast."

"All right." If she and Ben were going to make it, she was going to have to figure out Ben's brother. Somehow, she thought he wouldn't be an easy egg to crack.

She reached the staircase and took the steps as quickly as she could. The girls spotted her first. They were sitting together at a table in the kitchen. They flew out of their seats into her open arms.

"Oh, thank God." Daphne sniffled between sobs. "I've been so afraid. You were so still when Dad carried you onboard. I thought you were dead."

"I knew you weren't dead then, but I was afraid you would be," Ella finished.

"Thank God you're okay. We can all be together now."

"Girls, let Shiri breathe." Ben's voice caught her attention from the side of the room. He half-sat, half-lay on an ottoman across the room. He held a steaming cup of some kind of hot liquid in his hand. His eyes were hooded, and she couldn't make out his expression.

"Hi there." She smiled. He was so handsome. It should have been illegal to look that good in the middle of a storm. Behind her, she heard a whimper. She turned but didn't see anyone.

Ella sighed. "That's Aunty Addison. She's having a hard time with the sea like this."

"I'm having a little trouble with it, too."

Daphne gasped. "Are you going to throw up?"

"No, I don't think so."

Both girls sighed. "Thank goodness."

She couldn't help her giggle. When they spoke in unison, it was so clear they were twins.

"Why don't you go check on Aunty Addison, girls?" Ben stood. "I'm sure she would appreciate it."

"But Shiri just got here." Daphne put her hands on her hips.

"Don't talk back to me, Daph." Ben shook his head. "I don't want to punish you. I need to speak to Seven." Ben held out his hands in front of him. "I'm sorry, I mean Shiri."

The girls scampered from the room. Shiri scratched her head. What was this? Why was Ben being so distant? He hadn't even crossed the room to her, and they'd all thought she'd been near death's door for days.

"I don't care what you call me, Ben. You can call me Shiri or Seven." *As long as you call me something*, her heart cried out.

"I have to call you Shiri. It's what everyone calls you now."

"Yes, I can explain that..."

Ben held out his hand. "I don't need the details."

"You don't?"

"No. Look, I haven't the heart to tell the kids yet that there won't be a 'you and me.' If it's okay with you, I'll wait to tell them until we get to this island we're all going to hide out on."

Shiri's head spun. "Why won't there be an us, Ben?"

He looked down. "We both know you should be with Roman. He loves you. Go to him. We're not good for each other. Every time we get together, bad things happen. I'm not the man for you."

Oh no. This wasn't happening. No way, no how. She hadn't been through everything to have this take place now.

"How dare you."

He looked up, making eye-contact with her for the first time since she'd stepped into the room. "Pardon?"

"I said, how dare you. Who do you think you are? I don't love Roman." She stepped forward, shoving Ben hard on his chest. He took two steps backward as his eyes widened in surprise.

"Shiri, I'm doing the right thing for you."

"If you don't love me, that's fine. I can't make you. If you can't forgive me because I disappeared for five years, that's fine. I can't change any of that. But I have waited five years, thinking of nothing but you every second of every day. I did everything I could to stay in your life when it should have been impossible." She was screaming now. "You don't get to decide what's best for me. I love you. At least be man enough to tell me you don't feel the same way!"

TWENTY-ONE

Ben struggled with what he had heard. Shiri seemed furious. She was in love with him? She'd actually shoved him? His heart beat faster with disastrous hope. He couldn't let himself trust this too much. The fact remained that he hadn't been able to do anything for her when she'd needed him the most.

"Shiri, calm down. You just woke up from some kind of Conditioned coma. You can't get worked up."

Tears sprang from her eyes, and his heart skipped a beat. No, she couldn't cry.

He'd never be able to stick to this if she cried.

"Don't get worked up? I love you. I've said it a lot, and you have nothing to say. You've destroyed my heart. Yes, I suppose I'll simply *calm down*." She turned to leave.

"Shiri, wait."

"Why? Why should I wait, Ben? Haven't you said enough?"

"Shiri, please." Ben's hands shook. He could feel tears threatening in his eyes.

Truth was, he couldn't care less if he wept like a baby at that moment.

She threw her hands in the air. "Please, what?"

"Please, listen." He walked toward her when he knew he should be walking away. She was like air for him. Who was he kidding? He couldn't be near Shiri and not touch her. His hands shook from the effort not to stroke her face.

"I'm listening."

"Shiri, I love you so much I can hardly breathe from the all-consuming nature of it." He might as well get it all out. "I love you so much I couldn't do anything but try to avenge you for five years."

Shiri's crying turned immediately into sobs. She covered her face with her hands. Dear God, he hadn't wanted that. He crossed the distance between them and drew her into his arms with more force than necessary. He couldn't help it.

Ben needed Shiri.

"I'm sorry, Ben." She rubbed her face against his shirt. He could smell her unique scent. How did the woman always smell of coffee? When had that become his favorite aroma? "I wanted to come back to you every day. They told me it wasn't safe for any of us, but I should have anyway. Every day of my life has been dictated by fear."

"I wouldn't have wanted you to come back. Not if it wasn't safe. That's always what I've wanted. I love you. I want you safe. That's why you need to be with Roman."

Shiri's sobs increased. "Ben, how can you say that?"

"Because I love you. I want you to have the best, Seven." Damn it, he'd done it again. Part of him would always think of her that way. *His Seven.*

"No."

"I'm not a saint, Shiri. I'm standing here holding you and it's everything I want in the universe."

"Then what is the problem? Why can't we be together? Haven't we both had enough pain?"

He closed his eyes, rubbing his cheek against her hair. "You had to kill a woman because I couldn't stop her. I'm useless, sweetheart. Useless to you."

"Ben." She lifted her head and shook him. Her gaze met his and he wished he could lose himself in it forever. "No one could have done more there. You broke into a facility—I still don't know how—and retrieved me. The only reason I could get to Madame was because she was distracted by you."

"She took me down like I was a child."

"No." She stomped her foot. Ben stared down at her delicate looking toes in amazement. He'd never seen her this adamant before. The emotion added color to her cheeks and, to his utter amazement, his cock jumped in his pants. "We're all children next to her. That's how she got to be the Madame. You withstood her. You are here and not in a mental hospital. You got me out of there. So what that Roman showed up at the end? If he hadn't, you would have found a way."

"Oh, Shiri." When she said it like that, he could almost believe her.

"You're not supposed to be able to battle people like Madame. None of us should have to. It's this whole system of Institutions that makes someone like her possible. For five years, you made her miserable by throwing lawsuits at her. Trust me, Ben; you're more than capable. Besides..."

Her voice trailed off, and he pushed back to look at her. Her hair appeared windblown. Her face looked a mess of tears and fury. He'd never seen her more beautiful.

"Besides?"

"I had no heart until I met you, Ben. I was dead inside. I love you."

"I was dead, too." He sighed. "And then when you died—"

"I'm so sorry—"

"I thought I could never know happiness again. I love you. Forget it. I won't give you to Roman. I can't. I thought I could, but I can't."

She kissed him. Her soft mouth met his, and he shuddered. She was his, no matter what name she used. He'd never been self-sacrificing, and he had no idea why he'd thought he could be. Needing her like air, he pulled her closer against him. His excitement had to be obvious to her; he was as hard as a rock.

Her hand stroked the side of his face. She was such a loving, gentle being. If he could, he would make certain she never had another bad day. She should spend her life bathed in sunlight with only gentle breezes leading her way.

As if on cue, the boat lurched to port, sending them both flying backward onto the ottoman. She screamed and threw her arms around his neck.

"It's okay." He rubbed her back. "It's rough water, but Gene is really good at this. He sailed around the world, remember?"

"Through weather like this?"

Ben nodded. He really had no idea, but he was certain they hadn't been through everything they had just to drown. "Yep."

"Are you lying?"

He grinned. "Can you taste it?"

"Apparently."

"Come with me." He pulled her with him, trying to

resist the urge to slam her against the wall and take her until she pleaded with him to give her release. It had been five years since they'd been together. He was going to have to be gentle with her so he didn't scare her off.

"Tell me again." Her voice sounded barely above a whisper but it pulsated through his blood.

"I love you, and I won't give you up."

He might never be able to protect her, but he would die trying. That would have to be enough.

"Where are we going?"

Ben couldn't help the grin that crossed his face. She sounded impatient, and he was enormously glad she was as affected by their reunion as he was. "My cabin."

"How big is this boat?"

"Pretty damn large. Addison says her family had several this size, but it's the biggest one I've ever been on."

"Guy has a lot of resources behind our movement."

He slammed open the door, dragged her inside, and then closed it just as fast. Pushing her against the wall of his cabin, he sniffed her skin until he felt as if he could drown in her scent. It would be a good way to go. "I don't want to talk about Guy or the movement. I only want to focus on you."

Their lips met, and he plunged his tongue into her mouth. He'd waited so long for this, had doubted it could or should ever happen. Hell, he'd thought she'd died. There was nothing more important to him in the universe than laying claim to her body. Until he felt her quiver with pleasure beneath him, he couldn't believe it was actually real. Even then, he might not believe it.

"Shirt. Off." He couldn't speak in full sentences. His cock strained at his pants, begging for release.

Shiri did as he instructed, her eyes wild with heat. "I want your hands on me, Ben."

"I want them on you." He caressed her flat stomach. She was too thin. He would feed her until she begged him to stop. But first he had to possess her.

He tugged at her bra until the clasp came loose. The last thing he wanted to do was break it, but he would if it got in his way. The boat jarred to the port side again, and Shiri squeaked.

"Don't worry about it. It's nothing."

She laughed, running her hands through his hair. "You don't know that."

"Let me distract you." He lowered his head to lick her neck, desperate to have her taste in his mouth. "We'll make our own rocking."

Shiri laughed, her perfectly formed breasts brushing up against him. "That was cheesy, Ben."

"Sorry. I never promised you poetry."

She kissed him, hard. His lady was aggressive, and he loved it. "Take your shirt off and I'll forgive you the corny lines."

He laughed as he pulled his Polo off.

She ran her fingers down his chest. "Ben, you're always so buff. How much do you work out?"

"Not as much as I should, but enough that I can stay in shape." He kissed her nose. "Do you want to talk about this now?"

"No."

They embraced like two people starved for each other. Ben had never needed another person's contact as much as he required hers. He struggled with her pants, pulling the button apart and tugging on them until they fell to her ankles.

Her legs had gotten even shapelier in the five years they'd been apart. She must have taken up running.

"Shiri, I want to have you naked out in the sun. When we get to this island, I'm going to find a way."

She kissed her way up his chest toward his neck, stroking his erection through his pants as she did. "Couple of problems with that."

"You're going to kill my fantasy." He let his fingers play with her panties, toying with the edge of the lace but not really taking them off her. "What are the problems?"

"I'm a redhead. I know you don't like redheads."

He suddenly recalled his ridiculous statement. "You know that's not true. I like *you* an incredible amount. I love you. I was just trying to be contrary. I'm a big fucking idiot."

She grinned from ear to ear, showing off her perfectly straight, white teeth.

"You are forgiven."

Her sweet words made his throat close up. How was it that this gentle soul wanted him? He pushed away the question—he was keeping her. Somehow, he'd gotten her. He wasn't giving her back.

"What does your gorgeous red hair, which is really more of a strawberry blonde, have to do with nakedness and the island?" He swept a hand over her belly button and felt her shiver.

She raised an eyebrow. "The sun is not my friend."

Shiri had the most beautiful porcelain skin. He traced his hands down her shoulders to her wrists. "Yep, I definitely see some freckles that weren't there five years ago. You've clearly been spending too much time out in the sun."

She bit down on his shoulder, and he yelped. "I do not have new freckles. Bite your tongue."

He grinned as he unzipped his pants. Shiri cupped his

hard length, and he managed not to come in her hands through sheer force of will alone. "You said there was a second reason why I can't have you naked outside."

"There isn't a whole ton of privacy on the main island. You can be alone in your cabana, but outside of that, someone is always around, needing you to complete some kind of task."

"Seven..." He knew he'd used the wrong name but seemed powerless to do otherwise sometimes. "I'm very resourceful. I promise you I will find us some private shade at some point where I can have you alone and naked."

"This will be your project?"

"Yes." He finally slid her panties down her legs.

"How is it fair that I'm standing here naked and you still have your briefs on?"

Ben looked down as if he hadn't known he was still partially dressed. "Really? I guess you'll have to take them off me."

She bit down on her lower lip, which had to be the cutest thing he'd ever seen. Every unconscious movement the woman made caused him to get even hotter. He could spend days staring at everything she did. But for now, all he wanted was to be inside her, to feel her muscles clench around him as she cried out in pleasure.

Shiri yanked his briefs down his legs, and he stepped out of them. She cupped his penis, massaging it between her hands.

"You can't get me pregnant."

He nodded. "I know." He wished he could, but told himself it didn't matter. He wanted Shiri more than anything in the world, with or without babies. "There hasn't been anyone else for me in five years. No one."

She kissed his lips. "Ben, there could never be anyone but you."

"Do you trust me?"

"Always."

He picked her up so that he supported her weight up against the wall. "Wrap your legs around my waist."

With minimal movements, Shiri had her legs around him. Ben positioned his cock just outside her core. He could feel her heat calling out to him. Yes, this was what he needed, what he'd craved for five years. This was all he wanted in life.

"I love you, Shiri."

She bit down on his lip. "I love you too, Ben."

Shiri met his gaze. He didn't have to be told what she wanted. He tried to start out slowly, but every movement and moan she made drove him further into a frenzied pleasure he'd never known before. Their joining felt destined to him. He was supposed to feel like this. He was supposed to have Shiri as his own.

"Oh God, Shiri." He called out her name as if it were a prayer, because to him it was. "I love you, sweetheart."

Shiri yelled for him as she came. Her muscles grasped him and milked his cock until he came—hard. He cried for her again, knowing that nothing would ever be more important than that moment between them.

Somehow, he didn't drop her. He maneuvered them both down onto the bed, and then he knew nothing at all but blackness and happiness intertwined.

Sometime later—he had no idea how long—he opened his eyes. Shiri ran her hands gently through his hair. Her eyes were sleepy, but she looked happy and peaceful. Good —that was how he wanted to keep her.

"The seas seem to have calmed." She curled up closer to him.

He took a deep breath to take in more of her scent.

"I told you I would distract you."

"You did." She kissed his shoulder. "Can I ask you something?"

"Anything." He yawned. What he really wanted was to kiss her senseless, make love again, and pass out until morning. But he was pretty sure he was going to have to get up and relieve Gene from his captaining duties. Plus, he needed to check on his girls.

"How did you know you were going to marry your wife?"

He sat up a little bit. "How did I know I was going to marry Dana?"

"Yes."

"You want to talk about Dana?"

She nodded. "I do."

"I knew I would marry her within seconds of meeting her, because that's how it works for me. Just like I knew I would love you forever right away, too. I'm built that way." He pulled her up against him. "Why do you want to talk about Dana?"

"Because you married her."

Now he understood. He kissed her temple. "You want to know if I want to marry you?"

Shiri's cheeks turned a delicious shade of red. "Am I that obvious?"

"Yes."

"Okay, yes, I want to know if you want to marry me." She closed her eyes as she spoke.

"I do. I want forever, Shiri. Will you marry me?"

Shiri's eyes popped open. "You're serious?"

"God, yes."

"Yes, I want to marry you. It's all I've wanted for five years."

He rolled over to kiss her. "I don't have anything to offer you now. I'm going to have to start from scratch, and I come with two companions. They adore you, but we're a package deal."

"Then I guess it's a good thing I love them, too."

He'd known that to be true, but he liked hearing it just the same.

CHAPTER 22
THE ISLAND, ONE YEAR LATER

"Two things, Ben." Guy looked up from his computer screen as Ben came farther into the room.

It was always *two things*. Hiding his smile at the way that Guy always addressed him, Ben sat down in the chair opposite Guy's desk.

"I read your memo."

Ben nodded. He'd emailed it to him that morning.

"You're serious?"

He took a deep breath. "We can't blow anything else up. It's time to try winning the hearts of the people."

Guy sat back in his chair. "Do you think that's even possible?"

"I do. And if it doesn't work, we can always blow up the Institutions again."

Guy scratched his bald head. "I'm going to have to think about this. You make a good point. A lot of them. I can see why you were a good lawyer. I'm glad to have you on my side. Always have been."

It had been a little hard for Ben to warm up to Guy once he'd found out he had been the reason Shiri hadn't contacted him during their separation. However, Ben had always appreciated a good leader. Guy had an enormous responsibility, and he bore it well. He did his best. They'd come to some kind of friendship, even if neither of them would ever call the other man his closest friend.

"Thank you." He shifted in his chair, anxious to get back to Shiri and the girls.

"Was there a second thing?"

With a gleam in his eye, Guy spoke. "Our Seers tell me Shiri is pregnant."

Ben shook his head. "But she's infertile. How...? I mean... who changed that? Laurel?" It wasn't that Ben wasn't excited that Shiri was pregnant, but hearing about it from Guy had thrown him for a loop. Did Shiri even know?

"Roman. But if you ask him, he'll deny it. He's not exactly forthcoming when it comes to Shiri."

That was true. Ben couldn't blame him. There couldn't be anything easy about being in love with someone who didn't love you. Still, the former Fury behaved like a nice guy to him. Ben would always be grateful.

He grinned as Guy's words sank in. Shiri was pregnant with his baby. It was everything he'd wanted. The girls were safe and starting to find their feet in this strange place. It was weird not having to hide.

"You know that Gene, Ella and yes—you—are all Conditioned. I can always feel when someone is Conditioned. It's like a ringing in my head. It's why they wanted me to be a Fury. You may have hidden it really well or maybe it was subdued because you weren't able to push at your powers. Here, maybe you're more open. I don't know why it's obvious now, but it is, so I want you to know that."

Ben hadn't known that Guy could do those things, but

there were a lot of things about Guy he didn't know. He would suspect Guy's best friends didn't know him.

It didn't surprise him to find out he was Conditioned, and now that he was safe from the dangers of being labeled as such, he really didn't care.

"What's going on?"

Shiri stepped into the room behind him. Swinging around in the chair, he grinned at her, hoping she could see all the love in his eyes. Later, when they were alone, he would show her again how he felt, make sure he let her know how utterly irreplaceable she was to him. He could try to wait until they had a private moment to tell her but there was no such thing as privacy on this island. She hadn't been kidding when she'd told him that.

"You and I... we... we're pregnant."

Shiri gasped before a breathtaking grin overtook her expression.

Life was as close to perfect as it could ever be. He was a damn lucky man.

EPILOGUE

The President looked at the message that flashed over his computer screen.

How the hell had it gotten there?

We are the Conditioned. We are Human Beings held against our will. We will not be forgotten.

AFTERWORD

Dearest Reader,

Thank you so much for reading Illicit Connections. I am hard at work on the next book in this series. In the meantime, please join us in my reader group https://www.facebook.com/groups/rebeccasrandomness where you can chat with me and hear about all of my books. Please turn the page for a complete list of all my books and to learn more about me.

Thanks again
Rebecca

UNTITLED

Please Turn the page for a complete list of my books

ABOUT THE AUTHOR

As a teenager, I would hide in my room to read my favorite romance novels when I was supposed to be doing my homework.

I am the mother of three adorable boys and I am fortunate to be married to my best friend. I live in Austin Texas where I am determined to eat all the barbecue in town.

I am in love with science fiction, fantasy, and the paranormal and try to use all of these elements in my writing. I've been told I'm a little bloodthirsty so I hope that when you read my work you'll enjoy the action packed ride that always ends in romance. I love to write series because I love to see characters develop over time and it always makes me happy to see my favorite characters make guest appearances in other books.

In my world anything is possible, anything can happen, and you should suspect that it will.

I'd love to hear from you! Please visit my website at www.rebeccaroyce.com to sign up for my newsletter and learn about my books!

Here's where you can find me online:

Rebecca's Randomness Reading Group https://www.facebook.com/groups/RebeccasRandomness/

https://www.rebeccaroyce.com

https://www.facebook.com/authorrebeccaroyce/

www.twitter.com/rebeccaroyce

Instagram: rebeccaroyce79
MeWe: RebeccaRoyce
Cheers!!
Rebecca

OTHER BOOKS BY REBECCA ROYCE...

Dragon Wars (completed series)

Forever

Eternal

Always

Evermore

Endless

Wards and Wands (completed series)

Hexed and Vexed

Curse Reversed

Meow, Baby (novella, co-written with Ripley Proserpina)

Tragic Magic

Safe Haven

Everywhere and Nowhere

Dimension X (coming soon)

More coming soon....

Soul Bound

Prisoner of the Dragons

More coming soon....

Shadow Promised

Strange Days

Weird Nights

Bizarre Years

More coming soon...

The Warrior (completed series)

Initiation

Driven

Subversive

Redemption

Justice

Warrior World (spin off of The Warrior, completed series)

Deacon

Micah

Jason

The Westervelt Wolves (completed series)

Her Wolf

Summer's Wolf

Wolf Reborn

Wolf's Valentine

Wolf's Magic

Alpha Wolf

Angel's Wolf

Darkest Wolf

Lone Wolf

Fallen Alpha

Alpha Rising

Alpha's Strength

Alpha's Sacrifice

Alpha's Truth

Alpha Enticing

Hidden Alpha (coming soon)

The Capes (completed series)

Seductive Powers

Adrenaline Rush

Last Ascension

Illicit Minds

Illicit Senses

Illicit Connections

Illicit Danger (coming soon)

The Outsiders

Love Beyond Time

Love Beyond Sanity

Love Beyond Loyalty

Love Beyond Sight

Love Beyond Expectations

Love Beyond Oceans

Love Beyond Flames

Love Beyond Lies

Love Beyond Death (coming soon)

Cascade (completed series)

Haunted Redemption

Phoenix Everlasting

Fragility Unearthed

Persuasion Enraptured

Reverse Harem Story (completed series)

Unconventional

Unexpected

Undeniable

Kiss Her Goodbye (completed series)

Hard Truths

Dark Truths

Deadly Truths

Shifter World

Planet Bear

Planet Wolf (coming soon)

The Swamp

Hidden

Pursued (coming soon)

Stand Alone Titles

Under The Lights

No Quitting Allowed

Mr. Wrong

Bite Marks

Bitten Surrender

The Vampire and The Virgin

www.ingramcontent.com/pod-product-compliance
Lightning Source LLC
Chambersburg PA
CBHW011026260626
47153CB00020B/2955